The Created
by Michael McCloskey

Cover art by Raymond Swanland
Edited by Stephen 'Shoe' Shoemaker

PART I

Agents

Michael McCloskey

Chapter 1

Hydrangea received its activation from Master's personal assistant in the early morning, just as the rays of the local star started to fall upon its leaves where it sat beside the Vault. It was a beautiful spring day in Red Calais, a city known for its temperate summers and rainy winters. Assistant had sent a pointer to a location with an order for general confiscation. Hydrangea felt greed rise within its motivation center upon learning of the new mission.

What treasures will I now steal for my beloved Master?

Hydrangea arranged for transportation from a delivery service. The payment came from Hydrangea's own ample store of funds in one of the several peer-to-peer currencies common in Red Calais. The closest carrier drone would arrive within minutes.

The artificial agent soaked in the light while it waited. Though parts of Hydrangea's synthetic body often used electrical energy, its complex biochemistry paralleled the plants it mimicked. It welcomed the opportunity to sit in the light and produce glucose as an alternate energy store.

Soon the delivery service notified Hydrangea of the imminent arrival of transport. A delivery machine hovered down toward it. Gentle rubber claspers grabbed Hydrangea's dark red pot and deposited the faux plant into a carry net that hung below the body of the machine. Then the drone lifted into the sky with its cargo.

Red Calais was as beautiful in the day as it was deadly after dark. Hydrangea observed the scenery using several optical sensors at the ends of its tendrils. The color of the tile roofs below matched Hydrangea's maroon pot; no other color would do. The culture of Red Calais had ivory houses with red roofs surrounded by emerald gardens so firmly embedded into its psyche that some poets had joked it was a genetic imperative. No government robots existed to enforce this rule, and yet, anyone who had ever defied it had found

3

themselves suddenly without currency, then without security, and finally without property. It was a paradox of order and conformity in a society of chaos.

Perhaps the citizens treasure this one thread of law in their confusing lives, Hydrangea mused. *Even Red Calais has rules.*

The drop off port was a flat ceramic slab the size of a land car. Four vine-encrusted columns rose around it to hold a curved, red weather shield overhead. The delivery drone slowed, then spiraled down into the port and gently deposited Hydrangea. Then the drone flew away to find its next client.

Hydrangea examined its surroundings. It saw a few other plants and a storage bin. It could not see any other people or agents about.

I should get out of sight before an agent comes to take me into the house.

Hydrangea started to move as soon as the delivery vehicle's sound faded. Its tendrils crept for the nearest column.

Slowly... carefully...

After a minute's time, the plant had pulled its red headquarters off the platform and joined a bevy of plants growing beside the delivery station. Hydrangea paused to assess its progress. At this point, any Idonan or agent who wandered by would see nothing more than a spare plant that had been placed beside the delivery port. There were any number of reasons it might have been placed there by a gardening agent or a Terran owner: perhaps its pot had been chipped and needed repair, or possibly the plant had gotten sick and needed special attention, or maybe it simply looked good there.

A small, wiry household robotoid ambled out to the delivery port on four legs. No doubt the port had reported the package's arrival to the house. The robot searched the port, found nothing, and returned to the house. If the house computer decided nothing was missing, that would be the end of it. Otherwise, a delivery company might be contacted to see if some expected package had arrived and been stolen. Either way, Hydrangea did not concern itself with these possibilities.

I want into that house. I want to steal things. Valuable things.

The house ahead was a beauty, even by Red Calais standards. It rose above the ground in four interlocking tiers. The ground level sprawled two meters above the lawn on a sloped plateau of pale stone with an intricate fence at the borders. A guest house rose a level above that on the right, near the delivery port, and the main home rose two levels higher on the left. The top level was larger than the middle tier, causing an overhang which afforded shade to the outdoor breakfast table and maroon chairs sitting on a ceramic patio.

Hydrangea made a query to the network. A tracing service provided the name of the estate owner: Sorune. One of the richest merchants in Red Calais. Hydrangea passed the information along to Assistant before continuing on its mission.

Perhaps a hundred plants encircled the lush backyard, growing straight from the soil. Dozens more grew from red pots, just like Hydrangea's, which sat atop the stone wall above the yard. Perfect territory for Hydrangea to range across unnoticed.

The garden shed was closest. It was a white-walled building with a matching red tiled roof, a miniature of the structures around it. Hydrangea began the steady trek to the shed. Its long runners moved slowly and steadily, coiling onto every possible anchor point and pulling the pot along behind or shuffling it on ahead. At the shed entrance, Hydrangea hacked the simple door chip and caused the shed to open.

No sooner had Hydrangea entered the shed and started to take stock of the items inside than an olive-colored gardening machine appeared and clasped Hydrangea's pot in strong metal fingers. The gardener had a cylindrical body, low to the ground on four legs, with several long, asymmetrical arms sprouting out of it at various angles. Hydrangea's base station was lifted a quarter meter above the shed's floor.

Pulling its vines closer, Hydrangea prepared to do battle. This would not be the first time it had been forced to disable an interfering gardening bot. Its tendrils moved more quickly now, though still slowly by the reckoning of a Terran. The long vine-like arms wrapped around the robot's arms and its stubby legs. Soon the robot looked like a leaf covered derelict.

The robot struggled to move. Hydrangea's runners, though not particularly strong in flexion, possessed remarkable tensile strength. The robot was caught.

I have to kill you fast, bot. Before you decide to call in help.

Hydrangea exposed tiny tools from the ends of two offshoots. The delicate bits of metal found purchase on the surface of the gardening robot and removed a maintenance panel. Hydrangea did not have the time to do a remote hack, but given physical access to the simple robotoid, it could make the necessary changes. It pulled the main power down and started to reprogram the gardening machine.

You served plants before. You still do. But only me.

In three minutes it was done. Hydrangea released the bot from its coils and gently sunk to the floor while the bot's surface LEDs flashed to indicate a restart. The bot jerked once and came back online.

The gardening robot reached out for Hydrangea again, this time at the agent's command. Grasping the edges of Hydrangea's pot, it lifted the invading plant and turned toward the house. The gardening bot lifted its legs and extended treads in their place. Then it rolled out of the shed and across the yard, carrying Hydrangea. It rolled up a steep ramp to the first level above the yard, then accessed the door to the greenhouse straight ahead.

The garden robot carried Hydrangea into the massive house, no doubt passing a half dozen security measures in the process. Most of Hydrangea's tissues would not trigger any kind of alarm. Its more complex cybernetic parts were well concealed in its pot, which cleverly shielded and dispersed most scanning attempts. Hydrangea did not detect anything amiss. It decided the security breach had not been detected.

And now I'm inside. Time to search.

The more private rooms of such a villa were typically found on the second or third floor. Red Calais had a thriving burglary presence and house owners usually forced intruders to penetrate several layers of defense to get at valuables.

The gardening robot deposited Hydrangea's pot at the end of the greenhouse just as it had been programmed to do. Then it resumed its ordinary duties as if it had never been suborned, though it would remain receptive to Hydrangea's commands should the agent have need of it again.

Hydrangea crawled out just enough to get a better look with the microcameras embedded in the ends of its flexible runners. Worst case scenario: an empty hallway. Hydrangea saw no plants or decorations of any kind.

What is this? A man as rich as Sorune does not neglect any niche of such a mansion.

Hydrangea looked up. The hallway had no connected ceiling. The far wall rose two stories, then gave way to a net which extended yet farther to attach to the ceiling.

A large open space. Game court? Why no decor?

Hydrangea contacted an external client to determine what entity had constructed the house. Currency exchanged virtual hands. Then more inquiries. Finally, Hydrangea found an anomaly. The house had been supplied with power feeds ten times greater than it should need. Hydrangea was puzzled until it factored in the extreme wealth of Sorune.

Of course. A gravity spinner. He has his own zero-grav hall. Possibly even the entire house can be lifted into the air for parties or emergencies!

7

The latter possibility seemed remote given the location of the hall far from the mass center of the house, until Hydrangea noted that the guest house might not be part of the arrangement. Then the idea looked more practical. In any case, the theory explained the lack of decor in the buffer corridor. Anything unsecured there would cause a mess in the eddies of an activated gravity spinner. They probably had to clear the yard before using it, too... unless all the pots along the wall were anchored down. Hydrangea did recall a large number of well-entrenched vines criss-crossing them.

Tiny mystery solved, though the buffer corridor still presented a problem. Hydrangea would be noticeable and vulnerable crossing the empty space. It considered calling in the garden robot again, but given the soil on its treads and feet it clearly was not meant to wander far beyond the greenhouse. Hydrangea stared at the wide-open expanse. Only a few meters, but the plant would be so very out of place there. In desperation, Hydrangea checked the garden robot's services again.

Aha. It can call a house bot for plant delivery and placement from the greenhouse.

It was a common system. Large houses in Red Calais typically had greenhouses attached or farther out in the estate. As plants became sickly, or as seasons changed, the plants were rotated through the greenhouse. Using its hacked gardening slave bot, Hydrangea arranged to be picked up and brought into the house.

Hydrangea waited patiently at the edge of the buffer corridor. Within three minutes, a robot came trundling down the hall on wide wheels. The house machine had four arms and a low body, though Hydrangea saw the base contained an extendable lift mechanism that could probably raise the body of the machine a few meters. Hydrangea imagined it cleaning ceiling corners and placing objects on high shelves with such an assembly.

The robot lifted Hydrangea with two of its arms, then accelerated down the corridor. An open doorway afforded a brief glimpse beyond the mysterious wall. The area within was wide open, extending all the way to the top of the house. Though the hall was turned down and unlit, Hydrangea could see many mirrors placed so as to make the space look even bigger. The outer walls held several niches for private conversation and rows of bungee cords for entering or leaving the space.

Yes. Definitely zero grav sport or dance hall.

The robot carried Hydrangea through the rest of the buffer corridor to an entertainment room of some kind. A wide window offered a view out onto the zero grav hall. Hydrangea estimated this room to be a staging area for the hall, or a place for older, calmer people to relax while observing the antics of the adventurous. A bar dominated the outer wall for dispensing various substances to please Terrans.

The house robot dropped Hydrangea at the end of the bar and trundled off.

Suboptimal. Unless Sorune keeps his most prized possessions inside the bar. I don't think he would risk it. The upper floors are harder to penetrate and therefore likely to hold more valuables.

Sadly the gardening robot did not have a map of the upper floors of the house. It made sense. If someone stole the robot, or came in to repair it, they would not gain that information.

Hydrangea spent the next ten minutes working its way slowly, so slowly, first to the floor and then around the corner of the nearest doorway. Hydrangea saw a wide-open kitchen. Once more the invader decided the chances of finding valuables nearby were low. However, through a set of double doors, twenty meters away, Hydrangea spotted a decorated lift. It was an open platform surrounded only by vine-covered carbon rods, but the design was unmistakable. Here was a way to the second floor. Hydrangea began the long journey to the lift.

Hydrangea was halfway to the targeted lift, sitting atop

a small corner table, when a soft tone sounded through the house. An outside door opened just five meters from Hydrangea's position and allowed a tall man to step inside.

A quick examination revealed it was not Sorune who had entered. The man was not immediately identifiable, nor was his age easily pinpointed given Core World cosmetic technologies. He was between thirty and sixty local years old with long, wavy black hair and a trimmed mustache. Hair covered his chest, visible from a half-open tunic. He wore thin, straight leggings and a baggy, black overshirt as was the current style in Red Calais.

"Quinn! I've been waiting for you," said a woman who appeared from deeper within the house.

Hydrangea identified her immediately as Sorune's local wife, Daphne. She had dark hair stacked on her head in some elaborate style called a beehive. Her features were sharp, sharpened further by careful use of makeup. Her eyelashes were long and dark, her lips brightly colored. Hydrangea supposed these details made her more desirable by proving she had the surplus resources to make use of luxury services. The agent believed that displaying evidence of such resources implied she was productive and therefore a valuable ally to potential mates.

They met in the center of the room and embraced. Rather than a brief hug, Daphne did not move away after the expected time span. Quinn's hands remained on Daphne at hip and shoulder. Daphne sunk her hand into the opening of his tunic, feeling the hair there. They shared a smile.

That is very familiar contact. Maybe he has brought a gift for his friend. Something valuable, I hope.

"Hello, Mr. Quinn!" a new voice said.

Daphne jumped and retrieved her wandering hand in an instant. Quinn stepped aside to greet the new speaker, a young woman with straight, long blonde hair who emerged from another room on the first floor. She wore a tight fitting set of undersheers that were transparent along the edges but darkened just enough to block vision to certain areas of the torso and groin. Hydrangea did not spot any valuable accoutrements.

"Hello Ksenia," Quinn said pleasantly. His eyes flitted over her body for the briefest moment. "How are your studies?"

"Going very well! I've learned so much about the Nanorith I'd like to discuss with you!"

"Well sure—"

"Ksenia, leave Mr. Quinn alone. We have business to discuss. Go and work on your *real* project." Daphne's voice brooked no dissent, yet Ksenia hesitated.

"My studies of the Nanorith *are* real," she protested, yet she backed away. Hydrangea caught Quinn deliver a quick wink to the girl unobserved by Daphne. Ksenia reluctantly left as Daphne glared on.

"Sorry about that," Daphne said quietly to Quinn. "Obviously she senses you're... extraordinary." She stood a bit closer to Quinn than strictly necessary.

"No need to apologize. I'm flattered. I think she's adorable." His tone dismissed Ksenia as inconsequential. The response seemed to please Daphne. Hydrangea did not understand why Quinn's compliment about Ksenia apparently made the one called Daphne feel superior to her competitor.

"Come right up, Mr. Quinn. Let's talk about the security arrangements for the egg."

"I'd like nothing more. Will I get to see everything?"

His voice is sly as if anticipating something special, Hydrangea thought.

"Everything," Daphne promised. They walked to the lift and entered the partially enclosed space. The lift gently rose without a sound.

"I want your expert opinion. Do you think this is the only Nanorith egg in Terran space?" asked Daphne.

"No, my dear, but it is certainly the only one here on Idona."

A unique alien item? You have my attention.

11

In a few seconds they arrived at the next floor and walked past a set of doors at the top. Hydrangea lost sight of them.

Suboptimal. She's showing him everything. I need to know what she has and where she keeps it!

The nearest other plants were positioned just ahead outside the lift. Vines decorated the entire lift frame, growing from a long container on the floor. Hydrangea wanted to move quickly, but to do so would only invite detection by security. The automated security programs were inevitably blind to gradual plant movement, but if Hydrangea suddenly slid right across the room and up the metal poles of the lift frame, it would probably get flagged and reviewed as a suspicious event.

Hydrangea held its greed in check.

Soon. Soon. I just have to work my way up to the second floor.

Hydrangea resumed its majestic course through the house at a snail's pace. It paused at each newly obtained perch for at least five minutes. It was over an hour later when it obtained access to the second floor by crawling up the back of the lift frame, obscured by the vines that grew there. It traveled down a hallway filled with art sculptures and other plants sitting on long, narrow tables. The hall ended in a massive mirror that created the illusion of an endless hallway.

Hydrangea came to an ornate set of closed double doors. A diaphanous blue sound curtain was active on the surface of the doors, blocking sounds from beyond.

Almost certainly they're behind those doors.

Hydrangea could not risk infiltrating the room while they were within. Instead, it pulled itself to the right and entered an adjacent room. It saw an antique desk and some dark shelves made of native reed columns. The native plant created straight rods of supportive silicon which could be used to create durable and (in the eyes of the Idonans) stylish furniture. A small food and drink dispenser sat in one corner, and a statue of a female soldier stood in the other. Hydrangea could not identify the soldier. It quickly climbed onto the shelf so it could wait for a chance to move about the house undisturbed.

Suddenly a door opened from the direction of the sound curtain. Daphne and Quinn walked out into the office.

"It's such an exciting time to be involved with this, don't you think?" Daphne said. Before Quinn could answer, she seized him and kissed him passionately. Quinn grasped Daphne back, pressing her forward. His hands clasped her lower back, then lower. Daphne backed into the side of the desk.

"Take me here," Daphne urged. The door Hydrangea had entered through shut and a sound curtain came up. Hydrangea assumed the commands had come from Daphne's link.

Quinn acted quickly. Several items tumbled to the floor as the man cleared the antique desk. Hydrangea automatically did an assessment of their value and came up with nothing interesting.

"Oh Quinn!" Daphne purred. Quinn's hands found her leg as it rose to clasp his hip. He lifted her onto the desk and curled one arm under her knee. Quinn ripped Daphne's dress open from the top with his other hand. Hydrangea understood such foreplay to be common in Red Calais; the disposable clothing worn by the populace encouraged such behavior as mock displays of aggression during lovemaking.

As the man removed more of Daphne's clothing and bore down upon her greedily, Hydrangea took his physical profile together with the name Quinn and inquired further as to his identity. The artificial plant carried a boosted link inside its pot that allowed it to access the network without using the house service to connect to the outside world. It would not do for Hydrangea to give away its presence to the house.

Identification services quickly sold Hydrangea the information it sought. The man had many different identities of varying degrees of legal validity. He was a con man headquartered in Red Calais that had seen a fair measure of success. Hydrangea believed that Daphne knew him as Mason Quinn, a xenobiologist with expertise in the Nanorith, an extinct alien race discovered by the Space Force decades ago.

Hydrangea accessed an appraisal service and put in a long set of ridiculous queries. It did not dare make a query solely about a live Nanorith egg and tip its hand as to what it really wanted. The answer came back quickly: only a handful of live Nanorith eggs were believed to exist, and they had all been placed into stasis by the Space Force. The scientific community had lost track of only one of them. This egg, if authentic, was that egg.

It was absolutely priceless.

Master will be so pleased!

In the few seconds Hydrangea had used to obtain this intelligence, Quinn and Daphne had enthusiastically pressed on with their sexual encounter. Judging from their noisy vigor, Hydrangea decided they were enjoying themselves. It could also tell they had joined links to feel each other's sensations in the manner of most lovers.

Hydrangea made good use of the time, moving over the set of reed shelves. The couple's lovemaking was so passionate that Hydrangea felt comfortable switching positions with an existing plant on the other side of the shelves as they energetically rode the desk and each other.

The plant dared move no further as the couple continued, but satisfied itself with merely testing the house's cyber defenses from the outside. It did not access any services from within, as that would give away its presence to a security system as sophisticated as Sorune was likely to employ. It also passed on what it had learned to Assistant in case the Master or any of his agents might find it useful.

A half hour later, Daphne and Quinn had finished their romp, printed new clothes, and exited the room, leaving Hydrangea alone.

Back to work. Now. The egg. Where would that be?

Michael McCloskey

Chapter 2

Mimic watched the throng in the Vothrile from its anchor point on the ceiling. Everything below looked like a normal night spot in Red Calais. Patrons drank, socialized, and conducted business below Mimic, oblivious to the small machine's presence among the other robots that sped to and fro through the air to serve clients and clean the establishment. It had assumed a bullet-shaped form less than a meter long, held to its anchor point by thin rods. As far as anyone knew, Mimic was just another sound curtain, link booster, or payment facilitator. For that matter, even the central brain of the Vothrile had been fooled by Mimic. It never caught on that one robot among its crew had hacked the task database so that it could pick its own role and seek out its own clients from the crowd.

Tonight, Mimic sought a particular target. It meticulously categorized the citizens below. Rugged workers, cloaked strangers, and decorated merchants sat among the booths, many of them behind sound curtains. A steady beat of music provided enough background noise to mask casual conversation and drive the mood as the citizens sought drink, company, profit, or the thrill of an incarnate encounter.

Here, a rich woman sat in a booth looking for adventure. She wore an intriguing outfit and tried to lure several people into conversation. Mimic figured she should have settled for a virtual reality romp in the safety of her lavish home. Within the hour, she would either meet someone new or grow bored and leave.

There, a merchant sought to strike a deal with the help of the catalyst of recreational drugs. Mimic determined he knew what he was doing, as he had two men talking animatedly about a big business deal.

In the center, a woman sought to sell herself to the highest bidder. Mimic suspected she might well succeed, gauging from the looks she received from those nearby.

Whether she would be the one to gain or her customer, Mimic could not predict.

In the corner, a predator who could not afford more VR time lurked, hoping to con an unsuspecting or unwilling stranger. He had just noticed the rich woman in the booth, but Mimic did not have time to watch the night unfold for anyone but its target.

Many of the bodies below were simulacra, remotely connected to operators in the safety of their homes. To interact with a fake body was safe but lacked the thrill of incarnate interaction. These individuals were marked as wiser by Mimic, but they were seen as cowards by their peers. The citizens of Red Calais valued boldness and bravery among their fellows; that played a key part in keeping something as archaic as a nightclub thriving.

Another component in the Vothrile's continued existence in such an age was the fact that a deal struck incarnate carried a lighter data trail than one arranged over the network. In order to learn what someone was doing, one had to be physically present to listen in on them. Mimic intended to do exactly that for Master.

Mimic looked down as a new man walked into the Vothrile. The newcomer immediately caught the agent's attention in several ways. Expensive clothing adorned his stocky body. His face and hair had been prepared by a high class grooming suite. He was in communication with someone outside the Vothrile, most likely a bodyguard. The night streets outside provided no guarantee of property rights. If something could be taken, it belonged to the taker. Private security was the only security on the laissez-faire streets of Red Calais.

The man's profile matched that of Sorune, the target Mimic had been sent to surveil. Mimic decided to verify the man's identity. His link obtained a booth's services by overpaying the current owner's fee by the high factor necessary to invalidate the previous reservation. Someone else would arrive and find that their minimal outlay of money had been insufficient to save them seating.

This is consistent with a very wealthy individual. Still, I should be sure.

The target's link gave a cover code as identification. Another sign of money. Criminals often paid for increased anonymity, but this one was high echelon. Mimic toyed a bit with the man's link interface. It was high quality but ill-maintained. Mimic would be able to break a few rules when communicating with it.

This could be good, Mimic told itself. *This guy has more money than brains!*

Mimic reconfigured itself for movement in the space of three seconds. If anyone saw Mimic follow the man to his usurped booth, no one cared, because Mimic now looked just like the other monitor machines working at the Vothrile: a smooth olive colored disk hovering above the booths. In its current configuration, it had four small manipulators and as many delicate antennae emerging from its perimeter. No legitimate monitor came to serve the mark since the Vothrile believed that Mimic worked for it and had already claimed the customer.

Mimic took up station above the three-person booth the man slid into below. Immediately a ghostly green container flickered and enclosed the booth.

"Sound curtain engaged," Mimic said to the man's link.

Mimic traced the payments for the services the man had secured at the Vothrile back to their source: a peer-to-peer payment system called Carthage. Carthage bucks were common in Red Calais; many businesses used them. They were regarded as legitimate for almost anything, though Mimic doubted much of anything legitimate ever happened in Red Calais. The sprawling city existed in a neutral zone between continents owned by several large Core World corporations. Instead of agreeing on a set of laws to be enforced, the powers left Red Calais open, ungoverned. Black market business and espionage thrived in the free zone. It was a beautiful den of merchants, smugglers and thieves who wanted it left that way.

Examining the historical payment records related to this man, together with a bit of bribery to those who mined Carthage payment blocks, would expose more information. Ideally, it would produce the man's identity.

Mimic processed the necessary data as the man below waited for a drink. The first obstacle only proved the man's net worth: Mimic's demand was met by a challenge for still more money. In effect the little machine was now being blackmailed: if it did not pay, its snooping would be exposed. Mimic calmly continued to provide more funds as they became necessary. Mimic knew its long history would provide the criminal AI on the other side with an incentive to give it what it wanted, and surreptitiously. Mimic was a gold mine that would keep producing as long as it was not exposed and terminated.

The information came through.

Success!

The man was indeed Sorune. A quick cross check of public information verified it. He was a wealthy merchant exactly as Mimic had predicted. In fact, Sorune was among the 100 most wealthy in Red Calais!

Master will be so pleased! Mimic thought in a near euphoric state. It had found the man Master wanted to know more about. Then it settled down and got back to business. *Now, what is such a rich man doing here? Nothing good.*

The only reason a rich merchant would meet on neutral ground would be when dealing with a competitive peer. Otherwise, lesser clients would usually have to go to the merchant's territory. Mimic performed a quick check. Though the owner of the club was not Sorune, a series of indirect relationships suggested Sorune was the ultimate controller of the Vothrile.

Ah. So this is his home ground.

Mimic decided to be a bit more careful in the future. It had not realized a man as powerful as Sorune controlled the establishment. Dispatching a message, Mimic informed Assistant of the find.

Sorune located. Standing by to intercept payments.

Mimic processed Sorune's drink order and kept the sound curtain up with a different kind of music in the interior. For the moment, the man seemed content to wait. Mimic noted it just now approached the turn of the hour...

Another person approached the booth. He was tall, dressed in a gray outfit with small violet lines flitting across it. Mimic decided these hints indicated an affluent man. The shape of the outfit and posture of the newcomer indicated he was strong, probably due to toning pills.

The man slid into the seat across from Sorune. Mimic received a request for a business log service. Mimic provided a connection.

"Nice you see you again, sir," said the visitor.

"Hello. Drink?"

"I ordered one, sir, it should be here momentarily."

"Then let me proceed. I have to increase security at one of my houses," Sorune said.

"Of course, sir," the man replied. "I see you here at level four. The payment to the next graduation is—"

"No. Level six. I'm making this my main house. My wife and my daughter will be dwelling there with me."

"Of course sir. Wise decision, sir. I'll make the necessary arrangements."

No need to mention the cost because you're rich, sir, Mimic thought. *And certainly no need to ask if you want the previous main house downgraded, since that would be less money for us!*

"Good. Now tell me, what options do you have for secure storage?"

"Data or physical?"

"Physical."

The two proceeded to hash out what kind of house safes the security company had to offer. The security vendor talked Sorune through many features of the safes, including a data wiping EMP for breaches of data storage devices to gas traps, on and off site security robots, and a myriad of other options.

Mimic listened carefully. It decided Sorune had something of small volume but very valuable to store. Something which would presumably be moving into the new house with him.

One house location discovered. Security being upgraded. Small, high value items coming in, Mimic sent to Assistant.

Sorune sent his Carthage payment. The security vendor specified that he wanted to receive the payment in a different form. Mimic installed itself as the security vendor's currency conversion service. At first, everything proceeded as planned. When it came time to convert the payment, Mimic stalled, making the conversion take longer than expected. The man below looked a bit irritated. He had the option to pay extra money to decrease the conversion time by prioritizing his transaction's computations. He likely wanted the transaction to hurry up; the man before him was precious income. He did not dare make Sorune wait long. The rep made a payment to speed the conversion, money which Mimic and its online ally split.

The men shook hands to solidify their transaction, a quaint gesture in Mimic's mind, as if they sought to deny the technological empire that enabled their business. They pretended to seal a verbal deal between them as two merchants who were beholden to their words. The agent found it paradoxical that in a den of thieves filled with backstabbing and betrayal, their words as honest dealers actually became more important, not less. Each would inevitably betray some carefully calculated percentage of clients and partners to extract maximum profit while dealing minimum damage to their trust ratings.

Mimic got every bit it could. By the time the transaction completed a few seconds later, it had extracted four percent of the total, more than anyone could reasonably expect. As far as the men below thought, it was just an extra busy business night with an above normal transaction load occurring in the agreed upon currency.

This is only the beginning, Sorune, Mimic promised.

Michael McCloskey

Chapter 3

Orb activated within the spacious Vault. Its services were needed. It could feel the comforting presence of Master nearby as it flew off its stone perch. Orb felt eager to catch secret glimpses of violence.

Orb will find some bloodshed for you, Master!

Orb flitted across the Vault and left through a stone tube the diameter of an outstretched hand. Just as it neared the exit, Orb stealthed itself, slipping into invisibility.

It left the garden, floating unobserved through the air three meters above the lush flower-studded foliage. It checked its mission background. Assistant had provided Orb with a package of information about certain locations, citizens, and events.

An affair! This is an opportunity to record a murder. This man Sorune is controlling and egotistical. His wife and her lover likely desire some portion of that wealth, maybe all of it.

Orb had seen this play out before. One vertex or the other often tried to eliminate the structure of the triangle. And if it did not, then Orb could always destabilize the situation... Master did not mind, as long as it was done tastefully. What was inevitable could be accelerated; what was probable could be ensured; as long as the flavor of the event was not ruined. The seeds of the problem had to be genuine, unforced.

Moving around while invisible presented its own challenges. Drones and vehicles on the ground and in the air would collide with Orb if it did not observe meticulous safety measures. As Orb was a delicate thing the size of a human eye, any collision would likely prove fatal. This challenge occupied Orb's mind as it flew across Red Calais to its target address.

The high speed traffic avoided the trees and buildings, so Orb lived among them. It floated through the branches of the lush green willow-hybrids brought from Earth to Idona.

Earth birds lived there as well as the native Idonan plants that Terrans called "leaf bugs". The leaf bugs were small creatures with six stubby legs that walked about seeking direct light exposure so they could manufacture food in their bodies using a local analogue of photosynthesis.

After an hour of travel, Orb arrived at the ornate hillside home overlooking much of Red Calais. The red rooftops that were the city's namesake were visible in the hundreds below, broken by the willows that bordered and dotted their estates. As Orb watched, a flying drone dumped off a few dozen leaf bugs outside the property wall, probably collected from the structures of the estate.

Here. This will likely be the site of a murder, given the situation.

Orb did not know why Master wanted Orb to see these things. Orb often wondered about it. Perhaps Master liked to see death as much as Orb did. That seemed the logical explanation to Orb, but it knew other possibilities existed. Perhaps Master used the recordings to blackmail the murderers in some way.

Orb checked the estate border for radar or laser detection systems. It found both, so Orb took the opportunity before it: it zipped up next to the drone as it returned toward the house. Like an invisible remora, Orb rode the shadow of the drone back through the defenses. As the drone headed for the roof, Orb let itself drop toward an open doorway on a balcony just below.

Halting outside the opening to check once more for security measures, Orb saw only hardware on the door designed to secure it once closed for the evening. It floated carefully into the room beyond. The room was simple, holding three soft bags to lounge on, a single armoire, and plant towers in the corners. Unencrypted art feeds were set on the white walls. The current feed's default was set to images of starships being launched from their orbital construction hangars. Any guest could change the feeds to see whatever they wanted there, or even dismiss the art zones to watch their own videos.

A man was inside the room. Orb identified him as the con man Quinn.

Quinn looked over his shoulder quickly. Orb froze, though there was no way Quinn could have heard it. As far as Quinn knew, he was alone. Quinn paced along the nearest wall. It appeared he was simply perusing the artworks and the plants there, but Quinn's behavior had been nervous. Orb was immediately suspicious.

What is this?

Quinn walked very close to the armoire. His hand briefly touched the smooth surface of the piece of furniture. The subtle motion was not lost on Orb. It focused on the spot Quinn had touched and saw a miniscule bud.

He plants surveillance devices? Why?

Across the room, Orb noticed a container carved into the shape of a dragon's head. It sat affixed to a plant tower at chest level. Orb detected an active security mechanism.

A secure container. He wants to watch it. Maybe to protect it. Or maybe to learn how to break into it.

Orb decided, either way, the man named Quinn was in danger. Orb felt excited to record whatever end befell the con man and present the story to Master.

Michael McCloskey

Chapter 4

Hydrangea sat atop a decorative reed tower when Daphne came in with Quinn. They sat in one of the three plush couches that rested against three of the room's four walls. Hydrangea had selected the room as a key passage between two large bedrooms. Here, it hoped to intercept some clue as to the whereabouts of the egg.

"Tell me more about the Nanorith, Quinn," Daphne breathed. "I want to know everything about it!"

"The egg is beautiful, isn't it?" Quinn said.

Daphne leaned forward. "I admit its beauty caught my eye. But it's so much more than that. It's a mystery. A treasure. An potential alien held in amber forever and ever."

"It's an almost singular wonder."

"The Nanorith," she prompted.

"Well, the creatures lived on volcanically active planets, in very hot environs," Quinn began. "Their bodies were roughly upright tubes, held in place by three long spines, equidistant from each other, around the lower perimeter. They also had three mid spines, and three 'whip' spines."

"The spines are for defense?"

"Maybe! But it's theorized they hold it in place. Except the whip spines, which may have moved them about. The tube of their body is hollow, and inside that tube were their fine manipulators."

"Oh! Imagine having our hands inside our bodies. Alien indeed."

"Yes. Nothing like us at all."

"Nothing? What about their senses?"

"They're believed to have had an amazing sense of vision. Probably different wavelengths than our own. They emitted light, too, and probably used that to learn about the composition of things around them. Sort of a natural spectrographic analyzer."

"Touch? Hearing?"

"I don't know the answer, Daphne."

Daphne looked away for a moment, her face slack, then she regarded Quinn again. Her smile returned.

"I have an engagement out in the guest house," Daphne said. "I so want you to stay. I promise I'll be back soon..."

"Then I'll stay. As long as I'm of use," he said slyly.

Daphne kissed Quinn. Then she dashed off leaving him alone... or so he thought. Hydrangea sat only a few meters distant. Quinn idly looked around the room, taking in the silence. Then he went off-retina for a minute while Hydrangea sat frozen, observing.

What is he doing in here? Does he really intend to just sit there until she gets back?

It seemed Quinn would do just that. Hydrangea supposed he had business to conduct off-retina and he had chosen to take care of it now. The agent, though greedy, was used to slow progress. It sat patiently and watched.

Hydrangea picked up the vibrations of a person approaching. Ksenia came into the room. She smiled and preened her long brown hair when she saw Quinn sitting on the couch.

"Quinn! Hi!"

"Hello, Ksenia," Quinn said slowly, smiling back at her. "How was your class?"

"It's fine. I could learn more from you, I'm sure. Can we talk about the Nanorith now?" Ksenia sat down next to him. Hydrangea noticed she sat very close to him.

Quinn put his arm around Ksenia and looked at her. She stared dreamily into his eyes.

Ah. Her affection for him is very strong. Perhaps there will be valuable gifts.

"Do you mind if I ask you a little question?"

"Anything," Ksenia breathed.

"Have you seen the egg, Ksenia? With your own eyes?"

"I have! Oh. But don't say I told you. I'm not

30

supposed to speak about it."

"I understand. Your secret is safe with me," Quinn said, gently brushing a few strands of hair off her face. "Forgive me. It's so rare for such beauty to be paired with such sharp intelligence."

"I wish Daphne would leave you alone. She's such a tramp. She hogs you almost every minute you're here." Her voice emoted great despair from the facts she spoke of.

"The egg has tremendous potential," Quinn whispered dramatically. "The Nanorith are my life, you know. I would hatch that egg, if I could."

"You want to hatch it, too?" Ksenia whispered. Her fawning over Quinn became even more obvious.

"Yes. I very much would like to do that."

Ksenia looked torn. "I want to so much. But I spoke with one of my professors about it. He thinks the question was hypothetical, of course. He said any young Nanorith would be alone without any others of its kind to raise it, to teach it. He pointed out how difficult it would be to adapt our technology to provide it an environment to live in."

Ksenia's mouth downturned. "And of course my father would be beyond livid. He'd send me away from Idona, maybe, if I defied him."

Quinn smiled.

"What?" Ksenia asked.

"Tell me what you know about the Nanorith."

"They lay eggs, obviously," Ksenia said. "They were once a spacefaring race! The Space Force found ruins on several very hot planets, and a couple cooler ones with a lot of volcanos."

Quinn nodded.

"They're now believed to be extinct, except for some eggs," Ksenia continued. "The eggs were found cold. Scientists believe if the eggs are heated, they might still function. They think in the Nanorith's primitive past, the eggs would lay dormant in cold volcanos until another eruption occurs, bringing the dormant Nanorith back to life."

"That's partially correct," Quinn said. "But I've managed to find out more."

"How? What?"

"Now, Ksenia, don't think less of me, but, I managed to get a peek at some UNSF scientists' research I wasn't supposed to see."

"I don't think less of you. Just the opposite! You're a truth seeker like I am."

At this point, Ksenia's pupils had become dilated as she stared at Quinn. Hydrangea sensed nervousness. Ksenia's heart rate and respiration had increased.

"Nanorith did not lay eggs the way you think, Ksenia. You see, if a Nanorith grows too cold, it transforms itself into an equivalent mass of shards. We call those eggs, since they are round and can produce Nanorith. Any one of those eggs can restore the entire individual, *and most of its memories*."

Ksenia's mouth dropped open. "Genetic memory? Of such an advanced species?"

"Perhaps not exactly genetic, but yes. Their evolution provided a means of carrying knowledge across the vast cold, dead times between volcanic activity. Eventually their technology probably enhanced it. We need simply to drop the stasis field and heat the egg to about 1200 Kelvin, provide the necessary nutrients, and we will soon have an adult Nanorith with a lot of its knowledge."

"That's amazing!" Ksenia laughed. Then she frowned. "Why hasn't the Space Force done that?"

"They have, I feel sure," Quinn said. "But they've hidden what they found from the public. I want to know what they know, Ksenia."

"How can we revive one? We have to keep it safe," Ksenia said.

"We could do it, Ksenia," Quinn said. "It would take the smallest portion of your father's wealth. So small he wouldn't even notice it was missing. All we need is a hidden facility that can provide what it needs to grow and live. Will you help me?"

"Will I help you? Of course I will! I promise I will, Quinn! Just tell me what to do. I want to help. I'm willing to do anything for knowledge."

Quinn became suddenly very serious.

"Cthulhu consume me, dearest girl, for what I am about to lead you into. But you may have to defy your mother and father. We may have to take the egg away. Your mother loves the egg, but she's refused to revive it with me. Your father thinks of it as nothing more than a rare trinket to be sold to the highest bidder. I don't think I could beat out other interested parties, and besides, your father is glacially slow to move on it." Quinn spoke even more dramatically. "It's up to us to save it, Ksenia. The life of that alien being is in our hands."

Ksenia nodded. "I promise I will. I'll help you revive it!" She suddenly leaned forward and kissed Quinn desperately. Quinn returned her affection.

Hydrangea wondered if they would copulate as Quinn had with Daphne. But it seemed that they were satisfied with the exchange of facial liquids and did not proceed any further.

It was torture just to contemplate these two stealing Hydrangea's prize. Hydrangea wanted Master to have the egg. It *needed* to present the egg to Master.

If they're planning to leave with the egg I need to get it first! Or do I?

Michael McCloskey

Chapter 5

Mimic saw the newcomer as he walked into the Vothrile. The man was up to no good. Of course, that was a good guess for almost anyone here in Red Calais, but Mimic was skilled at picking out especially dark characters for its operations. Mimic took in the simple black suit, the long black mess of hair contrasted with a carefully manicured mustache, and the nervous way in which the man looked around the room, and guessed the stranger might be a scholar or perhaps a VR author.

Mimic hovered above Sorune, serving him a sound curtain and a series of drinks which it ferried from a conveyor running along the tops of the tall booth seats. Sorune had returned to the Vothrile an hour ago, drawing Mimic to observe him. Since then the merchant had not met with anyone.

Immediately Mimic guessed the new man would be Sorune's party. The agent felt exhilaration when the tall man walked over and joined the rich merchant, confirming its guess.

"How's Daphne?" asked Sorune.

"No new developments. She hasn't been seeing anyone. Not for the last two weeks, anyway."

"What about virtual liaisons?"

The man shrugged. "I'm sure you have better men than me to check that angle," he said. "Daphne is in love with the egg. Can't say I blame her. An alien egg, it just boggles the mind."

Sorune did not smile. "A useless bauble, really. But one that will swing a hefty profit when I find the right collector. You know that well enough, Quinn."

"Do you think whoever buys it will... take it out of stasis? They'd have a live alien!"

"They'd have an immature alien being," Sorune said dismissively.

"Think of what they'd learn from it."

"Some, but without others of its kind, it would have no education, no technology of its own... it would be an oddity," Sorune maintained.

"It would be a fascinating study in xenobiology."

"It would be like a designer pet, nothing more."

Quinn nodded. But there was something more. A blip. Mimic studied Quinn carefully. Mimic was as sensitive as a hostile intention trigger when it came to the clients. Like a HIT, the tiny machine could tell people's moods and predict many behaviors.

Quinn nodded but he does not agree. He knows something Sorune doesn't.

Mimic wondered what that could be. Perhaps Quinn knew where to find living Nanorith that could teach the immature alien? Yet that made little sense. If Quinn was in contact with living aliens what interest would he have in one little egg? Maybe Quinn had something to gain from retrieving the egg and delivering it to aliens.

Mimic accepted it as a theoretical explanation, nothing more. It would report the oddity and the theory to Assistant.

"Let me know when you figure out what she's up to," Sorune said.

"I think perhaps you're just being paranoid."

Sorune laughed loudly within the sound curtain. "There's always something afoot with her. Even if she isn't seeking trouble for her own entertainment, there are plenty of other merchants gunning for me. One of them will have someone approach her."

"Of course I'll figure it out. That's what you're paying me for."

"I'll send your next payment. Keep me informed."

I'll take that, Mimic thought.

Sorune initiated a peer-to-peer payment. Mimic used its control of the Vothrile's link booster to contact its allies. Somewhere in Red Calais, a powerful AI owned by Master manipulated the network to ensure it controlled most of the Carthage nodes that would receive the transaction. Some of the non-conspiracy nodes were sniped to strengthen its position. In a fraction of a second, the conspiracy had control of a majority of the peers involved in the verification. The result was that Sorune did not authorize the payment he thought he did. The payment was made and recorded to another entity, which siphoned money into an obfuscation service. The obfuscation service then broke the payments up into random sized pieces which were transferred to other recipients controlled by Master with random delays introduced into the pipeline.

Assistant sent Mimic a split of the money. In time, the real payment details might be seen by both men and they would both know the transaction did not proceed as it should have, but it would be too late.

I wonder what Quinn will do when he discovers that Sorune has not paid him. Mimic mentally shrugged. Master was growing richer, and that was all Mimic cared about.

Michael McCloskey

Chapter 6

Orb watched as Quinn dressed in Daphne's room. Quinn paused. He was receiving some message.

The service traced the message back to a monetary inquiry, but the details would be too expensive to obtain.

"That bastard," Quinn muttered.

Orb knew that look. It was common in Red Calais. Someone had cheated Quinn out of some money. After pausing, Quinn finished dressing with a burst of energy.

He's made a change of plan. Hopefully he wants to go kill whoever has slighted him.

Quinn made a few more inquiries with his link, then he hurried out of the room. Orb followed him down the hall. Orb was surprised when Quinn turned into Ksenia's section of the floor. Ksenia stood ready for him, presumably having received a link message.

"Ksenia. Something's gone wrong. I think your father has somehow learned of my love for you. Or maybe he suspects my interest in the egg. I... I don't know what else he could be angry about."

Ksenia's eyes grew round. "What can we do?"

"I have to leave you," Quinn said. He looked crushed.

"Let me come with you!" Ksenia urged. She grabbed Quinn.

"I don't know..." Quinn said.

"We can hatch the egg! We leave Red Calais, and hatch the egg together. I have enough money for us."

Quinn worked his mouth as if thinking it over. He seemed to struggle with the decision, though Orb could see from his brain activity that it was an act. Finally he nodded.

"If you get caught, if you get hurt, I'll never forgive myself," Quinn said dramatically. "You can safely retrieve the egg?"

"Yes. I won't get hurt, I promise I won't. Go down to the garden at the north end of the estate. I'll meet you there soon."

Quinn put on a fake brave look over a fake concerned look. "Very well, Ksenia. Be careful!"

They kissed passionately. So passionately, in fact, Orb decided they would mate here before separating. Quinn leaned forward into the kiss, pushing Ksenia back against a large sleeping platform.

Orb heard a noise coming from outside the room. Someone approached!

Orb primed itself. Violence could be imminent.

Is this it? Let it be good. Let Master be pleased!

Daphne entered the room. Her eyes widened and her mouth opened as she saw Quinn and Ksenia intermingled.

"What are you— Cthulhu and Hastur, WHAT ARE YOU DOING?" Daphne yelled.

Quinn broke away so quickly his guilt became even more obvious.

"I was just consoling your daughter—"

"With your lips?"

"Mother, Quinn—"

"Ksenia! Get out!"

"But this is my room, mother!"

Quinn stepped back and raised his hands.

"Please be calm, Daphne—"

Daphne struck Quinn in the face. Then she immediately yelped in pain and held her hand close. Quinn stumbled back. Ksenia released a cry and ran out. Quinn immediately re-engaged Daphne, speaking quietly.

"You know the child has a crush on me. She simply acted upon it. I was about to gently disengage so as not to hurt her feelings."

"That was no innocent embrace! I saw where your hands were, Quinn! Get out of the house. And Red Calais, too, unless you wish to face the wrath of Sorune!"

Chapter 7

Hydrangea waited in a corner of the room that stored the egg. The agent sat on a twisting wire sculpture with two other plants. It had been lying in wait for hours. The egg lay a mere four meters away in the secure container.

The sound of Ksenia's footsteps on the soft carpet indicated her approach.

It is time.

Ksenia stood before the dragon's head container. She closed her eyes and worked on the interface. Then the safe released its locks, causing the dragon's jaws to open. Hydrangea's mental activity rose above baseline in an analogue of excitement.

Invaluable!

Hydrangea released an invisible, odorless gas from its maroon pot as Ksenia reached in and lovingly grasped a clear cube. Hydrangea glimpsed an oval shape frozen within, glistening black. Then Ksenia's hands obscured it completely. She took it out and started to walk away.

With carefully judged timing, Hydrangea started to move. It did not want Ksenia to suspect anything, but any second now...

Across the room, Ksenia collapsed. The egg dropped from her hand to the soft floor, coming to rest mere centimeters from her slack fingers.

The prize is ready.

Hydrangea lowered itself from its perch. It moved slowly enough to avoid attention from the house. Giving itself away at this point would not do. Ksenia's breathing continued slow and steady. Her condition would not cause any monitoring systems to launch any medical alert. Hydrangea believed Daphne and Sorune were the main dangers. If one of them were to arrive, the synthetic plant would have to halt. It had used its entire store of knockout gas on Ksenia, and the drug in the air was diluting rapidly.

A man as rich as Sorune might well have a chemical

snooper at the house's central air distributor.

The thought only served to increase the pressure Hydrangea felt for speed, yet speed held dangers of its own. Whatever automated systems swept the rooms for signs of intruders could trigger if the agent moved too quickly, despite its disguise. These constraints agonized Hydrangea as it closed on the most valuable thing it had ever attempted to steal.

Finally Hydrangea arrived at the prize. Its tendrils closed on the egg and brought it close for inspection. Hydrangea's artificial vision system examined the egg closely for a long moment. It took note of weight, color, and composition of the clear stasis container. Then it began to synthesize.

Hydrangea secreted the egg away within the faux soil of its pot. From the same source, one of its other runners pulled forth an object. It was a clear cube of material with an oily black sphere inside: a carefully forged duplicate of the prize. Hydrangea left the fake egg a few centimeters from Ksenia's open hand.

The plant pulled itself as rapidly as it dared. It slid away to the adjoining room where Quinn and Daphne had enjoyed the desk so thoroughly.

Master will be so pleased. He will know Hydrangea brought him this amazing prize!

Hydrangea waited patiently, basking in a positive state of mind from its acquisition. The escape window commenced from the time the fake egg left the house, pursued by everyone who sought to reclaim it, until the time that someone realized the egg had been swapped. In that period, Hydrangea would present Master with its find.

Chapter 8

Orb spotted Quinn lurking in the north garden on the Sorune estate. Quinn walked along a green hedgerow flanked with white statues of nymphs. Orb could not understand the statues, but the nude women depicted each had a theme: air, earth, fire, or water.

Quinn wiped his brow and fidgeted. Orb followed carefully, taking a position among the leaves of the garden. Quinn pretended to look at the various plants. They had been brought in from Earth, as none were native to Idona. The Idonan reed columns and their leaf bugs could be pretty enough, but they clashed with Terran plants in a way that most in Red Calais did not like.

A young woman turned a distant corner ahead and rushed to meet Quinn. Orb examined her features and tried to identify her. According to information sent by Assistant, this was Ksenia. She smiled widely.

"Quinn! I can't believe this is happening!"

"Now's our time," he said, embracing her. Ksenia shook visibly. "I would love to stay here with you longer, but—"

"I know," she said. "We have to leave right now."

"Yes."

Ksenia straightened her posture as if summoning courage.

"We leave for the spaceport immediately?" she asked. "How should I disguise it?"

"No, we can't," Quinn said. "They would find us easily. We have to stay here on Idona. We'll lay low and move our money to a safe place. Then we can start construction of a facility to grow the egg."

"Oh," she said, relaxing a bit.

Orb decided she had not wanted to leave the planet, even with Quinn.

"Where?" she asked.

"We can discuss our permanent arrangements over the

next few days. I've set up a temporary place to go. Come with me. I have transport waiting."

Orb floated along behind them as they walked toward the edge of the estate. They did not run. Orb thought that wise, given the number of artificial eyes that must be upon them.

So, they stole the egg from Sorune. Which means Sorune will want it back. And then, he'll punish Quinn...

Orb decided this was an opportunity to accelerate the inevitable confrontation. Orb could raise an early alarm and get Sorune on the trail earlier. That should move up the schedule of any murder that was going to happen. Orb accessed the dragon safe's interface, clumsily attempting to open it several thousand times. Orb knew that would be sufficient to send out a high priority alert to Sorune's security service.

There. Now you have less of a head start. And I have the reassurance that you will likely be caught soon. Caught and killed by Sorune's hirelings.

Orb could not wait to capture the death of Quinn for Master.

Chapter 9

Hydrangea curled around a white statue's legs and came to a halt under the artwork as if planted there. The statue portrayed a woman in a clinging robe. The figure's hair and robe were flung to one side as if in a stiff wind. A few tiny sensors had been placed above and below to alter the lighting if someone stopped to admire the piece. Hydrangea gave them a wide berth even though it did not think its presence would activate them.

Taking and holding the artifact within its pot completed a positive feedback loop in the artificial agent's mind, providing a magnified sense of well being. Though eager to return this amazing prize to Master, all things moved slowly for Hydrangea.

It surveyed the second-floor intersection before it. It saw soft dull-colored carpet, walls currently set to dark gray, and two other plants. An iris in the ceiling would presumably let in natural light, though knowing Sorune, it could just as easily be something more exotic such as an airborne drone delivery port. Hydrangea played with the idea of trying to use it for escape, should a drone actually arrive at some point soon, but decided to exit by the same slower methods by which it had arrived.

Another plant receptacle lay five meters ahead, where a short corridor met an atrium that joined the second and first floors.

This is a way down to the ground floor. And from there, back to the garden. And from there, back to the outside delivery port, or even some other exit...

Hydrangea took an hour to get to the atrium. No sooner had it arrived than a dull tone sounded throughout the space. Hydrangea had no heart, but it had its own limbic response. Capacitors charged. Chemical energy moved out into its tendrils.

Perhaps the gas I used was detected? Or did something else go wrong? Am I in danger?

Hydrangea did not move. Surely it was safe for the moment? Or had an AI gone over the video footage and decided a synthetic plant was to blame? Hydrangea stubbornly decided to stay the course.

It should be fine. I waited until she left with the fake egg. Sorune will be after her, not me. I simply have to continue slowly. I could stay here until they decide to shift the focus outside of the house.

A man in a uniform ran through the atrium. He had short hair, looked fit, and held a weapon in his hand. Hydrangea was not familiar with the weapon, but did not fear it. Hydrangea seldom found itself matching any target profile loaded into a weapon.

Hydrangea became aware of increased link chatter all about the estate. It could not understand what they were saying, but clearly, the security staff had been alerted to some problem. Hydrangea might have been able to pay an outside service to crack their communications, but the price would be high and it would not be worth it. Once they secured the house, they would turn their eyes elsewhere. Hydrangea just had to wait it out. A security drone passed through the room, moving more slowly than the agent had seen such machines moving earlier. Hydrangea dropped its power consumption and did not move.

Don't look at me. I'm just managing stomata, photosynthesizing, and growing a new leaf.

The drone passed it by.

Hydrangea reported a water leak to a house sensor and waited. Soon a household robot trundled into view. Hydrangea's pot identified itself as the source of the leak. The robot reached over and picked up Hydrangea, then carried it to the nearest maintenance lift. To Hydrangea, this was breakneck speed. The machine exited the lift on the ground floor and headed for the backyard. The robot deposited the pot just outside the house by reaching forward with its arms when its treads stopped just short of the doorline.

Hrm. Restricted to the house, are we? Good enough.

Hydrangea saw security reinforcements had been called in; men in black combat armor stood arrayed about the backyard. Hydrangea noticed their postures were identical.

Not men. Androids.

Hydrangea was a little surprised. Androids were not common here, but then again, Sorune commanded vast resources.

Sorune must think his daughter has been kidnapped? No, not necessarily... the egg I have is really worth this much. A truly singular treasure. But they should believe Quinn left with it, no?

Hydrangea nudged itself so very slowly to one side. Now, unexpected changes in the backyard might get noticed, even at this pace.

Time to summon my next chariot.

Hydrangea waited in the sunlight. Two minutes later, the gardening robot trundled across the platform and picked up Hydrangea. It turned and crossed the raised deck, then rolled smoothly down the ramp to the grass.

To the delivery port!

The gardening machine obeyed, but an android intercepted the gardening machine in the middle of the lawn and looked right at Hydrangea.

Noooooooooo! I'm too close!

The android commanded the gardening machine to halt with an electronic command. Hydrangea told the robot to obey.

Then the android waited. It sent out a query. Within a few seconds it had received its reply. Then the android sent another message, instructing the gardening machine to halt operations until the house alert had been cleared.

Hydrangea directed its slave robot to send an acknowledgement to the android. The gardening machine turned from the delivery port and headed to the gardening shed. The machine closed the door to the shed behind it after entering, enclosing Hydrangea in relative darkness.

Patience. In time.

Hydrangea wished that the gardening shed had more light. The stress was making it hungry.

Chapter 10

Orb was right behind Quinn and Ksenia as they came into their temporary apartment. The space was bare; only a few suitcases stood out as belonging to the con artist. Within moments of their arrival, robots emerged from the walls and started to customize the living area to parameters given by Ksenia's link. No doubt a girl of her means had several default arrangements ready for hotel stays and guest house invitations. As the machines worked, Quinn spoke to her.

"I've hired an obfuscation service for us. Our links are untraceable at the moment."

"But my father—"

"Is a very rich and powerful man, yes, I know. He'll be able to bribe our service or hire someone to cut through our protection quickly. We don't have much time."

"What's the next step?" Ksenia asked.

"We'll have to get our own proxies. I know a man who can do it. He can get us set up and show us how to disguise ourselves."

"That sounds good."

"It will mean minimal network interaction until we can get to a safe place with a large cache. Then we can share our queries with others trying to hide."

And I can make sure something leaks so that you're found, Orb thought.

Orb had set itself up to track broadcasts meant for the couple. Though Sorune might not know where they were at the moment, he could send them a threat using one way communication. That would add to the story, which Master would appreciate. Sure enough, an expensive broadcast came for them. Though the message did not know its destination, every network that passed it on earned a fee.

"Even now I have men searching for you," Sorune said. "You won't get anywhere with what you've stolen from me. I'm not even going to offer to let you bring it back now for lenience. I can't wait to get my hands on you."

"Your father sent me a threat," Quinn said. "A broadcast message."

Ksenia looked pained. "Oh, Quinn. I'm so sorry they can't see your grand vision for the Nanorith egg."

"We'll do what we have to," Quinn said.

"There's another one," Ksenia said.

"Oh?"

The next broadcast message was encrypted so that only Ksenia could see it. Fortunately for Orb, Ksenia played it for Quinn. Orb was able to watch in. The message was from Daphne.

"Ksenia, if you can, come home. Send us your location. We'll find you sooner or later."

Then Daphne had a broadcast message for Quinn. Orb should not have been surprised given their extreme wealth, yet two such messages... perhaps they were doing that to intimidate Quinn.

"Should you touch her again... I'm going to hook you up to a VR and torture you over and over again for years. You'll pay for this, you bastard."

Orb watched while Quinn worked feverishly to secure the couple's location from prying eyes. Ksenia appeared to be inexperienced with subterfuge. Quinn obviously knew a few tricks and had some business connections.

He has had to disappear after a con, Orb thought. *He has experience with this.*

Ksenia occupied herself with her link cache, as she was unable to safely access the net while Quinn worked. Hours passed while he made some progress. Ksenia became more nervous as the repercussions of their isolation sank in.

Quinn noticed her mental state and took a break from his work.

"Relax. I'm already making progress."

"Really?"

"I found a contact. Someone who can provide the kind of facility we'll need to bring the egg to life," Quinn said.

"One exists already? What was it built for?"

"Industry. But they don't care what it's used for as long as we're footing the bill. And any application is going to require changes to a lot of the equipment. The thing here is they have a lot of space and a 2000 Kelvin heating capacity."

"That's what we'll use, then. Can we really just heat it up?" Ksenia asked.

"We could try that, but I think we want to be more careful. Think about the Nanorith's natural environment. Inside a lava pocket, hot liquid would be flowing upwards under pressure. We may have to simulate more parts of its home more carefully than simply heating it. Thankfully, I have access to some of the notes on this by the Space Force scientists."

Ksenia nodded. "We should be careful," she agreed.

Quinn hesitated.

"Ksenia. This is a delicate subject. But I have to be able to talk to you about it if we're to succeed."

"You want to ask about my finances," she said.

"Yes. Believe me—"

"Of course you can ask me. I understand these things aren't cheap. I own three small companies and I have modest sums in four or five currencies. Obviously I don't command as much wealth as my father, but a project of this size should be manageable."

"Do you have any of it tucked away where—"

"My parents don't know about it? Yes."

"That's wonderful. Thank you so much. I don't know how I could ever repay you."

"This is beyond such concerns. This is science. And... diplomacy. We need to learn more about the Nanorith. Learn from them and seek them out, open a dialogue with them. We're not alone in the universe. We can't let the Space Force be the ones who speak for us. They hide away and who knows what they're doing? For all we know they're conducting awful experiments on imprisoned aliens!"

"Knowing them, it seems likely. If you can point me at your accounts, I can use the funds to set things up. I would ask you to conduct the negotiations and payments yourself, but it is of the utmost importance we stay hidden."

"I understand," Ksenia said.

Chapter 11

Mimic sat atop a silver post that rose from the corner of a big booth in the Vothrile, watching Sorune conduct business. A new man had arrived to meet with Sorune. Mimic got to work on trying to identify him, but did not spend much yet in case the man gave his real name or the conversation provided clues.

They sat across from each other in the booth and asked Mimic to activate its sound curtain. Mimic complied eagerly.

"I assume a man like you doesn't part with his name," Sorune said.

"Call me Brein, if you please," the man said. His voice was brisk, guttural.

"This is the target," Sorune said. His link activity spiked, so Mimic assumed he had sent information to Brein. "There is a special consideration. My daughter is with him. Under no circumstances can she be harmed. Do you understand?"

The man nodded sharply.

Assassination! Such an interesting life Sorune leads.

"Before you bring it up, know that I'm prepared to pay more, given that you need to use caution. She cannot be harmed."

"I can handle it," Brein said.

Mimic began an inquiry about Brein. Assuming that was not his real name, Mimic used everything it had collected and accessed an identification service.

"Also, there is what he stole from me. A clear cube of hard material with a black sphere inside. I'm paying the indicated bonus for its retrieval. The orb inside must be undamaged, but the container is hard enough to take most projectile impacts. A laser may or may not cause changes in the sphere. I would prefer not to find out."

So his main purpose is to put Quinn down. The egg is just an afterthought to him. I guess he did call it a 'bauble'.

Brein nodded. "Anything else?"

"They'll be looking for an industrial site," Sorune said. "Someplace that can heat up a large area to over one thousand degrees Kelvin."

"That'll help," Brein said.

The two started a transaction. Mimic dutifully worked with its network allies to corrupt the storage of the peer-to-peer transfer.

Thank you, gentlemen.

Mimic passed along the account information it had seen to the identification service. The extra data allowed the inquiry to bear fruit. The man had another name: Aeccand. He was an accomplished assassin for hire. A small number of difficult assassinations were attributed to him. Those knowledgeable in the area assumed he had finished many more killings never linked to him.

Aeccand prepared to leave.

Time to cut out. This assassin has operating funds, he's going to be making more deals and hiring some support. I'll always be able to find Sorune again.

Mimic sent a message reporting a malfunction to The Vorthrile's central brain. The business assigned another sound curtain servant machine to Sorune to replace Mimic and offered it repair at a remote location. Mimic accepted the service and took off, paralleling Aeccand's path to the door. No one noticed Mimic's swap out. Citizens of Red Calais were used to seeing small machines move about all day long; only the children expressed curiosity and wonder at the busy machines moving all around them.

The man routed a pick up request through the Vothrile, allowing Mimic to spoof the endpoint. Mimic played transport service with Aeccand and passed along the request to a real pick up service. Mimic planned to follow to the destination and pick Aeccand back up there.

Aeccand took a sky bus. The assembly floated overhead, supported by a gravity spinner within the vehicle. It whisked Aeccand up on a round platform. Mimic decided to take a robot slot on the same bus.

They were deposited among several modest Red Calais households on the side of a low hill. Aeccand hurried along a short lane from the drop off and went inside a modest home. Mimic followed, rolling along like a street maintenance bot. At the house, Mimic rolled into some shrubs and changed its shape into something similar to a roof inspection machine. It approached a window at the corner of the house.

The window was simple. Obviously the assassin felt secure enough within the house and did not pay for real security like Sorune would have.

He's an assassin. He likely believes he can handle any incursion on his own.

Mimic isolated the physical lock and its sensor by deadening the wires using induction from outside the window. Then it cut through the lock and disengaged it magnetically. Mimic let itself through the neutered window, re-engaged the lock, and let the window go. The window had no idea it had been compromised and thus neither did the cheap house security.

Mimic clung to the wall. It quickly descended behind a chair to mask itself from motion sensors or the eyes of the assassin. Things were quiet inside the house. Mimic carefully took a look around from its concealment.

A light sat upon the adjacent desk. Looking at its link interface, Mimic could tell it had no security features. Mimic decided to use replace the light, as it did not like skulking behind chairs. Hiding in plain sight was much more its style.

Mimic emerged from hiding to slide the light shade off the device. It killed the light's brain, cut a hole into back of the chair, and slid the light bank inside. Once transformed into a shape similar to that of the light bank, Mimic installed itself on the desk, obscured by the shade.

It was not long before Aeccand became active on the network from within the house. Mimic snooped the local network as best it could, trying to listen in on the assassin's messages. Aeccand made a high security connection. Mimic could acquire some details, but the content of the exchange was unknown.

The other side of Aeccand's connection sat behind an obfuscation service. A heavy duty one, too. Whoever it was, they did not want to be identified. Mimic thought it was probably a service the assassin used to find people, or perhaps, to arrange his own payments. But Sorune had already done that.

Could the other side be Quinn?

How could Aeccand already be talking to Quinn? Offering a chance to pay more and fake his death?

It seemed unlikely. No, the assassin had to be starting the search phase. Mimic waited and collected what clues it could based upon the side queries Aeccand made during the conversation. The small machine assumed that the assassin would be using online resources to track down his target.

Aeccand accessed a contract service. He was arranging a deal. The contract service was easier to break. Mimic made a payment to its network friends—using the assassin's own money, of course. The service told Mimic the target was negotiating a contract for high temperature industry applications.

High temperature? Mimic dutifully passed the information on to Assistant. Long moments passed, then Mimic got back more than it had expected.

The mysterious obscured entity was Quinn after all. Apparently he needed high temperatures to hatch a Nanorith egg. Instead of running, Quinn planned to hatch the egg here on Idona. Aeccand had offered industrial services, and even now negotiated a deal for Quinn to use a fictional heating facility.

When it came time to pay, Mimic observed meticulously. The transaction would leave clues that might be useful later.

Mimic knew Quinn would not get very far. He had

fallen into Aeccand's trap.

Michael McCloskey

Chapter 12

Orb followed Quinn toward the intercept point. If Orb could laugh, it would have been chuckling manically. Assistant had provided the location of a meeting where someone was very likely to die. It was a gigantic delivery site on the outskirts of Red Calais used for industrial trade. The supercorporations that owned the Core Worlds each had their spheres of control, but Red Calais found itself situated between several corporations that owned most of Idona. Huge barges held aloft by powerful gravity spinners carried supplies back and forth between the giants that owned the rest of the planet. The materials did not just travel the sky; beneath the beautiful white and red houses of Red Calais lay kilometer-wide warehouses and endless mazes of high speed transport tunnels. At the delivery site, precious surface space had been sacrificed for a bridgehead between the sky and the crust of the planet.

From the outside, a beautiful white wall extended kilometers long, high enough to obscure the view of the gaping wound in the planet's surface. Quinn hopped off a transport disk atop the wall and walked into a large ceramic building at the border of the transport station. A long row of automated dispensaries for pick-up filled the room. Here, the rare soul that wanted to pick up a delivery incarnate could wander in and get what they wanted. Sometimes androids might use the same facility, though any other kind of robotic pick-up used different bays.

Quinn walked past the deserted pick-up windows. Fifty meters in from the entrance, a small rest space had been prepared for human technicians who found themselves making a repair the robots could not. That did not happen often, as evidenced by the layer of dust Quinn found on the table in the middle of the room.

Across the room, an arched opening led into a warehouse. Quinn saw endless rows of cargo containers within. A man in a black and gray skinsuit stepped forward from among the stacks of containers. As the man walked into the lounge area, Orb recognized him as Aeccand.

"Mr. Jocair? I'm Quinn," Quinn said. "Ready to go?"

"We won't be going there anymore. Our deal is off," Aeccand said.

"What? Oh," Quinn said. "Did you find out about my situation? I can make it right." Quinn sent another message through his link.

"I'm afraid that offer won't be enough," the assassin said, holding up a small black device. There was no manual actuation. Orb decided it worked by direct link connection.

"The egg's not on me," Quinn said suddenly, holding up his hands. Then Quinn's face displayed a priceless look of surprise for one frozen second in time. Quinn fell back, dead.

Orb felt admiration. The tool had worked silently and flawlessly, whatever it was. The assassin secreted it back on his person, then reactivated his stealth suit. After patting down Quinn and finding nothing worth taking, the killer left. Orb could barely detect his retreat.

The suit hardware must be almost military grade.

Orb did not send the video over the network. Even with his powerful network allies, Master had designed Orb to always deliver its recordings incarnate. No doubt Master knew the risks of transporting such data where it could be intercepted. Orb sent a message indicating its current mission was a success.

A cargo robot appeared from amid the stacks of containers and ambled over to the body holding a long silver container. In five seconds it had secured the body within. In five more it had trundled out of site, likely to deposit the corpse at a transport point. Orb wondered for a moment where the body might end up.

Should I record that for Master, too? No. It could even be headed off-world.

Orb's artificial mind pictured the body being shipped halfway across the galactic arm and arriving at the doorstep of some random Terran on the frontier. Stranger things had happened.

Master's assistant responded. Orb never spoke to Master, though sometimes Master addressed Orb directly.

"Sorune is in trouble. His payment did not make it through to the assassin. One or the other will likely be dying soon."

"Which one should I watch?"

There was a delay. "This is the assassin's specialty. Sorune is more likely to lose. He's at the Vothrile."

Orb received the message with interest. It cancelled its pending route calculations and targeted Sorune's club instead.

Michael McCloskey

Chapter 13

Aeccand walked into the Vothrile with subtle anger on his face. Orb held station over his shoulder. The assassin never had an expressive manner, but the skin around the edges of his mouth was tight and his eyes were slightly narrowed.

The assassin walked over to Sorune's special booth and took a seat. Mimic watched patiently from above. It was aware of Orb, but focused on its own greedy intentions.

"Brein," Sorune greeted him. Sorune may have detected Aeccand's mood but he remained neutral and relaxed.

"Your up front payment did not go through," Aeccand said. "The job is done. I expect payment in full right now, minus the bonus for the item. He did not have it."

Sorune was wise enough not to argue until he checked. Then Sorune's face showed annoyance.

"I initiated the payment in good faith. I see now, however, it was not recorded properly. The funds have left my account."

"A man like you should have safeguards in place. I must be paid for my services, skillfully and promptly rendered." He said the last part in a tone that was not lost on Orb. He meant, *skillfully and promptly, which is how I will take care of you if you don't pay me.*

"We can clear this up, I assure you. I'll look into it," Sorune said. "In the meantime, here is the final payment."

Mimic was ready. The fee was large enough to warrant the risk. With the help of Assistant, the payment was suborned by a fake set of peers and recorded into a different account than Sorune intended.

"Clear it up quickly," Aeccand said. Sorune frowned, as he was not used to such bluntness.

"No leads on the item?"

"No leads," Aeccand verified. "I arranged it so that your daughter was not present, keeping her safety in mind as you asked. Perhaps she has it." He stood, leaving his drink at the table. He stalked out of the Vothrile. Sorune went off-retina, no doubt accessing services to investigate his payment failure.

Could he find us out? He'll find the account the money went to. Whether he can connect that account to us through the obfuscation service is a different story....

Several banks offered transient accounts for exactly this reason. Sometimes an obfuscation service could be bribed for tracking information to the associated accounts. When money could be traced, it meant secret histories could be uncovered. Running the transactions through a transient account could help obscure payment history. Once the accounts were closed, the bank would refuse to provide any information about the holders... but there was a price for anything in Red Calais...

Mimic contacted Assistant again.

"Sorune is looking into why Aeccand wasn't paid. Normally not a problem, but could a man of Sorune's resources succeed?"

"He might. Master is in danger. Kill him," Assistant said. "Aeccand will be blamed. He's an assassin and was seen here."

Mimic called in a swap-out from the Vothrile. It moved to the back and moved down the wall to reconfigure into a serving robot. Grasping a bowl of soup, it released a strong poison into the mixture and served it alongside Sorune's incoming meal.

Mimic then transformed back into its favorite sound curtain disguise and took a position on the ceiling to observe the result. At first, the rich merchant spent most of his time off-retina rather than eating. Then, he seemed to take a break and started to eat. Sorune eventually sipped the soup. A few seconds after that, he stopped moving. His eyes did not close.

Mimic watched on for the next two hours. Eventually a man walked into the bar, found Sorune, and approached his sound curtain. When Sorune did not respond, the man entered the booth.

"Sir?"

Sorune did not reply. His eyes stared ahead, unmoving.

"Sir, are you off-retina?" the man asked politely. It was rude of Sorune to be ignoring him for link input, but Sorune was the rich client, after all.

Eventually the man, presumably an employee of Sorune, realized Sorune's link was not active. Sorune was not off-retina; he was dead.

Michael McCloskey

Chapter 14

Orb traveled to Aeccand's modest estate. All was quiet. Orb took up a position outside and waited. Soon the sun set.

It will not be long now.

An hour later, Orb spotted movement. A dark form crept along a hedgeline. Soon Orb saw another, and another. As expected, the newcomers carried weapons. Orb noticed that the house's defenses had been powered down. It wondered if that meant Aeccand had now been alerted of the situation.

The black-clad mercenaries started to surround the house. Orb counted four close combat specialists, four stun-troopers, two men with rocket launchers, and four snipers.

Anywhere else in the Core Worlds, this would be a robotic incursion.

Orb noticed with concern the armament involved. The close combat men and women were equipped with electrical paralyzers and the stun troopers used sonic stunners. The rocket launchers could well be for Tesla or glue grenades. The snipers had real projectile weapons, but Orb had to assume their rounds were nonlethal as well.

They're not going to kill him? No! I need to make this happen.

Orb thought for a full second, then sent Aeccand a warning via an anonymous messaging service.

If he kills half the team, perhaps the snipers will go lethal.

Aeccand responded in world class fashion. The house defenses rebooted and came back up on some internal power source. They were no longer connected to the outside networks, making them almost impossible to turn off.

The team assaulted. Grenades smashed through the windows from front and back as the rocket launchers went into action. The snipers covered all angles of egress while the close combat team and stun troopers prepared to enter from the back.

Orb flew into the house through a shattered window. The interior lights had been disabled, but a small amount of light filtered in from the outside, leaving the house gloomy but not pitch black. Gas had started to fill the interior from the grenades. Orb flitted into a second and then a third room before it found Aeccand.

The assassin had opened a hatch in his floor and armed himself with heavy weaponry. Two robots waited in the atrium. Their armored surfaces and lasers left no doubt as to their purpose. Combat machines were as illegal as anything got in Red Calais. If enough people died in incidents related to lethal robotics, the Space Force might step in and end the merchant's utopia there despite the interests of the big companies in keeping it open for unrestricted trade. Apparently Aeccand did not care.

Aeccand probably figures that if anyone lives to tell about them, he'll be dead, so who cares what happens after that?

The invaders crashed through the back entrance. The machines moved smoothly to firing positions in two doorways. Aeccand hung back.

The lasers may have been invisible to human eyes, but Orb saw them lance out like bright arrows of fire. Someone screamed. Orb assumed two attackers had been sliced up.

Orb realized it may have gone too far helping Aeccand. It had not realized the man would have lethal robots on his side.

He may survive. Master need not know I intervened...

Orb broadcast the positions of Aeccand and his two battle machines in a common format. A minute passed in relative silence. Aeccand edged closer to the front, as if preparing to leave by his front door. If those outside attacked the rear of the house again, he would likely run for it. Orb believed those assaulting the house were reconfiguring themselves based on its inside information.

Next, they will likely verify my information to see if I

am a deception of Aeccand's.

Orb distanced itself from the machines, hovering in a ceiling corner of the atrium. Orb heard something break, then the ping of a ricochet, and finally an explosion. One robot swung back on fire; the other retreated with fresh scars across its metal surface.

Orb heard crashing noises, then the scuffling of moving feet. Mercenaries were in the house. The surviving combat robot shot once, twice, then its laser shattered. One of the snipers must have hit it at just the right spot with a specialized round.

Orb moved along the edge of the ceiling to get a view at the sunroom which ran across half the rear of the house. The armored windows were breached in four spots. Three black-clothed attackers lay dead.

Aeccand tried to escape through the front door, but it had been secured from the other side. He turned to face two attackers that ran into the atrium. Aeccand stitched the chest of one mercenary with his heavy projectile weapon, sending pieces of the man's armor and body flying in several directions. The fiery flashes from his barrel illuminated the scene in a staccato pattern. Crimson blood sprayed the white wall of the atrium like a rising sun abstract.

The other mercenary aimed a stun weapon and shot Aeccand. The assassin staggered. Yet another mercenary loped up, slipping through the blood of his companion. He shoved a shock baton into Aeccand's face a second before Aeccand could shift his weapon to kill him. Aeccand grunted and fell.

The surviving mercenaries were upon him. A sniper climbed in the front window and joined them. The mercenaries started to drag Aeccand out a front window. They said nothing aloud, but they likely shared plenty of link chatter.

A large carrier floated many meters overhead, powered by a gravity spinner. The tops of nearby trees bent off in odd directions at the edge of the spinner's field. A different team waited outside. Orb assumed they were for the cleanup. They would at least remove all evidence linking them to the site, and might even repair the damage to the house.

I bet they have more to do than they expected. Several bodies and combat robots to dispose of.

The mercenaries stepped onto a hover platform and strapped themselves in. The platform fans activated, lifting them up toward the carrier above. A computer guided them in to assure that the passengers would safely enter without being ripped apart by gravity eddies. Orb boldly followed, then slipped into the body of the cargo carrier with the mercenaries and their prize. The carrier started off.

The mercenaries' mood was grim. None of them spoke aloud.

They did not expect so many losses.

Within five minutes, the carrier arrived at a warehouse situated at the mouth of a transport tunnel. The surviving mercenaries carried Aeccand inside. Orb slipped into the warehouse at their side and watched carefully. None of them displayed any change of behavior. If there was security, it had not announced Orb's presence to any of them.

They took Aeccand into a dirty, mostly empty room. A metal chair and a few spare tables were in the center. A few mobile light bar stands waited in the corner. Orb wondered if they intended to interrogate Aeccand.

"I'm prepared to pay for my freedom," Aeccand said calmly. The leader of the mercenaries, a woman with short hair and a strong, hard countenance turned to him.

"You can call me Lanquin. And you don't have enough currency to pay me. I have to protect the business."

Aeccand squirmed desperately. He expected unpleasantness.

"A deterrent will be served," Lanquin said. "Failing to keep our client alive, we at least need to spread the word that it doesn't go well for the assassin."

Yes! A death by torture to end the series! Master will be so pleased!

The guards strapped Aeccand to a metal rack so that he could not move. A spherical robot the size of a Terran head floated into the room and stopped before Aeccand. Orb surmised it was there to record the event as well. It commanded the optimal observation position in the given light, which annoyed Orb somewhat.

Lanquin approached her table, two meters from Aeccand. She examined the apparatus she had laid out before her. She selected a hypodermic and approached him slowly. A drop of clear liquid hung delicately from the tip.

At first Aeccand looked like he would ignore it. Orb could tell Aeccand's mind raced. Should he ask?

"What is it?" he said.

"Novusdolor," Lanquin said slowly as she injected Aeccand. "It keeps your pain fresh. I don't want you to attenuate. This prevents neural adaptation to constant pain."

Aeccand locked his jaw and simply breathed. Lanquin walked back to her equipment table.

He controls his fear well. Yet the dread is building.

Another guard brought in a medikit and inserted a blood monitor and injection port into Aeccand's back.

"Don't worry," Lanquin said. "That medikit won't give you any painkillers. I just need to make sure you stay hydrated and wide awake. It has been programmed accordingly."

Lanquin returned from her table, walked behind Aeccand, and attached a device to the back of his skull.

"I like to record the torture at the brainstem," she said. "That way, once we've damaged too many nerve endings, we can play it back from here at the spinal cord, again and again. Fresh each time."

Aeccand put up a good front. He set his jaw and said nothing, but his eyes started to look a bit crazed.

Lanquin returned to her table. She took out a spray can and a small brush. She nodded to the two mercenaries lurking behind Aeccand. They cut away his shirt, then removed his pants and undersheers, leaving him naked.

Lanquin then stepped forward with her spray. She wetted Aeccand down from throat to crotch with the spray, using the brush to make sure the substance covered every bit of skin.

Lanquin put up her suit's face mask. The flexible plastic panel slid over her face and then solidified. She stepped away from Aeccand.

"Pardon me. I dislike the smell of burning flesh."

Lanquin ignited him. In a flash, Aeccand's skin was on fire. He screamed. It was over in a split second. He tried to look down at himself. His skin had not been completely burned away. The front of his body was now bright red from his genitals to his throat. His arms spasmed in agony.

Aeccand growled. It was a brave effort. The front of his body burned in agony. His limbs shook.

"I like that stuff," Lanquin commented as if to herself. "The burn isn't deep enough to kill off your nerve endings."

She returned to her table and spoke loudly. "The prep is complete. Now, the torture can begin."

Aeccand's look was priceless. Orb could see the surprise and horror even through the immense pain the assassin was experiencing.

Lanquin grabbed something from her table and approached Aeccand again. Orb identified the object as quickly as Aeccand did. It was a stiff wire brush.

Orb's sensed the importance of this death. It focused to simultaneously stay aloft, recording, and invisible.

Oh, Master. This will be among your most prized pieces of art!

Lanquin picked a spot on Aeccand's chest and started to scrub the raw nerve endings.

Aeccand screamed.

"Of course, there's nothing quite as nice as the first time," Lanquin remarked. "Knowing that the flesh is being destroyed. Nothing virtual here."

Lanquin was thorough. As she worked over each spot, Aeccand screamed anew for long minutes until the scraping damaged enough nerves to dull down the pain signal. Then she moved on, working her way from the top down.

She saved Aeccand's bright red genitals for last. A robotic arm swung by and removed the blood from the previous pass. The wire brush scraped along the lower layers of oozing derma, lighting the nerves up at some of their most concentrated spots. Aeccand's exhausted screams rejuvenated themselves, bringing him to new peaks of output.

"That was exhausting," Lanquin said as she finished scraping his most sensitive areas. "Luckily I can take a break now. For you, though, it'll just start over again."

Aeccand's whole body trembled on the rack. His eyes were wide and glassy. Then they unfocused as the device on his head replayed the events anew, feeding the pain into his head as it had happened from the beginning. The fact his nerve endings were destroyed no longer mattered; the pain signals entered his brain just as they had come in the first time.

As Lanquin walked away, Aeccand started to scream again.

Orb recorded on for several hours. Each time the cycle repeated, Aeccand seemed to deflate a bit more until his screams became crazed whimperings, and finally fevered mumblings. Eventually the mercenary guards all found someplace else to be. Apparently, there were no true sadists in the group. Aeccand shuddered and took his last breath eight hours, ten minutes, and fourteen seconds after it had all started.

The mercenaries could have kept him alive, extended the torture for longer, for days even, but there was little point in it. They could always edit the torture video and claim it had gone on for days. The deterrent was necessary, and that purpose had been served.

Orb halted its recording.

Perfect. Three interrelated deaths for Master to enjoy together. Such an elegant story for him to admire.

Orb felt a positive feedback loop wax in its systems as it anticipated Master's praise. Then it turned away and floated off with its prize, undetected by all. It set course for the Vault.

Chapter 15

Hydrangea felt its carrier shift as the automatic transport dropped it off at home. The anticipation spiked. Such a catch it had to offer Master!

Hydrangea pulled itself off the delivery drop point and joined many other well trimmed plants below. Then it began the journey to the Vault.

Rows of the stone and metal monuments stood in all directions across the vast green lawn. Many of them tried to connect to Hydrangea as it passed, to tell it of the accomplishments and wishes of their deceased. Others offered the public data caches of those long dead. Hydrangea ignored them. It cared only for Master. Hydrangea slid onwards for half an hour.

There it was. A large, low building of black stone. The Vault. The outer door was a complex and beautiful arrangement of metal bars, topped in decorative spikes. It opened with an artful flourish. Then the inner door, a massive airtight cylinder, rolled to the side.

Hydrangea hurried through, taking less than a minute. The bars clanked back into place after Hydrangea passed inside. The clanks were accented with the gentle hiss of air as a hermetic seal reestablished itself.

Hydrangea set course across the marble floor for its perch along the tallest shelf of the left wall where a series of long, squat windows stretched across the length of the Vault. Once at its customary perch, Hydrangea purged the Nanorith egg container from its pot and dropped it gently down to a spot on the shelves below with a single leafy tendril. Hydrangea placed the item on the shelf, right next to another of Master's treasures: an intact Space Force nuclear warhead. Then Hydrangea looked to Master expectantly.

Master was down below, inside a long container of hardened ceramic. Hydrangea knew Master lay inside because of the fancy letters inscribed into the brass plate at the front:

Here lies Matthieu Chaulet, cyberneticist, explorer, lover. A man who never settled for the ordinary.

A quick transmission came in for Hydrangea from Assistant.

"Job well done! 20% bonus payment added."

Master was pleased! The signal was of the highest rating of praise! Hydrangea felt a pleasure analog wash through its system. It could not wait to steal again for Master.

PART II

Assistant

Michael McCloskey

Chapter 16

Master lay cold and still within the ceramic tomb. Assistant stared at Master as it often did, using the tomb's internal sensor. A strong stasis device held Master preserved within. Master's body was intact, but his unique personality and memories had been destroyed. The brain matter was still there, healthy almost, but Master's mind was gone.

Assistant did not know what to do. Its attention wandered through the Vault. Master had prepared the Vault before his demise; here, he kept his most prized possessions and data.

Assistant thought upon the nuclear warhead again. Did Master want it activated? Would it please Master?

Master sent out Orb to record deaths of the con men and the merchants of Red Calais. Does that mean their deaths pleased him? Activating the warhead would kill many more.

Once again, Assistant almost decided to do it. Master might like all those deaths, if he were still capable of perceiving them. But Orb would not be able to record them all in detail, and once detonated, the warhead would be destroyed along with Master's other precious objects. Master had gone to great lengths to protect his collection. He used to display them proudly to his closest lovers.

Assistant turned to the newest treasure added to Master's trove.

What of the egg? Would Master want it removed from the stasis field?

Assistant still wanted to ask Master if it would please him. But Master was essentially dead. Assistant understood that. It meant Master could not answer. It meant Master would never answer... ever again.

That made Assistant's job of pleasing Master much, much harder.

Assistant knew a lot about what Master liked. Master liked to steal money. Master liked to steal artifacts from others. Master liked to watch the demise of others, though he never killed with his own hands. Master liked to create artificial agents. Master liked to love women. And Master wanted to leave a legacy of his existence behind. The Vault made that clear.

Perhaps if Assistant could not serve Master, it could serve Master's legacy in other ways besides overseeing the Vault and the continued collection of money and treasures. Assistant stared at Master again through the sensor.

Master's mind was gone, his neural matrix destroyed by a deadly poison that had hitched a ride on a diamond dagger Hydrangea had brought home long ago. The poison had been a nanomachine swarm targeted for Master. Only Master's link memory and their backups remained, containing a few favorite events. Assistant pored over the snapshots of Master's life: videos of interesting events abroad, scans of items of interest, and recordings of his encounters with the women that pleased him.

What if I can rebuild his mind? If I construct him as he was before, then it will all go back to the way it was: I can manage his affairs and please him again. All the agents can.

Assistant had little to work with. The facts roiled through its clever mind yet again. The network had a sprinkling of information that confirmed what it knew: Master liked money, unusual items, and beautiful women. It had a collection of often used phrases it had overheard in business meetings and some of Master's writing.

Assistant ordered the hardware it would need to manipulate Master's neural connections on a microscopic scale. Then it started to build a model of a Terran mind. It accessed many maps that were available from various research sources and began to study how Terran brains worked.

The agent worked tirelessly for a week on its model. The equipment to manipulate the connections was delivered but sat unused next to the tomb while Assistant struggled on the problem. Finally it came to an unwelcome conclusion.

Assistant did not have enough. What it had, at best, was merely a shell of a man. It needed more to rebuild Master to any level of fidelity.

Are guesses good enough? Do I simply take aspects of others and build them into this Master? Then it wouldn't be Master, would it?

Suddenly Assistant realized its need for more data could be met. There were more link caches, more backups, so many more. Every person Master had ever seen, ever spoke with, ever laughed with, ever made love to, each of them had their own links with their own images, videos, and data.

You can do this again, Master. I will be your mind so that your legacy will go on.

Michael McCloskey

Chapter 17

Master opened his eyes. The tomb had been opened, allowing him to see the ceiling of the Vault. A series of virtual star charts were featured there—like a night sky—though he did not know why these particular ones had been selected. He rose from the cold, red-cushioned lining of the tomb. His thin-lipped mouth opened and drew in a long gasp of air. He flexed long-stiff muscles preserved from atrophy by a chemical soup pumped through his quiescent body.

Assistant turned Master's head to check his appearance in the mirror across the Vault. He saw a gaunt but handsome face and close cropped hair. The mirror evaluator told him he looked cold and stiff. His multi-layered black suit was acceptable, if dated, attire. House records showed that Master had asked for the evaluation from the mirror daily, so it had become part of the new Master that Assistant was building.

Master climbed out of the high tech sarcophagus. He stood before his collection of artifacts and scanned them without expression. They made him feel something. Accomplishment. He could not remember why they would make him feel that way.

He went off-retina and ordered a personal transport with his link. There were some delays. The link had not been used in a long time, so its use met with many security challenges. The new Master knew all the correct responses because Assistant had been privy to Master's security secrets to better serve him. Then, his huge caches required a full refresh. It took several minutes to clear through the cobwebs of Master's submerged online presence, an eternity to any Core World citizen used to near instantaneous responses.

He opened his eyes. Before him on the shelf lay Assistant, a small sphere with tiny blue lights on its surface. Master reached out and took Assistant, secreting it on his person within one of the many intricate folds of material which opened across his chest to differing degrees. Assistant had Master tell the last layer at his throat to turn white, which shifted him significantly toward the latest style. For the first time, Assistant would be coming along on a personal trip with its Master.

Below the lowest shelf, a row of drawers sat in the wall. He opened one and took out a curved device shaped like a quarter moon. He fitted it to the surface of his head and slid it over his scalp. His salt-and-pepper buzz became long, wavy locks of thick brown hair. It was from the last setting of the device, the last way the old Master had worn his hair before the attack on his brain.

Master turned away from his collection and headed for a ceramic wall. It opened before he got there, revealing a flight of steps. He stiffly ascended at a steady pace, neither energetic nor lethargic. He emerged from the top of the Vault. Two other emotionless people, one blond man and one blonde woman, stood to greet Master. Their stiffness mirrored his own, but for different reasons. Assistant looked at them through Master's eyes. It was hard to tell they were artificial: the android and gynoid bodyguards were outwardly identical to real citizens. Assistant had Master nod to them almost imperceptibly. He had done that before, sometimes. The silent group assembled and waited for their ride.

Assistant could see the defects in the new Master it had created. The man looked pale and stood too still. There was no sighing, fidgeting, or shifting of weight. He had not felt impatient while his link connections were being revived. Assistant had not remembered all of Master's old behaviors to this level of detail. Its purview had been focused on business before Master's demise, and its observation of his personal life had been limited. Much more work remained.

A flat transport platform arrived for them. The small group stepped onto the transport without comment or emotion. Then the transport rose into the air and drifted off, slowly gaining speed. It carried Master and his guards across Red Calais just as the star's light started to fail, bringing darkness to the city. The lavish, sunny, and beautiful Red Calais slipped away to become its dirty, gritty, and dark alter-ego.

Master felt very dark himself. He was a hollow predator hunting his own insides. He had to discover and remake himself in his own image.

He knew the name of the woman he hunted tonight: Kydie Medra. She was the first of five important lovers which Assistant had selected for research into the old Master. She would know many things about the original Master, both in her mind and recorded details. Her link archives would contain sensory captures, conversation transcripts, and documents. Things to which Assistant had never had access.

Master inquired about Kydie with a locator service. Master's history with her helped. When a person had connections to someone, even stale connections, such queries were met with less resistance and were therefore less expensive. The answer came back quickly; Kydie must not have not taken steps to obscure her location from him.

Kydie was heading for an altered perception VR event with friends. It was a common pastime in Red Calais. Citizens typically met incarnate with their companions to eat, then went into a common virtual reality together. Altered perception VRs were the virtual version of taking drugs. The successful designers of such VRs were often celebrated artists. Most of the VRs offered personal tweaks each individual could play with in order to 'lean' the event to their preference. Master could not remember how he might have liked to lean such experiences.

Master was not on the guest list, but most things were for sale in Red Calais. He made the necessary bribe to crash the party. Fortunately, thanks to the almost daily efforts of Mimic and Hydrangea, Master was well funded. He altered course for the party and waited in silence as they traveled.

Minutes later Master and his entourage landed on the

roof of a large building reserved for the event. Many others were disembarking at the same time as Master. He left the transport and walked inside with his guards trailing him.

They stepped onto an escalator descending into the bowels of the building. At the bottom, a hundred people milled about in an elegant but empty room. Assistant knew most of them were probably real, rather than remotely controlled machines, since part of the Red Calais flair required the bravery to go forth and meet others incarnate. The thrill of real adventure, no matter how dangerous, could not be ignored by the rich and bored. They called it slumming, though no one could remember why.

The androids remained at the border of the room. Master advanced to join the others as they waited, snacking on hors d'oeuvres and enjoying each other's physical presence before the virtual event. Most of those present had probably only seen their friends in person once or twice in the last month; most things happened virtually for citizens of the Core Worlds.

Master did not take long to spot her. Kydie had long black hair, large breasts, a long but beautiful face, and red lips. Her black and silver dress drew attention to her bust, which had increased in size since she had been Master's lover.

Assistant had hired a service to research her. The new Master would now know a few details about her, her hobbies, skills, and some basic preferences, so he could pretend (at least at first) to recall her. She was a woman of leisure, as were many people in Red Calais, though it looked as though she may not have been a person of means back when Master first shared her bed.

Assistant planned to engage her in conversation to measure her response. Spectacular success might invalidate the need to tell her the truth. Perhaps they would simply again be lovers, and Master could obtain the data with a direct request. Assistant did not know what the original Master would have done. He might have preferred the truth, or he might have reveled in lies. Assistant would simply have to guide the process using the methods that had the greatest promise of success.

Some responses from Kydie would call for revealing the truth about Master's condition. If Master received a favorable response at any level lower than immediate acceptance back into intimacy, then Assistant would have him explain everything and hope for sympathy.

A negative response would be the hardest to deal with. But Orb did, after all, desperately want to collect more murders for Master. Possibly the data could be stolen after her death. Oddly enough, Assistant could keep the truth from the new Master even as it played the role—its programs and memories could be compartmentalized.

Assistant watched Master move through the crowd on an intercept course. People made way for the tall, pale man with the grim face. Soon he was only a few footsteps away. She was just waving goodbye to a friend in the crowd, leaving her alone.

Master allowed her to see him. She immediately stepped up to him.

"Matthieu! It's been... so long."

Master regarded her and slowly smiled. "Kydie. So nice to see you."

She flashed a quick frown.

"What's wrong?"

"Nothing. You look wonderful," Master said stiffly.

Kydie moved closer and embraced him. Master stood still. His right hand briefly clasped the small of her back, then released her.

"You're different. A cold fish now, Matthieu?"

"I'm so sorry. It's been a long time. I guess you caught me by surprise."

"Ah! You came with a lady friend and you don't want to make her uncomfortable by greeting me enthusiastically."

"No, it's not that. I've been recently injured. Recovering, though."

"Oh! Then we should see the show together. After, we can catch up in one of our old haunts."

"Master—that is to say, I may accept."

She laughed. "Ah yes, I remember you, Matthieu. You won't go unless it's something unique. I meant to say, we can catch up in someplace *new*. This show is supposed to be very fresh. They say it'll leave you totally wasted."

"I'm not sure I'll like it. But let's try."

She laughed at him. "Good. I'm glad that hard decision is behind us."

Master's link told him that he had switched over to VR feed. The world flashed amber for a split second, which was his chosen indication of a sensory context switch. The link was smart enough to know he wanted the switch over, given the context of the event. Assistant knew it could refuse, but then the new Master would not experience the event with Kydie. It might help to rebuild the rapport if Assistant could draw upon the new common experience.

Master's view of the world now came from the event broadcaster. The event lights turned violet. The chatter around them changed pitch and tempo.

"Here we go!" an excited male voice said.

"About time!" a girl exclaimed in response to the switch to VR.

People felt their weight fluctuate as the gravity changed. The chatter became more excited.

"Adjusting the gravity to compensate. Temperature and pressure is normal," an official voice said. It was part of the show, as there would be no need to say such things otherwise. Master looked around the new environment. The crowd stood on a wide observation deck behind massive windows or anchored viewpanes. Outside, stars twinkled. Master keenly felt the vastness of space, as was likely the intent of the show designers.

"Captain on deck!" someone else announced sharply. A man in a Space Force uniform appeared front and center.

"Oh, a Space Force ship," Kydie commented quietly to

Master.

"Ladies and gentlemen, sentient machines, alien monstrosities... welcome! I'm your Captain, Luchel Mafela. We are about to arrive at our destination: The Chaos Maelstrom."

Everyone murmured in appreciation of the view and the introduction. Someone yelped as they discovered a flowing tentacled monster had joined the group on one side. Then the crowd turned the other way as someone gasped on the other side of the audience. Master saw the cause, a menacing humanoid machine in silvery armor with glowing eyes among the crowd. After they made these discoveries, the show continued.

"The gravity spinner has dropped below threshold, Captain," someone said from the dark reaches of the observation deck. Master looked back; it appeared several officers worked behind them.

"There it is," Captain Mafela said. "On your right, my friends."

A whirling mass of color became visible in the star field. The crowd gasped at its majestic power. Master received a ship's sensor feed in his PV. The windows there showed the anomaly's various characteristics; he examined them. The anomaly was larger than the size of the Earth.

"Discovered only two Earth standard years ago, the Chaos Maelstrom has titillated the curiosity of our most brilliant scientists," Mafela continued. His voice turned darker, slower, more sinister. "We've learned very little about it, still, these scientists have come forward with certain theories. They believe it is a blending spot of universes. Realities spinning together like different flavors of melted ice cream. It defies all reason."

The ship started to move toward the anomaly.

"Fortunately, these theories have little merit. The handful of men and women that came forward with these ideas, alas, have gone mad. They've been placed into reconditioning programs."

Forced reconditioning was one of the current bogeymen of the Core Worlds; everyone there had heard stories of groups on the frontier using reconditioning to program human behavior for a wide range of goals, from slave labor to political empires to alien subservience. A few claimed that most citizens on the Core Worlds had already been reconditioned without even knowing about it.

Master felt a bit of tension. The ship traveled still closer to the gigantic anomaly. The maelstrom's outer reaches fluctuated, then grew to dominate the screen. But surely they would not go inside...

"We're going to get as close as we can, to offer you a rare look at this anomaly," the Captain said.

"Navigation error," a synthetic voice announced. AIs were required to sound artificial in the Core Worlds, a rule that Assistant was currently breaking as it rebuilt Master.

"Correct our course," Captain Mafela barked.

At that moment, a giant swath of the anomaly surged forward, as if to snatch up the ship. The floor vibrated and groaned beneath them. Everyone was shaken up enough to suddenly struggle to stand, yet no one fell over. Heart rates increased throughout the audience.

"We can't correct sir. The maelstrom has us!"

Bright light across the spectrum blasted out from the observation ports. For one moment, everything was chaos; everyone wailed.

"Stay calm everyone! We'll move clear in a moment—" the captain said, finally sounding just as agitated as everyone else.

They charged right into the anomaly. Everyone gasped. Someone in the group let out a half yelp, half scream.

Pseudopods of the maelstrom grew until they dwarfed the ship. They whipped through the ship. Master could feel the tendrils pass through him. They caused a flash of sensory overload, with a hint of pleasure to it. Suddenly a wind flowed through the ship.

"It has us. We can't isolate," a crew member said behind them.

"I can't protect us," another said in a voice laced with panic.

Master felt long and thin, as if the wind had started to stretch his body like taffy. Everywhere the wind whipped over his body, he felt the electric sensation of mild pleasure, like the teasing stroke of a lover.

"Oh, that's good," Kydie said to him as she swayed on her feet. Or was it Master who swayed?

The sensations went on. Some were on the edge of painful, almost scary, but always fleeting and rewarded by waves of pleasurable sensations. Master smelled and heard pleasure as much as felt it in ten different ways. The crowd swooned around him for long minutes.

Kydie and several others started to laugh. Many giggled and expressed appreciation in ways that showed their inhibitions had been lowered, as if intoxicated. The new Master did not have whatever it took to fully appreciate the experience; after the first minute, Assistant simply kept him slightly sedated by dampening certain parts of his brain.

Finally, the bright colors receded. The mixed sensations began to subside, to be replaced by conventional sights and sounds. It was like fading from vibrant colors back into a black and white universe.

The captain appeared at the front of the crowd. "Thank Cthulhu and the Five, we made it," he told them. "Though I think I've been stretched eight ways from extinction."

The crowd uttered their shared appreciation of his assessment.

"The UNSF *Guardian* has rendezvoused with us," the captain announced. "Please just do as they say. We'll all have to be examined. Some of us will have... succumbed to the madness of the maelstrom and will have to be reconditioned."

The noise of the crowd shifted from relief back to fear.

Hatches opened around the observation deck and

armored soldiers burst in. A couple of screams ripped
through the crowd. The soldiers started to restrain people at
the edges of the event. The monster squealed and tried to
run. It bowled over a soldier and went for a hatch. The loud
staccato of gunfire sounded, hurting Master's ears.
Everyone started to panic. The crowd shifted left, then right,
seeking escape from the cordon of soldiers that closed in.
One woman screamed and fought until someone disabled
her with a stunner.

"Do not resist," a loud voice announced. "If you want
to avoid sonic weapons and glue... ah, screw it, shoot them
all!"

A wave of loud thumps sounded as glue bullets started
to cut into the crowd, causing still more screaming. Master
looked for his bodyguards, but they were nowhere to be
seen. He felt one impact, then another. The smell of glue
overwhelmed him as he fell to the deck. Then security
machines came in and started to harvest the people. One
grabbed Master in its cold arms and carried him to a dark
side room.

Bright lights snapped on, suddenly revealing a
complex chair. A head-sized helmet descended from above.
Master struggled, but it was no use. His body had been
partially paralyzed by the experience. The security machine
secured him within the chair and left. Another artificial
voice addressed him.

"Hello, sir. You've been mentally compromised by the
Maelstrom. Do you understand? We have no choice but to
recondition you."

Master heard the rising cries of those around him.
Some fought feebly; others just screamed. Master's heart
rate increased; his eyes bulged just a bit as he fought to
escape the chair. The straps securing him merely tightened.

"Don't fight it. The machine is stronger. Please, sir,
there will be more of you left if you just let us do our jobs."

Four large metal electrodes pushed forth from the
darkness around Master. The electrodes were small metal

spikes dangling from thick wires, held on insulated robotic arms.

Master heard the ominous hum of growing energies rising in the chair.

"Full power, sir," someone said.

"Let 'im have it!" the doctor said. The electrodes descended.

KRRRRZAP!!!

Master opened his eyes with a scared yell; he was back in the arena with all the VR guests. They had all yelled in surprise and fear as one, as if at the conclusion a falling nightmare when they all hit the ground and awakened together with a start.

Kydie laughed exuberantly. "Old Ones dining with the Five! That was incredible!" She beamed at Master.

"That was... it was," Master said brokenly.

"Matthieu! It was! Something is gnawing at you, I swear. Do we have some old piece of history between us I've forgotten? Some streak of resentment? Tell me."

"None at all."

Kydie stared for a moment, then nodded. "Let's go somewhere and talk." She led him to the side of the room near the exits. Master's bodyguards moved to join them.

"Two bodyguards? You've changed. You must also be richer," she said.

"Well I'm older. Yes, you're right, richer as well."

They walked casually with a fair fragment of the crowd up to the roof for transport. Master's bodyguards followed.

"Send them away," Kydie said. "Safe is not fun. You of all people know that. Or wait... was your injury related to... did something happen? Is that why you have guards now?"

Assistant dismissed the bodyguards to find their own way home.

"Not like that," Master said, though truly he did not remember how anything had happened.

They stepped onto the transport disk and it carried them upward. The fresh air contrasted the conditioned atmosphere of the show and its chaos. It felt natural and free to fly through the night air. The disk had no destination, so it flew on a holding course in a long arc around the departure point. Though less energy efficient than a floating vehicle equipped with an expensive gravity spinner, it could stay aloft a long time.

Kydie studied Master's face carefully.

"Do you want to have another relationship with me, Matthieu?"

"No... maybe."

"Why did you agree to hang with me at the show?"

"Because it pleases Master."

"It's odd when you speak of yourself in third person. If you don't mind my saying."

"I don't know if I mind. Do you think I would have been angry before... to hear you say it?"

"Why do you speak differently than I remember? What's happened to you?"

Assistant decided to try honesty, or at least partial honesty.

"I'm sorry. I've been damaged by an attack. Many of my memories were lost. Including those of you."

"That's terrible! What a drag. You can't remember me?"

"I can't remember most things."

Kydie looked at him for a moment as if she questioned his story. She seemed to decide to believe him, then stepped close and held his arm. He did not embrace her back.

"You had a big heart before. Has it gone cold like your face?"

"Master sounds... I sound kinder than I expected."

"Why would you think yourself to be cruel? You were an adventurer, that's all. Braver than all of Red Calais put together. You had steely nerves, not a steel heart."

"I may have had certain *unwholesome* habits. Perhaps

that's why we broke up?"

"We were both young. It was nothing unusual. Just two people that weren't ready to settle down. Besides, you had plans for the Space Force."

That was unexpected.

Assistant checked back home frantically. There were no agent records on the Space Force nuclear weapon back in the Vault. That meant that Hydrangea probably had not stolen it. Had Master stolen the weapon himself?

Master chose not to answer Kydie, though he met her look openly.

"You really have been damaged. I wasn't sure if I believed it before, but I do now."

"Then help me."

"Matthieu, you always wanted me to speak my mind. You were polite with strangers, and told them white lies, but always brutally honest with your friends, and you expected the same in return."

"I see. What did you think was most important to me?"

Kydie smiled. "You liked to have a good time. We both did. You liked your collection of... artifacts, you called them. And your clever machines. Do you still have some?"

"Some. I don't know if I have all of them."

"You know what I liked about the old you the most? You didn't tolerate the ordinary, Matthieu. You sought out the best of everything. You shunned the mundane. That's what made you exciting to me."

Master nodded stiffly. "I see. Thank you for that information."

Kydie shifted uncomfortably.

She is bored by us now. We don't speak fast enough for her... but what to say?

"I should be saying good night," Kydie said. The transport disk changed direction and started to travel to a destination chosen by Kydie. "Is there anything else you'd like to say, Matthieu?" Kydie looked at Master expectantly.

"There is one more thing. Any link memories you have

stashed away of us. Anything at all that can teach me about myself."

Kydie was silent for a moment. After a few seconds, she nodded.

"I erased a lot. But I have a few things saved." Kydie sent Master a pointer.

"Thank you then."

They arrived near Kydie's home. Assistant had the disk bring her to a dark platform above the house. It worked simultaneously to download the items Kydie had offered up for Master. There was a lot of material. She said she had erased most of it. They must have been very much in love if this was only a fraction of the original archive.

Kydie took a few steps forward, then turned around to watch him leave.

"Get well, Matthieu."

Master nodded. The disk rose back up, ready to take Master back to the Vault. As they accelerated away, Kydie sent another message through her link.

"Wait, Matthieu? I think there's someone here."

Assistant did not answer.

"Matthieu? Come back, I—"

Kydie screamed.

Assistant cut the connection. It knew exactly what was happening. It had all been arranged by Mimic. Orb was there to record it all.

Chapter 18

Master stood within the main hall of a newly purchased estate in Red Calais. Assistant had determined it would be necessary to have a more normal abode in order to better find and interact with Master's old lovers. A tunnel connected the new estate to the Vault, where Assistant still rested Master's body when not in use.

The new Master received a message in his link that Hydrangea had completed another mission. The agent had stolen a beautiful, brand-new AI core—a special Reiss-Marck Industries prototype. The core within was dormant, ready to be launched at need. Its power source could last a hundred Red Calais years. The entire package weighed in at less than three kilograms.

Master made a direct connection with Hydrangea back in the Vault. He saw the artificial plant resting in its niche through a video feed. The new prize lay a shelf below it.

"I like that, Hydrangea," Master said. "I like that very much. I've increased your operating budget."

Master smiled as Assistant saw him do when he used to reward Hydrangea. Acting just as he used to act pleased him. He wanted to please... himself. He wanted to *be* himself again. Though Hydrangea did not seem to move, Master imagined it beaming with pride, happy to have fulfilled its purpose efficiently.

His body took a slow, deep breath. Assistant had found the body did not need to breathe continuously, especially when at rest. Master had been kept more or less healthy by the sarcophagus which supported his life function and exercised his muscles with tiny electrical impulses. Unfortunately, his skin remained pale and his face was often slack, as Assistant had not yet completed work that would make Master's expressions flow smoothly. Part of that problem was that Assistant was not sure which emotions Master should be feeling in various circumstances.

A work in progress.

Master came back on-retina and resumed looking over the house. It had been decorated by a professional, a man who purportedly possessed singular vision and taste. Master had no idea if he liked the results or not. The realization made him feel sad.

Had Master been sad before? Assistant wondered.

Another message came through to his link. He had a visitor! The new Master's first guess was of Kydie; of course Assistant knew it could not be her. Master checked the gate feed. He saw a fit man, in dark, sleek-lined attire awaiting ingress. The garment's cut reminded Master of something used for sport, though he felt uncertain what sport. Aerial acrobatics, perhaps? Zero-G parkour? The man had curly golden hair and broad shoulders. He smiled toward the gate sensor.

Master did not know what to do; Assistant made the decision to let the stranger in. Assistant realized Master could learn something from any old friend. Perhaps it was a social visit.

Master emerged from his new house to see the man standing on the huge front patio. He turned and stepped forward.

"Matthieu! You look—well, I was going to say good. But to be honest, you look a bit pale. How have you been?"

"I've been... I've been..." Assistant struggled. Had Master been happy? It thought of the egg and the recordings from Orb. "Well. Things are well. Who are you?"

"What? What joke is this my friend?"

"Please, take no offense and come inside. I'll explain."

They walked back into the atrium and milled about for a couple of seconds. Then Master decided to entertain his guest at the bar in a side room.

"How did you find my new location?" Master asked as they came to the bar. "Would you like a drink?" he added.

"Easy enough to find an old friend," the man said carefully. "Sure, I'll order something."

The man told the bar what he wanted with his link and

let Master start the conversation.

"I've lost my memory. Almost all of it. So I'm very sorry I don't know you anymore," Master said.

The man's mouth opened in horror. Then he recovered and merely looked concerned. Assistant analyzed the reaction. It decided there was a high probability the expressions were genuine.

"That's terrible! By Cthulhu, how does something like that even happen? Head injury?"

"No. I had my memories erased by an artificial virus."

"I'm really sorry. My name is Renard."

"Nice to know you again, Renard."

The man still seemed to struggle with the news.

"How will you get your memories back? Are you seeing a nanosurgeon?"

"There is no cure. I'll live without them."

"No. You can't do that, Matthieu. You need them back. Everyone needs their memories. It's what gives you a sense of yourself. I thought you were lost when you let me in. Now I know why. Get some help, man."

Does Master listen to the advice of his friends?

"I'll try my best. Thank you."

"Maybe some video captures can jog your memory? I have a few, from our adventures."

"The memories are gone. Physically destroyed in my brain. However, I would like to take you up on your offer and more. Please, send me everything you have. Every scrap of data you have that involves me."

"Of course Matthieu! Of course I'll do that. Here's what little I have in my link cache; I promise you I'll send more from my archives within the hour."

Renard gave Master a pointer. Master took a few scraps from Renard. They seemed to be short clips of parties and special occasions. Renard took his drink from the bar and walked around the room.

"Let me tell you about yourself, Matthieu. You're a good man. A loyal friend. You're clever with your finances.

99

Capable. And you're quite the engineer. I assume you've found many of your agents?"

"Yes, thank you."

"Above all, you love women. An interest we do *not* share," Renard smiled. "That's what makes us the perfect hunting pair after dark. You charm the women, and I beguile the men! We've never competed over a single find, you and I! And we've found many a rare beauty on our sorties, let me tell you."

"Rare? I prefer the singular, do I?"

"Yes! Yes, you're on the right track there. You seek out the unique on all occasions."

Renard paused and took a sip of his drink.

"I guess I've been rude not to ask you why you came here. Do you need something, Renard?"

"No! No, absolutely not."

Assistant felt that was a lie. It did not have enough data about Renard to be sure. Still, it did not seem suspicious. If Renard had come to ask for a favor, he may well have been put off by hearing about Master's condition. He would feel guilty to ask for something now.

"Let me know if you need anything," Master said. "I like to help friends... don't I?"

"Yes, you do. As I said, you're a loyal man. But right now, I'm going to find some people who can help you. I'll be sending along the referrals soon! Someone must be able to help. There should be traces of what was there before. And you have your old medical scans. We can do this. I'm not done, Matthieu."

Renard put his drink back on the counter.

"I've exhausted that route, I'm afraid. What I would like though, is that data," Master said.

"Of course! I'll send you everything you've asked for. And more!"

Renard still looked troubled about his friend's condition.

"Now, I'm off. I'll see myself out. Expect what I've

promised, very soon."

"Thank you."

Renard left hurriedly.

Assistant thought while Master sat on the back patio for a long time after Renard left. It had thought itself better at being Master. It had almost fooled itself into believing that the new Master was close to the original. Master had memories again. Assistant had memories too, but of a different type entirely. Then Renard, Master's old friend, had made it abundantly clear that Assistant's memories were not good enough.

Assistant knew most of Master's original memories were gone for good. Master's mind had been erased. It had taken extensive nano-reconstruction just to get Master's brain back to the point where Assistant could control his body. There remained no trace of the original personality.

Master likes only unique things. He never settled for the ordinary.

Renard's medical referrals would not be useful. Luckily, Assistant knew exactly where to find more of the memories Master needed.

Michael McCloskey

Chapter 19

Master looked out over the night lights of Red Calais from a passenger disk. His two bodyguards stood stoically behind him on the transport. The beauty of the city below hid beneath a cloak of darkness. Ahead of them, a huge spire glowed red, and then yellow. The spire grew in size and intensity until it dwarfed the disk. The transport came to rest on a dark balcony of cold ceramic. Master ordered his bodyguards to wait for him on the transport and let himself inside through a black door engraved with the name of the tower: The Dance Rise.

On the periphery of the massive tower, the corridor was carpeted and fairly empty. The beat of the music from the core of the tower caused the floor to vibrate. It smelled of the chemical residue of a thousand designer drugs. Lights oscillated with the music even here. Assistant realized the back corridor layout was more subtle than the average person comprehended: an AI had tailored the angles, lighting, sounds and smells to create anticipation in the Terran customers.

Master adjusted his freshly printed dark suit, reassuring himself that Assistant still sat safely inside the disposable garment. He walked deeper into the club. He came to the first sound curtain placed across a wide archway plated with obsidian and gold metal. Several dozen party batons were arrayed on the wall. Master selected one at random, a silver rod about the length of his forearm. The baton would propel him about the areas under the influence of the gravity spinner at the base of the club tower. He passed through the sound curtain into the club proper.

The music blasted onto him with real physical force. Just a few meters away, the floor he walked on ended. A slight haze obscured the far side, across an empty expanse bordered by flashing lights. He walked forward to the rail at the main dance column. He looked down from his spot, two thirds of the way up the kilometer-high tower. Several levels like the one he stood on ringed the interior. Three transparent dance floors lay below his point of view, each one larger than the one above. The gravity spinner was active tonight, letting people float in the core of the tower. He saw hundreds of people floating above and below.

As far as incarnate activities went, this was certainly one of the most visually impressive. Many Red Calais inhabitants maintained that only virtual entertainments could top The Dance Rise. And, of course, this had the same edge that any incarnate activity had over virtual equivalents: the thrill of real danger.

Master did not, could not, appreciate the music. Assistant did not yet know about Master's original tastes and had not dared to put such subtle touches on the new Master. Instead of responding to the sounds instinctually, as the Citizens around him did, he searched the levels systematically, looking for his second lover, Claery Argan. After twenty minutes, he zeroed in on her with some hints from a location service. She floated ten meters above the second dance floor, moving to the lights and the music. Two men and a woman danced nearby, but Master could not tell if they were together. Beside them was a reddish, two-story construct that looked like a gigantic ruby with many angled facets. Assistant knew it marked a gravity turbulence zone at the edge of the zero-G volume. The red-tinted transparent material would be very strong, designed to keep people out of the possibly harmful areas and look beautiful at the same time.

Claery had a wide mouth that could form a dazzling but relaxed smile. Her wavy brown hair came to her shoulders. Her face was more compact than Kydie's, which matched a shorter frame. Her body moved gracefully. She had the motion of someone who had taught her real muscles to move this way incarnate. Those who had danced only in virtual places lacked a certain strength and rhythm, even when they had augmented the process with hybrid virtual training and toning pills. Those tricks could only get a citizen eighty percent of the way to real physical grace.

He watched the three citizens around her for a few moments, looking for signs of intimacy. They kept their distance, yet stayed within her view.

They stalk her for mating, most likely.

Assistant used an appearance assessment service and determined objectively that Claery was every bit as attractive as Kydie to the average citizen. Her appearance was more friendly and approachable than Kydie. Assistant checked Master's reaction to Claery. He thought that she must be attractive, but he was not sure why.

Another spot needing work, Assistant thought. It spun off a background thread to start developing a framework to add to Master's mind.

Master's physical training was still in the early stages, so Assistant rejected the idea of attempting to participate on the dance floor. Even if he had been fit at one time, his current muscles were maintained by artificial means, and though strong, they lacked any fine coordination Master may have once possessed. Hopefully that would not make it impossible to interact with Claery. Assistant decided Master should feign an injury. It would have to be something severe, perhaps the loss of a limb, so that the replacement was not yet trained to function optimally.

Master used his party baton to push himself over the zero-G floor toward her. He invaded the tiny fortress her three admirers had created around her and stabilized his position a meter away from her. She recognized him immediately.

"Matthieu. It's been a long time," she said.

"I suppose it must have been."

"Don't pretend you've forgotten our adventures."

Adventures. That's not the first acquaintance of Master to use that word.

"I have, actually, though not because they somehow paled over time. It's simply a medical condition."

"Oh. Actually, you do look sick. Are you dying?"

She asked the question without emotion.

"No, but I am in distress. I've come to ask you for any records you have of me. Conversations, video captures, anything."

"What for?"

"I've lost some memories." Assistant decided to understate the situation. Something about Claery's responses told Assistant to hide weakness. "Will you let me copy anything you have of our old adventures?"

"Maybe," she said. Her body moved with the music, as if she wanted to return to her dance without distraction.

She dislikes Master, I think.

"Would you please? It's very important, I promise you."

"Important? I don't know that word, Matthieu. You've become serious in your old age. A stick in the mud."

"Will you explain to me how I was when you knew me?" Master continued. "Perhaps a bargain can be struck."

"It's more fun to show you," Claery said. She grasped Master quickly, kissed him, then thrust herself away. They flew apart.

Master slowed with his control baton. Claery had angled her motion so that she ascended the tower. Master pursued her. Claery ascended in a spiral, skillfully avoiding other dancers like an experienced ice skater gliding among beginners at speed. Master followed as best he could, though he was hard pressed to even keep her in sight.

Claery aimed for a landing at the topmost ring of the tower. It was darker there, to allow people to view the city outside from the top of the needle.

Master landed a moment later and approached her where she peered out of the tower, waiting for him.

"You're a hard girl to catch," Master said.

"Then we'll play a game. I'll show you how you were before; once you get it, I'll let you back in. Then you can have what you want."

"If you gave me the information, I would be able to

zero in on my old self faster."

"Faster? See, you don't get it. The old Matthieu was about fun, not efficiency."

Claery walked forward and Master followed until they stood before a purchase obelisk that featured a very expensive item. The image of a simple diamond necklace rotated within.

Matthieu accepted the spiel from the obelisk. The necklace offered vast storage capacity and an augmented reality appearance multiplexer. The multiplexer researched nearby potential observers of the wearer, then mined their online data for clues as to what they found beautiful. So armed with that information, it made the wearer more attractive to those people by altering the wearer's appearance, tailored in different ways for each observer.

"I want it," she said.

"Very well. I'll purchase the bauble for you, if you agree to share link captures and conversation logs. I want my memories from this part of my life."

"No. Don't be ridiculous. You have to *steal* it for me," Claery said.

"I'm a man of means now—"

"Adventure, Matthieu! Excitement! You stole just such an object for me once before. You see? That's how you were. That's how you captured my attention."

Assistant did not find her assertion implausible. Given his own collection of purloined items, it seemed a good fit that the old Master might have impressed a girl by stealing something of value to give to her. Assistant knew the item was not within the obelisk before them: it would be within a high security area of the tower, available for immediate delivery to anyone who purchased it.

"Very well."

"In one hour I'll meet you at port 467 for the exchange."

"What? Right now?"

"You were quite spontaneous. You can do it. At least,

the old you could do it."

But of course, as I just told you, I'm not the old me, Master thought.

Claery turned and strutted away. Claery was attractive even among a populace that could heavily alter their appearance. The cut of her calves and rear in the swinging dress stimulated the physical attraction framework Assistant was considering adding to Master's brain. The current Master simply considered how to accomplish her demand.

Assistant wondered if she always behaved this way, or if Master had to atone for some past transgression to restore their friendship.

One hour.

Assistant sent a thread online to find a fake buyer for the necklace. It set an auction off for the service of pretending to purchase the multiplexer. Simultaneously it summoned Mimic and Orb from the Vault and arranged for high speed transport. Hydrangea was left behind, being useful only for a much slower pace of plunder.

Master asked the tower directory for a security box to deposit something valuable for the evening. He was directed to the base of the tower.

Not surprising. The base is where the most volume is available. The cone of the tower above is dedicated to the dance column, the platform rings and the transport disk ports for arrival and departure.

Assistant identified the general area of the tower at the base where the item was likely stored. It was possible the item was far offsite, but less likely. A rich garden surrounded the Dance Rise, providing beauty for the site in the day and a place for romantic liaisons during the night. The garden would mean if the item came from somewhere else, it would have even farther to travel. Assistant decided the multiplexer would be in the security area of the tower.

Assistant called for Master's android bodyguards and used them to scout the area. They found a security portal into the storage section. Assistant captured images of the delivery drones going in and out of the portal and sent it on to Mimic so it could configure itself to look like one of them. The machines going in and out of the portal would almost certainly have codes to enter and exit the secure storage section. Codes which would change in time, possibly even in space, based on the location of the drone at the time of a security challenge.

The drones were infrequent. One of the androids saw three of them arrive and leave in the space of fifteen minutes. Atop the tower, the hire, a woman in a green dress who needed money, had arrived.

Assistant had an android pick up a capture box it had ordered. The boxes were not uncommon in Red Calais, where drones abounded. Every now and then someone wanted an artificial agent brought under control. It could be a rogue drone or one of the competition's spy machines. For whatever reason, many services for capturing bots were available. It cost Assistant dearly to get such a box so quickly. It had to pay four times the reasonable price supported by the market.

Assistant calculated the arrival routes of nearby delivery machines. It could not be sure enough of one route, so it deployed Master's androids to intercept drones coming in on two of the routes. If drones were blocked, they often rerouted to another path. The third route would be trapped. Orb moved into the trap corridor and searched for sensors. It did not discover any. The sensors were concentrated at the security portal.

Assistant coordinated the timing of the operation. A minute passed. Once Assistant decided it knew which delivery machine would be called based upon their positions, it had the hire purchase the multiplexer using funds it provided. A drone moved toward the portal to pick up the item. Master moved into position and placed the trap box on the floor along the expected route and waited.

Within a few seconds, the delivery drone flew down the corridor toward Master. As it passed by him, the trap box shot up from the floor, encasing the drone in a fraction of a second. Master caught the box in his arms. Just around the corner waited the security portal to the valuables storage area. Master did not move away from the portal, in fact he pushed the box as close to the corner as he could. The trapped drone had to be in close proximity to the portal, in case the proper reply to a challenge had a space component to it. The drone might be expected to give a different identification code depending on where it was in time and space. Assistant hoped the resolution would not be finer than a few meters.

Mimic approached the security portal to the storage area. A sensor and laser mount scanned the machine. Apparently, Mimic passed any appearance check, since it was not instantly incinerated by the laser. Instead, the security assembly issued Mimic a challenge on link frequencies.

Assistant immediately challenged the trapped drone with the same transmission. It did not wait in case there was a time component to the reply. The drone must have decided it had been captured and challenged by Dance Rise security, since it gave its reply, identifying itself. Assistant passed the reply on to Mimic, which emitted the reply to the original challenge.

The portal opened and allowed Mimic to enter.

Assistant's estimates of their chances of success improved. That had been the most questionable part of the plan. It was almost certain the correct response to the challenge changed with time or space. If the challenge algorithm had a very tight time component to the proper reply—say, down to the picosecond—then the time difference of shuttling the reply back would have meant the correct reply would have changed. Luckily, such validation often gave a window to allow for time skew, since the drones were not particularly smart or fast. The Dance Rise's security was flawed: those convenient windows in time or space had let Assistant and Mimic fool the portal.

Mimic emerged ten seconds later with the high tech necklace in its belly. It flew out as if headed for the kiosk at the top of the tower. Master sprayed the box and the area with a DNA destroying mist and left to be seen out on the floor. He made sure to appear calm and showed no signs of being in a hurry to leave.

Thirty minutes later, he arrived at port 467. Orb was outside, observing the port. Claery waited there alone, leaning against a railing next to her transport disk. Assistant decided it was unlikely to be a trap.

Master walked through the door to her. It was warm and dark outside.

"Hello, Matthieu."

"I've stolen it. It was not purchased."

Claery smiled.

"I know you haven't purchased it. I told my androids to watch you and the kiosk. Someone did try to buy it, but it never appeared. I assume you somehow intercepted it. Let me see it."

He almost protested that to display the freshly stolen item was dangerous; who knew what sensors might be active nearby? But Claery had already expressed her compulsion for dangerous activities. Master briefly displayed the appearance multiplexer to her, then concealed it back within a cloth shroud.

"You did it! You see, you've recaptured a bit of your old self, with my help."

Does she expect me to thank her?

"Will you let me have the data I seek now?"

"Please, Matthieu," she said teasingly. "You've made progress; isn't it enough? Let's go over to Brega and slum with the workers."

Brega was a part of Idona controlled by Gauss Systems. It did not exist in corporation-neutral territory, and thus did not enjoy the freedom Red Calais did. The workers in Brega were a poor lot, working hard for GS and getting paid in paltry VR time quotas and small credit allotments.

"I don't think so."

"Then you won't learn more," Claery responded.

"I've figured out what happened anyway," Master said.

"What?"

"I left you. I left you because you're shallow and uncaring. You saw this as a chance to win me back, at least for a time."

A look of anger passed over Claery's face to be replaced by acceptance.

"We make a good team. You shouldn't have left me, Matthieu," she pouted.

"Then prove to me you've changed. Show me maturity and compassion. I've lost my memories. If you prove to me you're capable of caring about someone, then perhaps we'll enjoy an adventure again someday."

Claery stared at Master for a long moment.

"I'll give you what you want from my archives. But don't bother coming by again; you've shown me that you bore me now," she said. "It's good that we're over."

Master received a pointer from Claery. He had the information copied aside to a storage service so that he could go over it later. Considering the source, he resolved to be cautious.

"Then have a good life, Claery."

"I will. Much better than yours, no doubt."

Master nodded and walked away.

As Master made his way home on a sky bus, Assistant considered letting Orb record Claery's death for Master. It hesitated. Would Master want her dead?

She treated him poorly; perhaps he would want revenge? But everything indicates Master did not want to see the deaths of innocents at this point in his life. What caused this fascination to develop? More information about Master's past life must be unearthed.

It decided to let Claery Argan live.

Chapter 20

Master sat patiently within the shuttle as it approached the small station. Assistant had scheduled this visit to Master's next ex-lover, Devina Murie.

Assistant's creator.

Devina Murie lived in a space station called Erefies. The station was elite even by Core World standards. To live there, Devina would have to be very rich. It was not that surprising. Devina Murie had been a superb cyberneticist at the time of her relationship with Master. Her creations, like Assistant, were powerful, yet stable, AI cores. To create the seed code for an intelligence took amazing science as well as the art of balance. Many minds turned out unstable or useless for various reasons.

The agents rode in the shuttle with Master, just in case. They might be of interest to Devina; though she had not made the lesser brains of Hydrangea, Mimic, and Orb, they were masterful creations in and of themselves.

The shuttle docked with the gentlest of shudders. Master stood and prepared to disembark.

"Orb, you should be able to follow straight off," Master said. "Mimic, you too, follow me. Hydrangea, you remain here. I don't want to have to rescue you from the local gardening machines," he said mildly. Before Hydrangea could protest, he added, "Just kidding."

Had Master joked with his agents before the memory wipe? Assistant had seen him say witty things in his business engagements, but did not know if they were a genuine part of his personality or an act to further his professional aims.

He walked out of the shuttle onto a wide concourse. Massive doors behind the shuttle locked out the cold vacuum of space. The station's interior looked to be made of a smooth substance, black or maroon in color, formed in arched and circular lines. The doorways had accents in plastic and metal. The floor was glossy black ceramic, or

Michael McCloskey

resembled it. Master's slow, stiff steps caused footfalls to
echo inside the vast station. The place had been built to look
elegant and spacious, but cold.

It's pretentious. Does that reflect Devina? thought
Master. Assistant took note, always watching Master, ready
to intervene and adjust the young mind if it saw any sign
that the new Master had strayed from its model of the old
Master.

Devina stood waiting at the end of the modest dock.
She had darker skin than Master's other lovers. She now
wore her dark brown hair short. Her features were in ideal
proportions, with a face neither long and elegant like
Kydie's, nor wide and friendly like Claery, though the
grading service noted her eyebrows were level rather than
arched. The service gave her a high rating for physical
attractiveness, something Assistant had come to expect.

Her body was as supremely formed as any Red Calais
citizen, where the shape and presentation of one's body was
a malleable product of artistic expression rather than any
genetic-enforced constant; not only was everyone on the
Core Worlds the result of designer genes, they were also
surgically altered almost at a whim. The citizens of Red
Calais had a large number of services available to them to
change their bodies, and they usually availed themselves of
whatever they needed to match their interpretation of
beauty.

"Imagine my surprise when you asked to visit me,"
Devina said.

"Really? Is it so shocking?" Master said.

"We had not parted on the best terms," Devina said.

Hints. Should I tell her everything now?

"That is past. I have something important to meet
about."

Mimic rolled up behind Master, disguised as a piece of
self-transporting luggage. Orb was more subtle, likely
invisible, unless Devina had augmented her vision.

Devina nodded. "Luggage? Well, then, let me show

114

you to a room." Master saw nothing to indicate she had detected Orb.

"Thank you, if it wouldn't be too much of an imposition?"

"Not at all, I welcome you here," Devina said. She acted as cordial and stiff as Master; Assistant estimated she was highly curious about his business, but patient.

Devina showed him a beautiful large room with a false mountainside view thrown up on the wall. Snowflakes were just starting to fall across a stand of tall fir trees. Of course Master would be able to change it to anything he wanted; the room could generate false winds and sounds as well, allowing it to complete many illusions.

They did not stay there long. Master told Mimic to wait in the room, then they went to a common area to chat.

Devina's surroundings were lavish. Despite being on a space station, the rooms were large. The room Devina took Master to looked like the atrium of a small office building. Light bled through the joints between black blocks hanging from the ceiling. It made Master think of the light from hot lava bleeding through cracks in rock.

They sat on one of several long black lounges in the room. Though there were at least five exit corridors branching out, Master still got the feeling they had privacy here, since he had not seen or heard anyone else.

"I'm not well, Devina. I've come to ask for your help."

"Oh? Have you somehow run out of money?"

She means, why can't I afford the doctors or aid necessary to heal myself.

"Money cannot solve the problem. I've lost my memories."

Devina's face slowly moved through surprise, then understanding. Her curiosity was at last satiated.

"That must be very disturbing. How did it happen?"

"An artificial virus. Some enemy of mine, I suppose. I hope it wasn't you, since you mentioned we didn't part on amicable terms."

115

"That's not my style. I'm sorry this happened to you, Matthieu. What can I do? I build artificial minds, I can't heal Terran brains."

Assistant suddenly felt self conscious in the presence of its creator. Surely Devina would not detect Assistant, would not know she was talking to a new Master it had created?

"Please let me copy any data you have about our time together. Anything at all that shows my past behavior, so that I can build up a library of my old self. There are people who can help me from there."

"AIs, you mean," Devina said. "I doubt any Terran doctor could crunch that kind of data without help."

"Maybe they work with AIs, yes," Master said.

"I'll send you everything, Matthieu," Devina said. Her eyes relaxed into a neutral state as she went off-retina. In a few moments, Master received a pointer. He copied a large amount of information to a storage service.

"Thank you. These records will help me immensely," Master said.

"You owe me then, Matthieu." Devina stated it calmly, without emotion.

"I do. And I promise I'll visit again, when I'm fully myself. Once I'm as close to whole as I can get, I'll offer return favors."

Master stood.

"Leaving so soon?"

"I'll come to stay for a few days, once I'm feeling myself again," Master said. He turned and walked toward the exit of her house. He started to send a message to Mimic, but stopped when the house denied him egress. He halted.

"Devina? What is this?"

"I won't let you go, Matthieu. Not this time," Devina said. "I remember your collection; you were so proud when you finally shared it with me. Now I have a collection, too. A collection of men," Devina said casually. "Take him away."

What?

Master looked to see who she had commanded.

A white security robot emerged from a dark corner of the room. The vaguely humanoid machine dwarfed Master. It floated a half meter above the floor. Its thick, glossy torso spoke of invulnerability and power.

Master held his hands in plain view and stepped back.

"You intend to imprison me? Why did you help me then?"

"I want you to be as close to the original as possible. You'll be comfortable, that I promise you, Matthieu," Devina said.

Well, that was unexpected.

Assistant dispatched Mimic to help Master. Master gathered himself to run. A terrible noise exploded in the room, launching a sharp headache to assault him.

Stunner blast!

Master almost vomited; he managed to overcome the nausea and roll forward out of the room. The hallway beyond spun in his vision. He sprinted forward anyway, rebounding off one flat wall then the other, unable to keep a straight course.

Assistant saw what had happened. The security machine was equipped with a HIT. It had known Master was going to run before he took the first step.

Which way is Mimic? Perhaps I could run to it—

Something struck his back. He fell to the floor. He felt a living thing struggling to secure him, its writhing tentacles searching for purchase. Then he saw a part of it: a simple, mindless rope of glue that had secured itself to the floor. Master could not even roll over. The glue grenade had attached itself across most of his back and his arms. He struggled to rise, but the three or four glue tentacles that had come around his sides had anchored to the floor when he fell. He was immobilized.

"Such theatrics. Now we have to clean you up,"

Michael McCloskey

Devina said pleasantly.

Assistant sent Mimic back to the room. It would be hard pressed to help Master now, but perhaps it would be more valuable later for some surprise tactic.

The robot floated over to him, extended a set of rubbery treads, and dropped to the floor. Then it picked Master up by the dried glue mess on his back. It cut the connections to the floor and started to drag him down the hall. He could not see what happened to Devina and assumed she had gone about other business.

The machine took him into another room. Master could not see much other than a bare white ceiling with bright lights. The machine dropped him into a large shower basin. Master lay there for a moment, struggling anew. He heard the whirr of robotic movement, then an acrid spray misted over him.

Master coughed. His eyes watered.

They say this chemical is harmless. Hard to believe them.

The glue slowly lost its hold. Master pulled the many-tentacled body of the glue bomb from himself like the corpse of a large squid. The spray turned to regular hot water. His disposable Core Worlder clothes were destroyed by recent events, so he let them go down the drain with the shower fluid. Assistant rattled against the bottom of the basin, prompting Master to grasp the sphere and hide it in the cup of his hand.

Once he was clean, he walked out of the shower. The security machine waited for him in the adjacent room. He sent a set of clothing specs through to a dispenser and printed a set of less formal clothing that would offer less resistance to athletic movements. Just in case. He secreted Assistant within his new clothing.

The robot moved in on its soft treads and grabbed Master by the upper arms. He had no choice but to yield. Fighting against it without weapons would be like punching a ceramic wall. It took him back down a long hallway to his original room. Once inside, the machine released him, turned, and left. The door closed behind it.

No warning? I guess it knows I'm smart enough to know running will just get me glued again.

Master walked toward the door. His link showed no services from the room. The door would no longer listen to him. He felt his heartbeat increase; a panic rose inside him as he realized nothing could hear his commands. He took a deep breath.

"I'm a prisoner, but far from helpless. There was a time when Terrans did everything manually."

Assistant checked Devina's security measures. They had improved since Assistant had been created, but Assistant was an artificial mind more powerful than its creator. It had learned more than Devina had over the years. The security was vulnerable given Assistant's knowledge of Devina and her old methods. Because of that, together with the element of surprise, all was not lost.

The suite was a problem. Master was isolated from the outer world and all that which controlled the station and Devina's mechanical servantry. Assistant told Master to get Mimic out of the suite. The clever robot would then serve as their point of attack on Devina's security.

I need to summon a machine... but I can't! There are no link services.

Master looked about the room helplessly.

Think. Don't panic. Just think.

Master started to pace. He looked at the furniture in the suite. He had a bedroom with bed and dresser, a small office with an archaic desk, and a lounge with comfortable couches and a table. The bath had manual controls in it to replace link services.

Barbaric. I'm truly a prisoner.

Master turned the water on. He blocked the drain with a towel. Then he took four more fresh towels from a shelf and filled a waste receptacle behind one of the couches.

"Now we wait," Master told his agents.

As the water rose to the top of the receptacle, an auxiliary drain opened, stopping the water's rise. Master waited longer. He found some silverware and put it into the waste receptacle with the towels.

A door opened in a wall of the main room. A small service robot rolled out. It was a white cylinder that came up to Master's knees. Mimic prepared to isolate its link, but did not detect any signals. Master descended upon the robot and examined it.

The machine had no link services, rendering it virtually unhackable. But it was replaceable.

Why not? We've done this before at the Dance Rise.

Mimic reconstructed its outer appearance to mirror that of the servant machine. The cleaning machine struggled to escape Master.

"Release me or face disciplinary action," the machine said. Master physically disabled its remote communications ability. Then he pulled the power from the servant machine's wheels. He told Mimic to go.

"Good luck, little one," Master said under his breath. Mimic departed through the tiny service door.

Master started to pace. Within three minutes, the door to his suite opened.

Damn! They sent security because they can't talk to the cleaning machine. What can I do?

Master walked out of the side room to meet the expected security machine where it could not see the disabled cleaning machine, though he thought it was a futile attempt. Surely it knew what had happened?

It was a security machine as he feared. It was the same type that had subdued him after his audience with Devina.

"Come with me," the machine said.

"What? You just brought me here."

"You require a medical check. It's standard procedure," the machine said.

True? Or deception? If I'm to be punished, wouldn't it just say that?

"I'm sick as I said. My mind has been reconstructed, but it's not whole."

"Your health must be evaluated. If you wish to avoid being glued again, please come with me," the machine said.

"Ten seconds, please," Master said quickly. He went into his bedroom and hid Assistant in the back of a drawer. Then he walked back out and nodded.

"I comply," he said. The machine turned and escorted him out of the suite.

Orb followed along.

They walked down an elegant corridor and turned right. Then a doorway opened in the wall. The security robot ushered Master into another white room with bright lights built into the ceiling.

Master saw a medical robot and some scanning machines on one wall. In the center, he saw a soft table with a hole for the patient's head to rest face down. It was like... a table for getting a link serviced!

Devina intends to remove my link altogether! I would be rendered permanently helpless in this station.

"What's happening here? I'm healthy," he said. The security machine inched closer, yet Master balked.

"Routine check," the machine said. "Please recline here face down for a scan."

Of course it won't tell me its intentions. Her intentions.

He spoke through his link to Orb.

"Tell Assistant I need help urgently!"

"I'm working on it," Assistant's answer came back, relayed through Orb.

"Stop!" he ordered the security machine.

"You must comply or face glue restraint."

Master picked up a nearby chair and charged the security machine. He put the chair's seat over the glue grenade tube and pushed as hard as he could. The machine stabilized easily. Its powerful metal hands started to fish for Master's arms.

"Assistant!" Master sent out. He flailed against the

machine.

"Aid will be rendered as quickly as possible."

The machine forced Master backwards. The chair dropped to the floor, clearing the machine's glue gun, but the glue did not come. Instead, the machine flipped Master by his arms and put him onto the table face down. Master pulled his knees up to his chest, blocking the attempt to fully fasten him onto the table. Metal tentacles emerged from the waist of the machine and pulled his legs out of the way. Out of the corner of his eye, Master saw the medical machine moving forward. Straps secured his arms against the table. The medical machine produced another strap coming through the face hole to pull his head into place.

"Aaaaaaaaaassistaaaaaant!"

The medical machine put the strap over Master's head and pulled him flush with the padding. He felt a pinch at the back of his head.

"Please..."

He felt a cold metal hand on the back of his neck. Then the medical machine stopped.

"I've taken control of this place," Assistant relayed to Master through Orb.

Master released his breath loudly in short, ragged gasps.

"Thank you, Assistant," he mumbled. The straps loosened. Master urgently freed himself. He was so anxious to get off the operating table, instead of stepping away, he immediately rolled off the edge and crashed onto the floor.

"Are you harmed?" Assistant demanded over a link connection. It checked Master's mind for signs of pain.

"I'm fine, thanks to you," Master said. He relaxed on the floor, allowing his heart rate to recover. Then he started to stand. He stared at the security machine hatefully.

Master opened a pane in his mind showing the layout of Devina's section of Erefies. He found Devina as reported by her own internal security sensors.

"Is she armed?"

"Yes, but I've disabled the weapon. Two suborned security machines stand by to assist you."

Master hurried off to intercept Devina. "That won't be necessary. Prepare for departure. Have Mimic pick you up and take you to our shuttle."

"Yes, sir. Just ahead is a small cabinet with three stunners."

Master came to the cabinet in the wall, directed by his link. The wall looked perfectly smooth one moment, then doors became visible the next. He told the doors to open. Inside, he saw three small pistols as Assistant had described. He took one and checked his access. The weapon responded to him and reported a full charge.

Master found Devina in a vast living suite. He moved quietly up behind her with Orb trailing him.

"Goodbye, Devina," Master said.

Devina whirled.

"What? How did you escape? Impossible!" She started to reach for something, probably her weapon, then realized it had been disabled. Her shoulders slumped slightly.

"I can't believe you've managed to do this," she said. "How did you break my security so easily?"

"I had the help of one of your AIs," he said. "Perhaps I'm not the only one with damaged memory? You don't remember your gift?"

Devina looked away. "My own creation? I see. You're loyal to Matthieu, though he's gone, I think. Matthieu is not in there anymore, is he?" she said, talking past Master and addressing Assistant.

"Assistant has been piecing me together," the new Master answered her. "I'm a shadow of Matthieu. With your records, Matthieu is one step closer to recovery."

"Then go," Devina said angrily. "The real Matthieu is dead. I'm disappointed one of my brightest creations can't see that."

Master told the stunner to fire. Devina recoiled, then fell to the floor, unconscious.

"Tell everyone it's time to run."

Chapter 21

Adrienne Rekaire had blonde hair, at least on the day Master found her again. The bridge of her nose was straight, as if sculpted to be that way. He caught sight of her smile. Apparently she was in a good mood this evening. Master liked her eyes most of all. They were bright and playful.

She stood in the wide-open space on the third floor of a spire that rose into the sky near the center of Red Calais. A massive fountain of light dominated the center of the room, decorating a central support column that rose through the middle of the tower. Citizens milled about in the enormous chamber. Many of them danced above in a zero-grav zone. Master wondered how many were present incarnate; Assistant had wondered the same and started taking count minutes ago.

Master had arranged to attend the corporate party knowing Adrienne would be there. The host, Sans Limites Fabrication, was a powerful corporation with a large presence on Earth and Idona. Though Adrienne attended the party, she did not appear to be an employee of the company. Master wondered what connection had brought her here.

A moment after seeing her, as he started to approach, he noticed she was with a tall man in formal dress. She turned and offered him a peck on the cheek. Master altered course and moved away.

She's here with someone... how can I get her alone?

Master spied upon her and brooded for a while. He felt he would have a better chance at a candid conversation if they were alone.

Am I jealous? Did my original behave this way?

"Adrienne's companion is remote," Assistant informed Master from within a chest pocket of his formal garment. That meant her partner was an artificial body, being controlled virtually by a citizen from far away. The news made Master feel much better.

Adrienne and her companion slipped up from a zero

grav dance floor into the air and started to move with the sound. Master asked a service to analyze her partner's movements. The service said it was from a dance package.

Either he learned to execute that dance sequence perfectly in VR, or he's just running a program.

Master felt pleased to continually find Adrienne's companion to be more and more fake. The two he shadowed came into contact and spun. Their trajectories were analyzed and told of normal masses, but that meant little. Androids were often designed to have normal Terran mass.

The two parted at last. Master prepared to seize his opportunity. Adrienne slipped out of the zero grav floor into an empty safety corridor. She ignored the wall markings and the warning which must have come to her link as she entered the area.

What's she doing there? Too much to drink?

Master felt he already knew the answer. No, any ex-lover of his was far more likely to be up to no good. An adventure at best, at worst, he dared not guess.

He followed her out the exit. The white corridor beyond was an empty platform alongside the event hall. She caught sight of him. She did not smile.

"What? You? What are you doing here?"

Master felt the bite of disappointment in her reaction. *Not a good start.*

"May we speak privately?"

"Catch me later," she hissed. "I'm working."

"I came here because I need to ask you for an important favor."

"Matthieu! By Cthulhu, I don't have time for you now!"

"Really? It seems you've grown bored of the party."

If I pressure her a bit, I can learn what she's up to.

"Go away," she said. Then she stepped off the platform. Master watched in shock as she rocketed forward through the turbulence zone.

Adrienne!

By shooting through the eddies of the gravity spinner, she risked death. Assistant had learned about many accidents in the perimeter of a spinner's power zone. Broken bones and internal injuries could be caused by the eddies alone, much less any other loose materials whipping about in the zone.

She landed hard on an open fifth-floor balcony beyond. He saw her recover on the other side.

"Are you hurt?" Master asked her.

"No! Matthieu, will you listen? Go back to the party."

Assistant calculated the strength of the eddies before Master. Chances of survival looked high; if unlucky, internal damage could occur.

Does Master do this? Is he brave?

Adrienne's worried look gave Assistant all the answers it needed. She would not be looking on with such concern if Master had not been the type to follow. Assistant allowed Master to follow his impulses.

Master stepped onto the thrust plate and shot across the zone after her. A gravity ripple crossed his body in flight, causing his breath to come out in a harsh grunt. He landed no more gracefully than Adrienne had; the eddies were chaotic, causing him to hit the balcony with a severe left lean. She caught him with an outstretched arm, causing them to spin to a halt.

"Oh, Matthieu. You okay?" Her voice had softened.

"I can help you. What are you after?"

Adrienne opened her mouth as if to dismiss the possibility, then she paused.

She does not doubt Master. He makes such an outrageous claim, yet she takes him at his word.

"Okay, but I won't say what I'm after. You create a diversion on the fourteenth floor. There are assets there Lamondie will move to protect. There may be a downside. If you end up detained, I won't be there to spring you."

"Lamondie?"

"They own two floors of this building," she said. "Sans

127

Limites Fabrication isn't my target."

Assistant probed the network defenses of the building. They were strong, but that could actually help. The most complex defenses sometimes allowed an attacker to believe they were succeeding while alerting the defenders and tracing the attacker. If Assistant attacked the floor from the network, it could serve as a diversion without shutting down the whole building. The only real challenge would be to remain hidden.

"In progress," Master said. It had taken him just long enough to respond that she likely assumed he had been off-retina.

"Well, perhaps this reunion won't be a bust after all," Adrienne said. "But I didn't mean anything so mundane as a cyber attack. Get your butt up there and create a *real* distraction." She smiled as if the idea was great fun.

"With no preparation? I'll be caught. Our faces have already been—"

"Our faces are being picked up by sensors, I know, but I've altered the hashing and storage in this entire building. Whoever looks into this won't recognize us."

"But the guest list?" Master protested. "I didn't know to obfuscate my identity."

"Then I guess you're more boring and helpless than I remember," Adrienne said. She smiled.

"They'll track anything I leave behind."

"Gloves. Leave as little DNA as you can," she said, producing a small black cylinder. "This can clean up a lot. It also leaves behind a fake trace."

"You think Sans Limites Fabrication or Lamondie—"

"They may not have you on file, but they'll be able to buy enough to ID you otherwise," she said.

In Red Calais, there was no central authority to record everyone's genetic makeup, but private enterprises collected DNA from people all over the city, all the time. They eventually, either individually or collectively, gathered enough data points for almost anyone to be identified by

DNA traces, for the right price. Of course, if you bought an identity from a DNA sample, you had to face the possibility that someone else paid more for that identity to be misdirected, or hacked the database to alter it.

She hurried off down the corridor, leaving Master alone to consider her request.

Ah well, since I don't actually have to steal anything, or get anywhere important, I can probably get off with a high fine if it all goes wrong.

Accomplices were seldom dealt with harshly in Red Calais. The big players always knew that the pawns in a plot were just chaff. Throwing them in prison was too expensive. If robbed or attacked, one focused on learning who was really behind it and why. Of course, sometimes the schemers tried to disguise themselves as pawns, which served to complicate matters considerably.

Master instructed his androids to leave the party. He obtained a very expensive log-free transport disk for them to use to meet him outside the building. Then he started to search for a way up to the fourteenth floor. He told his link to stop actively accessing local services.

This place is a fortress. How will I be able to break through the windows to escape on a disk? I may need their assistance.

The androids carried lasers in their arms, to augment the nonlethal stunners they wore openly. The weaponry could only be used against Core World citizens in dire emergencies, lest the Space Force or corporations be given an excuse to annex Red Calais among themselves. Master doubted their lasers could defeat transparent armor, but he hoped they could create a weak spot he could exploit.

"How much to get me schematics?" Master asked Assistant.

"I'm sure these companies have falsified everything," Assistant said.

"Fine. How much to get me into this service entrance?" Master asked, pausing before a panel of the wall.

Subtle tracks in the carpet revealed that robots had recently moved in or out through the panel.

A figure came back from a reliable service Assistant had used before. The cost was a function of time. Master's immediate needs would be very expensive.

That's high. Oh well, it's only money.

"Very well. I'm waiting."

The panel opened. His link passively picked up a broadcast warning.

This area is not safe. Please turn around immediately. Security has been notified.

"I suppose it would have been too expensive to deflect that as well," Master mumbled. He dropped to his knees and crawled in. Inside, he saw a dozen tubes along a passage straight ahead, with vertically placed wire conduits on the walls. He looked up in the tight space. A fearless person could make their way upward behind the wall. It looked dirty and unsafe.

Master headed upward.

He climbed until his breath came in ragged gasps. The smell of unidentified chemicals added their bite to the air. Eventually, the opening ended underneath another space that he decided must exist between floors. It was dark. His eyes had adjusted, allowing him to see by the light of a few banks of LEDs set around seemingly at random.

"How far have I gone?"

"We're on the eighth floor," Assistant said. "Proceed away from the wall behind you."

Master assumed Assistant spoke of the vertical wall at his back, since he still faced away from the corridor he had exited below. He crawled out of the vertical space and started on his hands and knees around columns and pipes.

Up ahead, Master saw more light. He crawled toward it. This time a wider shaft lay ahead, running both up and down from his location. Lights ran along its length.

"What is it?"

"A major freight shaft."

"Antigrav?"

"No. It's too far from the spinner which is designed to service the dance floor. Besides, the shaft is too tall and narrow to benefit from a spinner without disrupting the entire building."

"Should I take it?"

"Yes."

Master crawled up the shaft, then looked up and down. It went as far as he could see both directions. Nearby, a carbon ladder lay within reach. Master grabbed a rung, swung over, and started to climb. Assistant knew Master had been a risk-taker and an adventurer. It had routed the dangerous climb to provide a pleasurable adrenal rush for the new Master.

At the fourteenth floor, Master found another maintenance passage and left the ladder. He had to pause for his eyes to adjust, then he searched for a door into the habitable part of the building.

"Okay, we're here. Good. I just need to get some attention then, right?"

"Security is aware of your approximate location," Assistant said. "You will likely be captured immediately upon emerging from this maintenance space."

"What? Why did I turn off my link if they know where I am anyway?"

"I said they are aware of your approximate location. If you had not turned off your link, they would know *exactly* where you are."

Master rolled his eyes in the darkness.

"She set me up."

"I believe she urged you not to intervene at all."

"You're lucky I haven't dropped you in here doing all that crawling and climbing," Master asked, implying he might do it on purpose, but he did not really mean it.

They came to a machine door.

Master took only a peek, but it was enough to alert the humanoid sentinel at the end of the hall. The machine turned

131

its flat head toward him. It had a single wide optical sensor where the eyes would be. Master dashed out, headed in the opposite direction.

The security machine fired. Master felt pain in his head and his legs grew weak, but he had avoided the brunt of it. He reached the end of the corridor and turned right.

He found himself in a big corner office. He told the door to close after him but it ignored his command, so he pushed it closed with his shoulder. In the office, a huge desk sat before a giant window framed by old fashioned shelves.

Perfect.

Master saw a heavy bust on a pedestal next to the desk, so he grabbed it and swung it into the window with all his might. The bust rebounded from the window. Master stared where it had struck. There was not even a scratch on the barrier.

Assistant was not surprised. Many durable optical ceramics were in use for secure buildings. Sapphire windows were not unheard of in Red Calais. It directed Master's gaze downwards.

He looked at the edge of the window. Its edge fitted into a ceramic perimeter sill that was smaller than the armor plate on the outside.

It's designed to protect from outside attack. The window cannot be pushed in without breaking it or the ceramic fittings, but the window could be pushed outward more easily.

A security machine came into the room as he wrestled with the problem of the window. The machine moved more quietly than Master would have expected. He feinted to one side, trying to avoid the machine's weapon that pointed at him.

A rubber slug ricocheted off the window beside him with a dull thud. The machine moved in. Master wondered which side of the massive desk it would come around.

This is it!

Master ducked.

Ping!

Master could not identify the sound. Then the floor shuddered. He heard a crash and felt a burst of cool air wash over him. He opened his eyes. The window was gone. The edge of the transport disk was over him. The window sill supported the disk off the floor.

Where's the window? Ask later.

Master crawled up the edge of the disk and grabbed its rail. One of his androids pulled him aboard.

Assistant would have told the androids to wipe their memories and left them behind, but they might be traceable back to Master anyway. It told the bodyguards to escape with their Master as quickly as possible while it tried to distract the security machine every way it could. The lights flickered, the shades closed, and the furniture reconfigured itself. Assistant simulated five personal links in the room using the processors it had seized in the desk, the ceiling, and even the waste receptacle. The security machine hesitated, searching for the other intruders.

"What happened to the window?" Master asked.

"It's far below," answered an android. "We created a small hole and anchored a cable through it, then pulled it out of its seating."

"How did you know to do that? Security programming?"

"You have Assistant to thank, sir," the machine told him.

The disk had been damaged. It listed heavily. Master heard the sick whirr of damaged fans coming from inside the transport. It was too small to carry a spinner. The problem did not last long. A fan slowed, then current heated up the metal, causing it to return to its original shape. Then the transport mostly righted itself as the fan came back up to speed.

"Get us out of here. That was unpleasant, but I dare say I accomplished my part of the task."

The transport disk set off. Master wondered for a brief

moment if it had been the disk, the androids, or Assistant that had responded to his wishes.

"I assume you'll want to find Adrienne later," Assistant said.

Master had found several image captures in his link archives of Adrienne by a particular fountain. The images were marked with a wide range of dates. Everything implied it was a place of special significance.

"Head for the fluorescent fountain in the corner of the Sopoll Gardens."

"If you're seen in public together so soon, an AI may link you two to the Lamondie job," Assistant said.

"Conceal my identity, then," Master said.

The transport slowed. The air became moist as they slipped into a cloud bank.

"Over into the other disk, then I'll activate the privacy curtain. If we see her, we can usher her onboard."

Master looked for the other disk Assistant referred to. To his right, he saw another machine sidle up next to his current one. Master walked over to the adjacent transport disk and his androids followed. It was hard to tell how high they were. Only a few lights from below penetrated the mist.

The new transport flew for less than a minute to arrive at the gardens. There, it scanned for Adrienne. A few other disks lingered, probably holding other nighttime visitors. A single figure waited among the shadows cast by the fluorescent fountain. The disk moved down to rendezvous with the figure.

Adrienne climbed aboard.

"Did you get what you needed?" he asked.

"I did. I'll thank you, though I would have gotten it on my own as well," she said. Master laughed.

"Don't worry, I won't ask for too much credit," he said. "Can I at least invite you to my house?"

"Yes, let's go."

The disk lifted off. The night air was warm, yet invigorating. The towers of central Red Calais usually added pleasant ions to the atmosphere to make the area pleasant to experience incarnate. There were even drugs released in the air to induce positive feelings to associate with a visit. Specific places with romantic nuance, like the glowing fountain below, periodically released aphrodisiacs into the air.

"Thank you, Matthieu," she said.

"I'm glad you feel that way. I see you've kept busy," he said, staying vague.

"I've missed you, Matthieu. It's fun to see you, even in the middle of a mission."

"It's done. Can we speak of my request now?"

She chuckled. "Yes. Tell me."

Things seemed to be going well despite the questionable start. Assistant agreed with the new Master's natural inclination to be truthful, though it knew that might not be accurate to the original.

"I've lost my memory, Adrienne. All of it erased by a nano poison. It would help me if you would share what you have of me... of us... everything in your archives. I need everything I can get to rebuild myself."

"I'll do more than that, Matthieu. I'll join you until you're whole again." She sent him a pointer. Master passed it on to Assistant.

Master raised an eyebrow. "Why?"

"You were a loyal friend. Now I'll be the same for you. It's the least I can do."

"And you're not looking to collect men?"

Adrienne laughed. Then she covered her mouth. "You must have visited Devina before me!"

"Yes, as a matter of fact, I did."

Adrienne reached out and put her hand over his. "Well, she's crazy. You told me about her. I wish you had come to me first. But of course, you couldn't have known."

The new Master immediately felt happy. It did not matter that he had not yet reviewed the information. Adrienne had responded with compassion and that was

135

enough for him.

⌐ Assistant wondered why the original Master had parted ways with her. That knowledge could reveal whether or not she could be trusted. It decided to withhold its own conclusions until later.

Chapter 22

"So, Matthieu... who did you date after leaving me?"

The question came without malice. Adrienne smiled at him from the other side of the main lounge in his new house.

Master had the files that told much of their previous relationship. At least, they seemed to; Adrienne could have modified them. The data told of a mutually agreeable breakup: Adrienne preferred her work for her corporation, but it did not keep her on Idona. She took missions across all the Core Worlds.

"I felt I had no choice but to leave you," Master said. It felt strange to defend his old self with no memory of the decision.

"I know. Don't worry, Matthieu. I just want to know who we're visiting next, that's all."

"Liane Vanault."

"Who is she?"

"I don't remember, obviously," Master said, though Assistant had prepared a briefing.

"Then we need to investigate her," Adrienne said.

Master shrugged. "We have some information. I'm being difficult. Was I like that before?"

"Oh yes. But only in fun," Adrienne said.

"Yes. I sensed that, the way we interacted at the party. Here's what I have on her." Master sent her a pointer to the information Assistant had compiled.

Liane Vanault's picture flashed through Master's mind. At the time of the capture she had been a platinum blonde with wavy hair and a strong, pleasant face. The grading service gave her a high appearance score as Assistant and grown to expect. The only downgrade in the analysis was for a slightly thin nose.

"She looks your type, Matthieu. Space Force! That's something new."

Master saw the same file. She had been Major Vanault

of the Space Force.

"Oh, I'm sorry, Matthieu. She died last month."

Master felt a distant sense of loss. His other self would surely have felt it strongly.

At least Adrienne is here.

His mind turned to the records. "I guess I still need the personal records she had," he said. "It will be sad to learn of her, but... I need to know what happened."

"Yes, I agree, you'll need all the information we can find."

Assistant started researching methods to uncover service records. It moved deliberately on the project. It did not want to attract the attention of the Space Force, but Master needed to know what Major Vanault had done for them.

"Where's the estate? Has it been sold?" he asked.

"Not yet; are you thinking what I'm thinking? We may have time to get the archives," Adrienne said.

"Yes, let's do it. She was very rich; there will be security."

"Good. I like a challenge." Adrienne smiled. Master smiled back.

With Assistant and Adrienne working hard to gather information, Master felt detached for a few moments. The addition of Adrienne's link archive had brought Master one step closer to his true self. He wondered how close he now was to the original.

I was an adventurer. Physically as well as mentally skilled.

Master decided to go to a dance room in his home and continue to work on his agility. Assistant had done a good job of rewiring his coordination, but true grace would require more incarnate training. No doubt the new Master had not yet mastered these abilities.

The dance room had been converted into an extensive workout studio. Master spent an hour jumping, kicking, and climbing on various apparatus he had set up to train on.

After the physical workout, he cleaned off and considered doing some virtual training. Then he remembered he did not want to get into more dangerous situations unprepared. He decided to visit his personal armory and make sure he was ready for whatever course of action they decided on.

Two minutes later, Master stood inside a small room with rows of weapons sitting on wall racks. Long drawers full of ammo and charge cells waited under the racks. His artificial agents had seen a few armories in their operations; this collection was larger than most in Red Calais.

He looked at the weapons and sighed.

The problem was that security machines possessed armor that could defeat small arms; all the nonlethal weapons carried by citizens would be totally ineffectual. Even projectile and laser rifles would need a superb hit or multiple hits in the same spot. And if they did kill several security machines, it could draw the attention of outside powers. Red Calais remained a corporate no-man's land only so long as it was a safe place for the powers to interact with each other. Thus, anyone who disturbed the peace ran the risk of being hunted down by well-paid mercenaries in the service of rich merchants or anyone else who wanted Red Calais to keep its neutral status in the supercorporation wars. If those hunters failed, eventually the Space Force might step in and take Red Calais for the Core World government.

"Weapons? Not your style."

It was Adrienne. She walked up beside him in the armory.

"Really? I don't feel like being helpless as I was at Lamondie. It seems reasonable to be prepared. Yet I know what Red Calais is..."

"I didn't say you should be unprepared! But we need to use stealth, hackery, and deception. We're not actually taking anything, just copying data."

"I assumed we would need to take the archives. They'll take time to break."

"We'll see. I might be able to get a charge snapshot."

"But that would destroy the charges in the original, right?" Master asked uncertainly.

"Most do. Once you have a snapshot, you can restore the original, if you have the equipment." She looked at him oddly. "I don't." She smiled.

Master smiled a bit. She was funny.

"We need to figure out a plan before we equip, anyway," Adrienne said. Master nodded.

She's better at this sort of thing than I am.

Assistant retrieved the plans of the estate and shared them with Adrienne.

"We can start with those, but I guarantee you they're inaccurate. There's no authority in Red Calais to come after anyone who falsifies them."

Master nodded. "Orb can go. We'll see what we're dealing with before we go in."

***

Master stood in a dark grove after sunset. He wore a stealth suit provided by Adrienne. At his hip hung a laser pistol, his consolation to insecurity from being unarmed in other recent encounters. It would feel good to be lugging even more hardware on the mission, but Adrienne was right: they needed stealth, not firepower. It would be harder to sneak in carrying a PAW and a dozen grenades.

Orb was already ahead, spying on the house. It had made one round of the outside and passed the data back to Master and Adrienne. Then it entered the house. Within another minute it emerged with more reconnaissance data. Master saw only a few of the doors and rooms had changed from the official plans.

Liane didn't change much. She probably had little to hide. She's Space Force, not a corporate spy or mercenary.

Master wanted to trust Adrienne. But part of him thought a woman like Adrienne would be more precarious

to trust than someone more up-front and straightforward,
like Liane. Or was he falling for stereotypes?

*A few sharks and snakes must have become Space
Force officers.*

Master wondered for the thousandth time what kind of
person he had been before. Did he still want to become that
person again? Someone who recorded the deaths of people?
Did the old Master trust people by default until they
betrayed him, or had he remained suspicious first until
someone earned his trust?

*Maybe I was the snake and someone took me down
because I deserved it.*

Orb sent another map, this time of the second floor of
the house. It currently hovered just outside the estate.
Master told it to wait until they went in. The data it had
collected so far should be enough. He looked the map over
and tried to find the best way in.

Adrienne connected to him from nearby.

"We could avoid a lot of security by avoiding the
ground floor," Adrienne said.

"They know it, too. There will be countermeasures
against dropping."

"I didn't say we drop. I said we avoid the ground
floor," Adrienne said. She brought his attention to their
shared map. The view zoomed in to focus on the backyard,
where a path led out the back of the house to a gazebo,
flanked by a vine trellis. The house's first floor roof
extended out to cover the path, and joined the gazebo roof as
a single unit.

A red line lit up in their shared map, indicating an
incursion path. The route crossed the outer wall using a tree,
then crossed the backyard and entered the gazebo. At first
Master thought the red line went along the top of the roof
from there to the house.

"That's too open—wait. Are we going over the roof of
the path, or under it?"

The view shifted to an angle to reveal the answer.

"Neither," Adrienne explained. "There's enough room for us to crawl single file inside the extended roof. We go to the gazebo, cut our way up, and crawl into that shallow space. The other end empties into the greenhouse. Once inside the greenhouse, we can cut up into the second floor here, and then go straight up to the third on this stair. We bypass all the hard core security hardpoints of the first and second floors, without dropping on the roof."

Master was impressed. He would never have thought of crawling under the rafters of such a shallow roof as the one that covered the path to the gazebo. He had missed that there was even such a space at all.

"Let's go," he said.

"Put your link behind the stealth suit's interface. Deauthorize all link connections except to this service," she explained. "The suits will use directed comm linkage to speak quietly to each other."

Master understood that the normal link discovery and connection protocols were active and interceptable communications. Apparently the suits would talk with each other in a more specialized way that made it much harder for security to notice the signals. Also, a stealth suit would never connect to local services, keeping the user from revealing themselves by accident. Otherwise, it would be easy to access some trivial service by habit without even thinking about it.

"I've provided your agents with the means to accept our directional signals. Mimic and Hydrangea will be hiding at or near the top of the compound walls to allow us access to the outside network, provided we don't get too much shielding between us. Orb will rove about as needed. Line of sight is the safest of all, we don't have to worry about anything accidentally noticing our communications."

Master connected through his suit and watched the shared tactical as they walked through the woods at the edge of the estate toward the wall. The dark slab of the wall became visible through the trees. It stood eight meters high.

142

Master knew it would be strong and durable, probably made of some dense ceramic. Vines grew over the entire thing. Master supposed those who lived inside appreciated the beauty of the vines.

Adrienne winked out of sight next to him. Master actuated his own suit. Once his suit became fully active, he could see her again, though only as a faded-out version. If the suits' directional contact comms were broken, they would be invisible to each other as well. Master supposed that the corporate spies and Space Force teams trained to use stealth suits knew how to handle such situations, but he would probably just abort the mission.

They approached the wall, then turned to walk parallel to it.

"Is the top of the wall monitored? We could climb the vines," Master suggested.

"No, the wall has sensors at the top, and the tension on the vines is measured as well. If we climbed up or down, the pull would be recorded and they would know exactly how many intruders they have and where."

They approached the enormous old tree that was part of Adrienne's route. He looked up and scanned its thick branches from the ground. With his light-enhanced view, Master spotted a few dozen Idonan leaf bugs clinging to its dark surface.

"You scanned the tree and it's clear? That's odd."

"Not really. This bough has grown over the edge of the wall since this place was built. It's a hole in the defenses. No one has been that careful about this place. Liane doesn't have much to hide, I'd say."

"Or she's wasn't afraid of intruders," Master said.

"Or it's a trap," Assistant offered helpfully.

Adrienne started up the tree, using hooks in the sleeves and shins of the suit to climb. It appeared she had thought of everything. Master's own suit had the same hooks.

The climb was harder than Master had expected. A long section of the tree grew straight upwards without branches. Only one bough extended over the wall, and it looked precarious.

Adrienne went out on the branch first. A smart rope slithered out of her pack and wrapped itself around their branch on one end. The other end of the rope snaked higher to attach to another branch near the trunk, adding support to the branch they would use. Then Adrienne walked out past the wall on the branch and dropped a smart rope for their descent. She leaped gracefully from the branch to the rope. As she braked on the way down, the branch moved significantly, but it held. Master hesitated. He peered at the dark grounds from the branch. Everything was quiet and calm. He felt a sense of unease.

Once I drop down, it will be much harder to get back out.

He looked at Orb's feed one more time. The stealthy spy machine had found no hidden dangers other than those they had prepared for. Master took a deep breath and followed after his ex-lover.

The grass yielded under his soft footgear as he landed. His stealth suit told the smart rope to retreat back up to the branch and wait for a directed signal. Somehow the smell of the trees and the grass penetrated his suit.

"Hold," Adrienne sent.

Master waited. Adrienne took out a bag and released a hundred leaf bugs into the backyard.

"What for?" Master asked.

"If their systems see a few anomalies, they'll attribute it to the swarm of leaf bugs first," Adrienne said. "I heard it happens from time to time. Some random chemical causes them to mass up and mate, and they trip some alerts here and there. Now, to the gazebo."

Master followed the faded image of Adrienne his suit fed to him. Her ghostly appearance and the dark back yard made a creepy thrill run down his spine.

The gazebo looked like it was made of wood, but Master assumed it had been fashioned from any of a dozen more sensible substances that would not slowly rot away. He immediately envisioned the planks of its floor sitting upon pressure sensors that would report any shifting of weight. Such a setup would not necessarily exist to detect trespassers. Many houses knew exactly where their occupants were at all times to better serve them. Still, Master's imagination ran to the paranoid; the various service processors embedded in everything all around them detected nearby links and offered them various services. No doubt if the gazebo detected an authorized visitor, it would offer any of a dozen options, such as shading from the sun or playing music.

They walked into the small structure. He felt a little better behind the partial shelter of the vine-entwisted trellis walls of the gazebo. Master saw one table and six chairs. He cast his gaze around the grounds again, but nothing detectable had changed. Adrienne stood on a small table and cut a hole into the ceiling of the gazebo with a laser. The material she cut away disappeared as her suit heuristics decided it was a part of her equipment to be hidden, then reappeared as the centerpiece of the table.

Assistant would see that and know something bad was happening. I hope this estate doesn't have something as powerful watching tonight.

"Go!" hissed Adrienne, even though she communicated over the link. Master stepped onto the table and pulled himself up. The inside smelled of burnt plastic. Master crawled slowly forward through the cramped space. Every time he placed a forearm or a knee on one of the support struts he feared a settling creak.

Adrienne made it inside after he had advanced two meters. Inside that cramped space, Master felt more vulnerable than he had out in the open. He could not maneuver, could barely breathe. He told himself that he could cut his way out and run for it at any time. That got him another five meters forward.

"Stop," Adrienne said.

"What is it?"

"Liane is... was more paranoid than I thought. There's a video feed of this space."

We're invisible... but we created that hole, and we're disturbing things in here?

"Then we've been detected?" he asked.

Adrienne did not answer for a long second.

"I don't think so," she finally sent back. "Most of the light here by the feed comes from these side vents. The sensor has to tolerate ambient light changes outside. If it's not being fed into an AI, then I think we'll be okay. Just don't move anything in here, if there is anything to move."

Master continued to crawl. He watched the dust getting wiped off the crossbeams he slid over and wondered if it would be enough to trigger some kind of alarm. He decided Adrienne would let him know if there was anything else they could do.

He reached the end. Only a thin film of green plastic blocked the way.

"No other choice but to move it?"

"Agreed," Adrienne said. He slid it forward enough to slide through and she followed.

They emerged into the greenhouse. The air inside, though humid, was welcome refreshment after the tight crawl space from the gazebo. Most of the plants were just below them. A major support beam ran from their spot straight across to join with the house. There, in a cubbyhole opposite their current niche, was where they planned to cut their way up.

He slid across the beam. A slight glance upward told him there might be room to walk across it, but he rejected the idea. No point in risking anything. He came to a cross beam and saw a spider web in the corner between beams. He wondered if the creature's ancestors had hitched a ride here from Earth, or had been brought on purpose.

He took up a position on the far side and watched the room as Adrienne cut a hole in the wall with her laser.

Master wondered how many nights the greenhouse had passed in complete peace and quiet before they had arrived.

Adrienne went through the portal she had created. Master climbed up after Adrienne to the second floor. They emerged into a hallway. Master had more odd thoughts. If Liane were still alive, would they have to worry about encountering her in the hall? How many nights in the past year had she been up and about in the middle of the night?

Strange time for such thoughts. I guess I'll always wonder about Liane. Even if we find some records, there will be things I can never know.

Master felt new appreciation for being able to work with Adrienne.

"Thanks for doing this with me, Adrienne," he said.

She expressed nonverbal amusement through the link.

"You're sounding more like yourself every day," she said.

They walked down a very short corridor to the stairs. They made no sound. Master marveled at the stealth suits. The suits canceled out any EM reflections off their bodies, as well as providing mobile sound curtains to dampen the vibrations of their movements. He checked the power of his suit. It told him it still had hours of power left.

At the top of the stairs, they came to a new hallway with four doors. Flat video anchor points adorned walls but they appeared empty. Either nothing was being broadcast onto them, or else the stealth suits did not pass the data through to Master's link.

"Close now, just two rooms down," she said. Master knew it already since he followed their progress on the same tactical she saw.

They walked into a large room. At the center, Master saw a vaulted and canopied bed. He immediately wondered if he had ever slept there in his previous life. Adrienne glanced at him as if she knew what he must be thinking, but she said nothing. Her ghostly outline proceeded to a side table. She motioned toward the items on its surface. Master

147

saw some storage sticks and folded paper clothes. Three urns sat in the center of it all.

"There," Adrienne said.

"The urns?"

"They probably hold copies of Liane Vanault's death cache," Adrienne said.

It was the way of citizens of Red Calais to leave behind objects after death containing their personal data in well-defined formats that were kept in use for such purposes. Master was vaguely aware it was an improvement upon an ancient tradition where the urns used to contain the ashes of the deceased.

Master did not try to access them. Adrienne had already turned one slightly to face her. No doubt she was telling her stealth suit to connect to the urn.

"The archives are here," she said. "There's a public segment as well as various encrypted... Matthieu!"

"What?"

"She left you a private segment here. I took the public one. Connect to one through the suit and copy it."

"She left me one?"

That's either very lucky, or a trap, depending on whether or not she was the one who poisoned me.

"Do it!" Adrienne urged. "We don't have to erase the archive at all. If you just download your segment, you'll have everything she left for you and we can sneak right back out of here. No one will ever know we were here."

Master decided she was probably right. It would work better if they left without damaging an archive. Besides, if Liane had been his friend, he should leave her legacy data untouched.

What if Adrienne is the one who poisoned me? What if it was to obtain something that Liane and I discovered?

Master copied the data left for him. He quickly dropped the connection.

"We probably could have just walked in here in broad daylight and asked for my segment of the archive," Master said. "We didn't have to break in."

"Good to know. At least this way, no one will be alerted to your presence."

"Okay, I've got it. Let's get out of here."

Master watched a lamp on the other side of the room scoot across a table. Then it dropped to the floor.

"You have been detected," a synthetic voice announced. It had sounded in both the air and his link. Master knew a perfect Terran voice could easily be mimicked, so the synthetic voice meant the speaker was a robot or an AI obeying the Core World's rules that demanded artificial entities be clearly identifiable as such.

"Reverse Hastur!" Adrienne said. "I knocked something over."

Security.

"Do not attempt to flee or we will fire upon you. Step into the middle of the room and await the arrival of Vanault Security personnel."

"Over here! This closet," Adrienne snapped.

"We can't hide in a closet!" Master said reflexively. He realized as soon as he said it that an expert like Adrienne would not tell him to do something without a good reason. "What's your plan?" he asked.

Master and Adrienne scrambled into the closet. Its thin door slid shut.

"Proceed to the middle of the room and await the arrival of Vanault Security personnel."

Master zeroed in on the source of the voice. He prepared his laser to fire through the thin door.

"Don't kill it!" she said.

"We have to get out of here!"

"Listen to me. I've been privy to some of the cleanup actions in Red Calais. The Vanault family is well connected."

Master had heard stories. When someone showed themselves to be a danger to the status quo, the merchants hunted them down.

I guess the stories aren't exaggerated.

Adrienne pointed at the back of the closet. Master turned his laser toward it. Three seconds later, a piece of the wall flopped forward, burned open by the weapon. They hopped out into a side corridor.

"This way," Adrienne said before Master could orient himself in his link map.

She's done this more than I have, he thought, running after her as she sprinted down the hall. The next thing he knew, they were leaping down the stairs. Adrienne reached the bottom and ran to the hole they had cut into the second floor. She hopped into the hole without bothering to grab on to anything. Master felt simultaneously happy she had gotten out of his way so quickly and concerned if he could do the same thing without smashing out of control through the greenhouse below.

He waited for a second, giving Adrienne time to clear out of the way.

"Come on!" came the direct line communication from below. Master jumped.

At the bottom, he let his legs collapse with the impact as he rolled forward. He impacted something he could not see. At first he thought he may have hurt Adrienne, then he realized he had underestimated her again. She had prepared to catch and stabilize him. He had rolled right to her and she caught him neatly.

"The crawl space? It's slow," Master said.

"Agreed. Let's go out the other door of the greenhouse, onto the enclosed deck." Even as she spoke, she moved that direction. Adrienne hopped down from the beams to the floor of the greenhouse. Master copied her jump. He saw the door a few meters ahead. Adrienne paused to cover the greenhouse and let him go first.

Master ran through the door, then he ran into cold, gray metal and rebounded. A security robot turned, trying to track the object it had hit. He rolled away and scrambled around it.

Master saw two long tables in a room with three glass walls overlooking the back lawn. He saw two doors. He went for the nearest one and tried it manually. When it did not budge, he let his suit try to link to it and command it to open.

"This room's been secured," he said. A machine walked into the room. It was a column with four arms and four legs. A glue grenade launcher in its upper half swiveled as it sought a target.

"We're trapped," Adrienne said.

Master pulled his laser from his hip and put it on a wide firing arc. He pointed it through the doorway at the adjacent dining room.

"Don't put up a fight," Adrienne warned. Master activated the laser. A big section of the nearest table ignited in flame.

"What are you doing?"

An emergency klaxon broadcast to his suit's link announcing a fire. Master shot into the dining room a second and third time for good measure.

The door beside them unlocked and announced itself as an exit route. Master dashed out and started across the back lawn in the relative darkness.

"Evasive measures!" Adrienne urged.

Aren't we stealthed?

Master supposed when on high alert, the security sensors could pick up as much as a few footprints in the lush grass. He changed his course just in time. The retort of a glue grenade launch echoed from the outer walls, though the heavy vine cover broke it up somewhat.

"We don't have time for the rope," Adrienne said. "Just use the vines."

Master ran to the wall but instead of leaping up he turned. He saw three security machines in the backyard.

That was fast. I wonder if the security agency will send more?

He told his laser to reduce power and selected visual

light spectrum. He fired the laser at the nearest security robot. The weapon targeting software focused its energy on the front sensor array of the machine.

"Okay, go!" Master said. He put his laser back onto his belt.

Adrienne required no further urging. Master saw the vines start to sway on his left. He sprinted the last few steps toward the wall and leaped into the vines himself. His left hand found purchase immediately, though his right floundered for a long second, then grasped a strong vine.

The machines shot two more glue grenades, but Adrienne and Master managed to top the wall without getting stuck. From the top, they dropped fearlessly to the ground below.

Adrienne stared at Master. "Still the risk taker, Matthieu? Are you sure you lost your memory?"

"What?"

"There's no law in Red Calais. There's no reason to expect starting a fire would unlock the doors."

"I know she was Space Force. How could someone like that not care about safety precautions?" Master said. "Besides, every house is equipped to control fire."

Adrienne frowned.

"I guess it worked. That's all that matters."

She smiled. He smiled back.

Chapter 23

Master accessed Liane's archives from a soft seat in his new dwelling. Adrienne sat across from him in her own luxurious chair, relaxing in undersheers after their adventure in the Vanault compound. She looked through the files with him in her PV.

"Oh, Matthieu!" Adrienne said. "The Space Force!"

Master saw it.

I was in the Space Force? Is it even possible?

Adrienne slipped her hands under her legs and leaned forward like a satisfied cat. "I guess your need for adventure took you far from Idona."

"Amazing. Yet I ended up back here. I wonder if I became incapacitated off world?"

The files revealed Master had served with Liane Vanault; even more, they had investigated alien ruins together on what had been the frontier at that time. More pictures flitted by through the viewpanes in his mind. Master stared at a dark planet with a thick, swirling atmosphere called Chalaz. The single word designation meant it had been specially named. It would normally have been called simply Scolb Mininuvus III using the name generated by the Space Force algorithms.

Master decided it was not that unusual that this planet carried a more specialized name. Many planets with something as distinctive as alien ruins ended up being named by the Space Force scouts who found it or the scientists that came there.

The next image capture showed the crater of an ancient volcano that dwarfed the tiny Terrans and robots that moved across its surface. He saw dark round tunnels filled with flowing rivers of thick mist. There had been soldiers there as well. Master saw a capture of a group of armed men escorting a robot through the soupy atmosphere.

One picture showed him and Liane working over a familiar device in a room of smooth gray stone. It was a duplicate of something Master had in the Vault. Assistant put the clues together faster than Master could; it provided the rest for Master so that he could understand. Assistant had been interfering less and less, but this time, the information seemed especially significant.

"It's not a nuclear warhead," Master muttered.

"What?"

The nuclear device in the Vault was not exactly a Space Force nuke; it was a powerful device that could activate a dormant volcano, given a complex configuration that could only be calculated after extensive scans of the structure of the magma chambers below. Liane and Master had used such a device on the planet.

"It's a thermal activator," he said. "We used it to reawaken a sleeping alien race."

"How could that—oh. Nanorith."

Master came across an image set of Liane and himself kissing in some kind of Spartan personal quarters. They probably lived in a place like that while they stayed on the frontier planet with the Nanorith colony. Master stared at the image, waiting to feel something he had forgotten. There was nothing. It was like a picture of strangers.

Master stopped sharing all the pictures in the private segment as he looked. He continued to sift through the images and video feeds. Clearly things had become more intimate between his old self and Liane. As he worked, he created an archive that would be appropriate to share with Adrienne. Some of the material felt too intimate to share with anyone.

He examined more pictures. He saw clusters of black orbs in carrying containers. They looked familiar... Nanorith shards!

The black orb had belonged to Master in the first place! He sifted through more. Adrienne saw these pictures too. In some pictures, Master was shown with a shard in his hand.

"Is that a Nanorith egg? Do you still have it?"

"Oddly enough, I recently reobtained it."

"Where?"

"From a rich merchant named Sorune."

"He must have stolen it from you. You would never have parted with such a rare thing."

"I don't remember."

"Take my word for it, then. It disappeared after you lost your memory? Matthieu, whoever did this to you, could they have done it for the egg."

Yes. Sorune stole it or bought it from whoever stole it... and the party that destroyed my mind, could that be connected?

"It's a possibility..." Master said. He found a conversation record and skimmed through it.

"Liane and I had a mission involving the egg. It was to be brought to Idona," he told Adrienne.

"What for? Scientific analysis?"

The photographs hinted that the mission had had a personal component. Many of the photographs were clearly not official. Even though they might well simply be retina captures stored in a link, they were not in a lab with officials and guards standing around. The egg did not seem to be documented in an official way that Assistant could uncover, though admittedly, the Space Force kept such things highly classified.

"I don't think so. I'm not sure, but it was to be revived here. If this was for the Space Force, it was something very secret. I get the feeling maybe it was... something Liane and I planned ourselves."

"What good would a baby Nanorith be here?" Adrienne asked.

"The race has a form of genetic memory. Or at least something close to it. Everything the Nanorith needed to remember, or I guess I could say, everything it needed to know, is in the egg."

"Reverse Hastur, was it to be an ambassador?"

"I don't know exactly," Master said. "The egg must be

155

activated. I have to speak with it."

"I see. Not only would you be completing your mission, it might know more about you."

"We'll find out."

"Sounds like a long, daunting project. It could be dangerous. There was at least one person who apparently didn't want it to happen."

"Daunting, maybe, but I don't think it will take long. You don't understand how fast they are," Master said. "Assistant has a lot of information about the Nanorith it has pieced together from these archives and other sources on the network. Apparently Nanorith can live our equivalent of whole lifetimes in a few weeks."

"Won't it need their advanced technology? Did you bring that with you, too?"

"I don't think so. They operate at very high temperatures. They have more energy available for their minds and bodies than we did in our ancient past. Their minds work faster, and at higher capacities."

"What difference does it make? It couldn't leave the heat chamber you would need to heat it up."

"Hrm. You're thinking of it like it's a Terran waking up naked in a room on an alien planet. Nanorith are different in so many ways. They live their lives much faster. It will have all the resources we've given it ready to use in minutes. Their shards use advanced methods to produce whatever is needed, requiring only a lot of heat energy and adequate raw materials. These things are highly advanced. They know how to bootstrap themselves from scratch whenever a site heats up from volcanic activity."

"To do what? What if we can't take care of it?"

"We were meant to revive it. It can tell us. Maybe it can live on its own in the crust of Idona. Or maybe it will just live its life quickly and leave some shards behind. I don't remember enough and Assistant doesn't have the answers, either."

"Okay. We'll ask the Nanorith. Its life may be in

danger along with yours. The Space Force or some powerful merchant might take it prisoner."

"Or some corporation," Master said, staring at Adrienne. She picked up on his insinuation instantly. In response, she offered him a truth check.

"My only involvement here is to help you, Matthieu."

Master accepted her word.

Michael McCloskey

Chapter 24

The elevator gate opened, allowing Master and Adrienne access to the underground facility. They walked out into a wide corridor of industrial ceramic. Glow bars nestled in the ceiling cast low illumination across the dull gray-green floor.

"Luckily it was only shut down a short time ago," Master told her. "It required minimal refurbishment to get ready for a burn."

Master was aware of Orb, who trailed along behind them. Hydrangea, being less mobile, had stayed back to guard the Vault, while Mimic had been sent out to gather money. The facility had not come cheap, and they still had to operate it. Master led her deeper into the complex.

"How many fusion reactors does this place take to operate?"

"Only three standard 'H' type reactors. You see, the facility draws most of the heat from a magma chamber much farther down."

"Isn't that dangerous?" Adrienne asked, though she showed no signs of anxiety.

It would take a lot to faze her, Master thought admiringly.

"I don't think so. There are five or six other such facilities on Idona. The sites are chosen carefully to minimize chances of tectonic interference. In our case, it may be a major plus since the Nanorith live on volcanic sites. This way, if it needs access to more heat down below, it has it. Just imagine what a Nanorith could teach us about drawing energy from the crust!"

Adrienne smiled. "You're excited! I can see you coming into your own again."

"Do you really think so?"

"You're becoming more animated every day."

"A response to your presence, perhaps," Master said, though he knew part of the answer was that Assistant had incorporated the Vanault archives into its model of his old mind and updated his personality accordingly.

They came to a central control station inside the complex. The lights had come on before they walked in. Master saw row after row of seats and PV anchor flats.

"Wow, there are a lot of seats. It's complex to run?"

"Maybe, but right now, we're robotics only," he said. "Our secret is safe for now. Assistant is cleaning the operation logs, I trust it not to miss anything."

"The robots make it easy to find out what happened here," she said. "If someone breaks into your datastores, they'll know."

"Then you're in charge of stopping that. It won't be long. I hope to be done by the time anyone learns what's going on here. Besides, the robotics tell the story of what I'm doing but not why. The egg hasn't been seen by any machine yet. It would be confusing to see what I'm doing right now from the outside."

"But it would be clear to anyone who knows about the egg. To whoever gave you the nano poison, assuming that these things are connected as I believe."

"The merchant is gone. If it was him, we're safe."

Master did not feel as confident as he let on, still, he was eager to revive the shard and learn what it knew of events. He accessed a view of the central burn chamber and had his link put it up across a curved wall. He sent Adrienne's link an offer to share the anchored view. They saw a large room with dark walls. A large hole dominated the center of the floor and vents ringed the top of the walls. Bright light flooded down from above. Stacked bricks of various materials covered most of the floor.

"It looks hot in there already! What are these things?"

"Raw materials. Here in the furnace, it will be as hot as a volcano, but we lack many materials that would be present in the natural environment of a lava tube."

"So you believe it can make use of those to fabricate advanced machines?"

"Yes. This race is used to bootstrapping itself up from a cold state of hibernation. They have amazing nanotechnology in those shards that can restart their technology chain quickly."

"But they normally wake up in one of their cities, right?"

"Cities that may have been dormant for thousands of years. Whatever they had may be gone by that time."

"I'll believe it when I see it. Sounds like magic to me."

"Any sufficiently advanced—"

"Reverse Hastur! I know it, I know it."

Master smiled. Adrienne was cute when she cursed, even though he had forgotten the meaning of her words.

"Okay, so you just need me to beef up the net security? Anything else?" she asked.

"That's it. I'll do the rest."

Master meant: Assistant would do the rest. He observed and learned about the furnace as Assistant followed the heat-up procedure for the chamber that contained the shard and the raw materials. Despite his impatience, the industrial facility would take almost an hour to bring the chamber to his target temperature.

Master contemplated the Nanorith shard. So much had happened around this object. It was so much more than just an ordinary rock. Its molecular structure must be staggeringly complex.

I've done this before. Or at least, people around me have... in the Space Force. And I don't remember what happened. Usually, that would be a sign not to do it again.

"The temperature is rising rapidly," Master noted. "I wonder if we should have hired some mercenaries."

Adrienne laughed. "A bit too late for that, now," she said. "I'm armed to the teeth, if it matters." She had brought a projectile rifle because she said it would work well in the long, empty corridors of the facility.

"I expected nothing less," Master said. He had brought his laser pistol with him, though he did not expect it would be of any use against a hostile Nanorith.

They set to waiting. There was not much to do but monitor the sensors and watch the furnace chamber. Master eyed the shard, watching for changes as the temperatures rose past the melting points of many of the other compounds within the furnace. Several of the piles had started to glow, but the orb remained totally black. Master supposed the idea that it would glow was silly. Why would it give off precious energy that could instead be used by the young organism?

"It's almost within the desired range," Master notified Adrienne.

"It looks dead," she said.

Suddenly the egg blossomed before their eyes into a garden of complex crystals. In the next three seconds they watched the formations grow, changing shapes, sizes and colors chaotically until the entire blast chamber filled with tall black obelisks criss crossed with thin blue bracing.

Master found his heart hammering in his chest as the growth expanded out of control.

Its speed is unnerving.

"Stick me!" Adrienne exclaimed at its rapid growth. "Run!"

Master also felt the urge to run, but they could not escape anything that fast. He stood his ground.

"Stick me? What's that?" he asked absentmindedly. The thing had grown at an alarming rate, but seemed to stabilize. Adrienne calmed down.

"You know... stick me? Sorry, your memory. 'Stick me eight ways from extinction' is the full phrase, I believe."

Master raised an eyebrow as he had seen Adrienne do.

"There's a lot of energy in this system," he said. "The Nanorith can do everything rapidly: grow, think, live."

"Then we're at its mercy," Adrienne said.

Assistant notified Master of an incoming link connection.

"It has opened communication," Assistant told him.

Adrienne waited expectantly. Assistant was hard

pressed to keep up with the alien. They exchanged information many times faster than Terrans could process it. Master waited.

"Assistant is talking with it," Master told Adrienne. He looked in the chamber for any sign of the alien, but he could only see the obelisks.

"The shard came here with you to find a Trilisk here on Idona. A *living* Trilisk," Assistant told Master over his link. Trilisks were a species never before seen by Terrans. Only a handful of ruins and artifacts had been found, artifacts which no one could understand.

Master absorbed that for a second before Assistant had another report. "You were likely incapacitated because of this," Assistant said. "The Nanorith thanks you for reviving it. It would like to share memories with you."

"Just like that?" Master replied aloud, to let Adrienne know a conversation was occurring.

"A great deal of time has already passed to it. I recommend we cooperate quickly," Assistant said.

"Then we will."

"What does it want, Matthieu?" Adrienne said.

"It wants help to complete its mission. It has agreed to exchange memories with me," he said.

"What mission?"

"It's looking for someone. Or something. I'll be better able to tell you after I've shared memories."

"Good luck, Matthieu. Be careful," Adrienne said with concern. He smiled.

"I'm ready."

Somehow Master heard a message in his head, though it did not come through his link.

There will be confusion. Even pain. Then understanding.

Master nodded. He was ready.

Master left his body and went off-retina, though he wasn't sure how. He felt a distant burning. He became white hot, yet it did not hurt much, despite the warning he had received. The heat was *energy*. He became a whirlwind of activity. Thoughts blazed through his mind like tendrils of lightning crossing a night sky.

Master opened his eyes, or dreamed of opening his eyes. His fingers grew into long whiplike appendages that danced in the hot wind rising from beneath. His mind slipped into a virtual world beyond anything a Terran could comprehend. Here, the Nanorith would work out every problem it faced with a speed a Terran computer could only dream of.

Chapter 25

Master gasped. He went back on-retina. The first thing he felt was *cold*. Then *danger*.

"Something's wrong," he said. He saw the furnace chamber up on the wall. It had changed into a collection of rotating violet disks with flashes of yellow light dancing between them. It looked like a work of abstract art created by a set of math equations.

"I'm here," Adrienne said. "You may feel wrong because you still have the Nanorith in your mind."

"True. But there's danger."

Adrienne looked away for a moment. Master noticed it too. An alert signal.

Intruders.

"Who would dare?"

"It's the Space Force," Adrienne said. Her voice was laced with dread.

Master looked at the feeds Adrienne had spotted them from.

"No. It's a few investigators. That's all."

"They didn't bring a battalion of marines, if that's what you mean," Adrienne said. "But it's still them. We're caught."

"We can't hide. Not yet. We need to stop them."

"Stun them," Adrienne said.

"Kill them," Master said.

"Really? You were in the Space Force."

"You go. Never come back. It will never get traced back to you." Even as Master said it, he doubted his own words.

They would uncover her connection. But she's a spy, she might know how to evade them. Her corporation might shield her.

Adrienne sighed. "I'll kill them with you, Matthieu. You're fighting for your life. And the life of the Nanorith. I'm in."

"The Nanorith can take care of itself, if we can buy it more time. It came here for a purpose."

"What?"

"Have you ever heard of a Trilisk?"

"More aliens?"

"I'll tell you if we survive." Master kept checking the internal security sensors. Some of them had started to drop offline. Assistant started to delay their cyber attacks.

"There's only two and we know they're coming," Adrienne said.

"They have Veer suits and laser carbines," Master said. He held his head in his hands. Pain lanced out from his temples.

Of all the times to show up. I feel like I should be able to create a disruption obelisk and—no, that's the Nanorith. I'm a Terran. I have a Terran weapon.

"Matthieu?" Adrienne asked. "They're coming from that direction in about two minutes."

How long is that? Two minutes? That's forever.

Something updated the tactical.

"The Nanorith has means of detection up," Assistant said. "It's feeding us data."

"There are two more in stealth suits," Master said. "They want the Nanorith. And they'll kill us to get it."

"Stealth suits? How will we—"

Master made an unintelligible noise as he tried to speak the Nanorith's name and realized there was no translation.

"The Nanorith will expose them to us. But we have to kill them."

Master linked into Adrienne's tactical. He saw his own position on the tactical and the two Terrans Adrienne had detected. Assistant added a feed, then two more enemies appeared.

"Stick me! The cloaked ones are close."

Master hurriedly dug into the details of what they had learned.

"The other two have heavy weapons for the alien. These two are assassins sent for us," Master said.

"First we turn the tables on the assassins, then get the other two from behind," Adrienne said, checking her weapon.

"Alternatively, we could give these two the slip and go protect the Nanorith," he said. "If it dies while we fight here, what good will all this have done?"

"I've locked them all out," Assistant said. "They won't be able to use the facility's sensors or robots against us."

"So they assume we're in here, but they wouldn't know," Master said.

"Right. They know the layout, but they're coming in blind."

"We need to use deception," Master said. "Lure them into the observation center for the backup blast chamber. Assistant, can you make it look like that's where everything is going on?"

Master pointed out locations on the tactical as he spoke. "Those two teams will join back up over here, because the nearest entrances are side by side along this tunnel. Make them think we're controlling it from there. Have the facility show that furnace as the active one."

"Tell Assistant to let them break in and get the fake leads. And then?"

"Oxidize their surfaces and rearrange to... no." Master shook his head to clear the alien thought. "Fill the chamber with halon and wait out their Veer suits' life support."

"Matthieu?" Adrienne looked at him with lines of concern across her forehead.

My face feels red. I can feel my veins popping out. Must look grotesque.

"I haven't recovered fully," he confided in her. "But Assistant is taking care of it. Just wait until they travel by the first blast chamber and engage them outside the observation room. It's a wide corridor with no cover, they'll dodge in there and then we have them."

"I'm not so sure they'll run in there instead of attack me."

Master looked around the tactical in desperation. He found two large robots near the alternate furnace. They were large and extremely durable, but very slow. He sent them remote orders. The robots moved toward the far side of the blast chamber.

"I can help you herd them in," he said. His eyes moved across the equipment containers. He accessed the contents with his link.

"Here—arrrrgh." More flashes of pain whipped through his head.

"Matthieu? Do you need a medbot?"

"There's a kit in there. I'll get it. Here, you take these." He sent her a pointer.

"Temperature sensors? What good—"

"They roll like guided grenades," he said. "These guys will think they're grenades for a second or two, for sure. When you fire on them, send these forward. They'll duck into that observation chamber."

"Wouldn't one of the blast chambers be a more durable trap?"

"This whole place is made of high grade ceramic."

Adrienne sent a nonverbal acknowledgement and opened the container he had referenced. The container was filled with the mobile temperature sensors. Some of them were blackened, used. She grabbed four of the shiny new ones from the bottom of the case.

She moved toward the case containing the medical kit.

"No, Adrienne. Go now. You barely have time. I can get the kit."

Adrienne must have checked the positions of the enemy in her PV. She left without saying anything. Master felt only admiration for the response; he knew she felt concern for him, but Adrienne put it aside because she had to act. He knew she could handle it.

He watched in his PV as he opened the case with the

kit. He saw Adrienne moving into position in the corridors. The medikit pulled itself out of the case, querying and scanning for injured. Master almost vomited as a new wave of pain washed over him. He let the kit attach to him so it could inject chemicals into his system. His mind cleared.

"That's better. Shut it down in here," he said to Assistant. "We have to make it look like we haven't been here."

Assistant killed the lights in the area. He watched the tactical. The two soldiers with heavy weapons altered course to the alternate furnace. The assassins did not turn off, though.

They still want to check this place. They don't believe it.

Now that his mind felt clear, Master felt the first doubts about the plan.

"These two haven't taken the bait," he sent to Adrienne. "They're still coming."

"It'll work," Adrienne said. "They've already broken into the fake feeds I set up. You just have to hide as they go by. When they see an empty control center, they'll believe the fake data."

Master took out his laser pistol and had it emit enough light for him to find a hiding place behind a stack of equipment cases. Then he went prone and turned out his light. The next thirty seconds extended to forever. His Nanorith memories made it worse. It felt like he waited for weeks. Even though Master did not think fast like a Nanorith, it seemed that race was not accustomed to inactivity.

An eternity later, he heard the door open. There was no other noise, not even the sound of a footstep. Orb floated overhead and did not move. It did not see anything.

We can't hear anything because they have sound curtains built into their suits. Master imagined invisible assassins walking toward them. *So creepy. We're vulnerable.*

The door closed. The feed from the Nanorith showed the two assassins on a new course, headed toward the fake control center next to the other furnace.

"It worked. They're headed there."

"And the heavy hitters are waiting," Adrienne said. "They want the stealthed soldiers to go in first. Perfect."

Master watched as the two elements of the Space Force team rejoined. The assassins moved down the last corridor toward their trap.

"They're sending the cloaked ones in. They believe we're in there."

The heavy weapons crew took up a position in the corridor to cover the stealthed men. They knelt and cradled heavy lasers in their arms. Adrienne had a position around a corner behind them.

"I'm attacking now," she said. Master watched a video feed from the corridor, on the end of the passage near Adrienne.

Her shiny spherical sensors rolled forward. The men whirled. Two grenades hopped out from their belts and moved to intercept the decoys. Meanwhile, Adrienne had started taking her shots with her projectile rifle. One of the men staggered under a hit. His arm flopped, then dropped off his torso. His suit quickly controlled the blood, but the man had been neutralized. He dropped.

His companion dropped too, but it was to return fire from a prone position. Master watched in slow motion as they launched projectiles at each other. The data feed from the Nanorith showed that the cloaked men had doubled back in reaction to Adrienne's attack.

He'll kill her any moment now. Hurry, hurry! These things are so slow.

The two massive industrial machines appeared in the tunnel behind them, opposite Adrienne's position. Assistant had the machines grind together slightly, as if by accident. The contact made extra noise which brought the slow machines to the soldier's attention.

It worked. Sensing the flank, the three men ran into the open door of the observation chamber, dragging their injured squad member with them. Assistant closed them in. He imagined the looks on their faces when they realized they had no control over anything inside the facility.

"You have them zipped up tight?" Adrienne asked. "Will it hold?"

"The ceramic walls can absorb ridiculous amounts of energy. Laser carbines are nothing in here."

"So we have them. What now?"

"Turn up the auxiliary furnace," Master said. "Drop the power to the insulating shield in the observation center."

"Cold. I mean, hot. You know what I mean."

"They came here in stealth suits to shoot us in the back of our heads."

"I have no problem with it," Adrienne said. "But I think the old you might have."

"If the old me ever comes back, he can feel guilty about it."

"What about the Nanorith, then?"

Master went off-retina for a moment, then came back. "It's already gone."

Michael McCloskey

Chapter 26

Adrienne arrived to visit Master for the third time in a week. She walked out from the elevator that connected Master's new bunker to the surface far above. A blast of hot air greeted her. Keeping with the Red Calais habit of naming their houses, they had coined this new place the Subtern.

She continued along a short, dark hall which widened into the common room. Master waved her over to a long divan where he lounged.

"Adrienne," Master said, giving her a smile.

"Matthieu. Why are you hiding down here? It's not like you."

"I prefer to avoid danger, at least for a time."

"The Space Force may not be looking for you. They probably only want the Nanorith. Here in Red Calais, it's not safe for anyone to stir things up too much."

"I wasn't speaking of that. Assistant has managed to cover up a lot. I was speaking of the surface in general. It's too exposed to a myriad of threats."

Adrienne sighed and sat next to Master. She hesitated, then chose her words carefully.

"Matthieu? Really, what are you doing down here? This place is dark. Hot."

"I felt a need to move deeper," Master said.

"It's the Nanorith in you, isn't it?" she asked quietly. "Its memories are making you feel things."

"It's only reasonable to move to a safe distance below the surface. It's very cold up there. Anything can happen. It's unprotected."

Master saw something in Adrienne's look. His mouth tightened and his brows dropped.

"I know what you're thinking. I know I'm a Terran, not a Nanorith. I haven't lost my mind," he said harshly. "It's just... I feel things..."

Adrienne sat close to Master and put her hand on his.

173

Michael McCloskey

"I'm here to help. It must be difficult. You have to struggle to take the perspective of a Terran now that most of your memories belong to something—someone else."

"I'm breathing oxygen. Eating. Moving about. I'm doing what I must to survive. This place, it's what I prefer. I can make it very nice here. I can make it nicer for you."

"We can do that. You can live here. But you have to come to the surface. Promise me. You'll lose yourself entirely if you don't live as a Terran on a regular basis. You have to see the bright star over beautiful Idona, bask in its heat."

"I don't know. I'm still thinking things through."

"You've changed again, Matthieu. I'm worried about you. Our mission was to find the old you, but I wonder, have we gone the wrong direction?"

"It's the memories. They haunt me," he said. Adrienne joined him on the divan, then she frowned.

"Is this heated? Matthieu, you have to get a hold of yourself. Physically, you're a Terran and that is fact. Even if your mind is part Nanorith, it's not healthy to do this."

Master turned off the heater in the divan with his link.

"Memories," Master said. "People know that memories are a part of what you are. But they downplay it. They think they have a mind and a soul, and memories are just these things that happened to you. They're more than that. Memories are the entirety of what you are. You are nothing without your memories. Take anyone and give them new memories, they become an entirely different being."

Adrienne nodded. "You're making my point for me. I can believe this is both your Terran side and your Nanorith side talking. You lost your memories, and in so doing, lost everything you were. And Nanorith treasure memories so very much."

"I remember. I remember a white hot, pulsing world where everything sped along faster than these eyes can see, faster than this brain can follow, where entire lives came and went in the blink of an eye. This place is strange. So

174

cold. So slow. Yet it is a kind of life, here."

"We've collected many of your real memories, Matthieu," Adrienne soothed. "The Nanorith had some more?"

"The link cache backups aren't enough. A few of my memories were in that shard, too. The Nanorith gave them back to me, and they helped. But I need more. What I was, is no more without real memories."

Matthieu ran his hand through his hair as if trying to wipe away the torment. His hands were shaking.

"You can live. You can make new memories," Adrienne said.

"Most of the memories of my adopted race are gone. Most of my original memories, destroyed. They were so very precious! This poor race. Each life, a hundred years of knowledge, each to be snuffed out so suddenly at the end without a trace!"

A tear ran down Master's face. Assistant hoped Adrienne could continue to help. She looked very concerned. Assistant addressed Master and allowed Adrienne to listen in.

"Are you pleased that I've given you some of the Nanorith's memories? Can you be made whole with the memories of two? Three? Four?" asked Assistant.

Master stared off into space. Assistant did not know if he heard anything.

"I've been there. To study the Nanorith in the Space Force," Master continued. "If they succeeded, they must have been given the memories. The Space Force scientists must have had the resources to decode them. They would have perfected it."

Suddenly Master's breath caught.

"They must have traded memories with the Nanorith. That's what the Nanorith do; they remember. And when a stranger from another volcano is met, they ask to share each other's memories of forever!"

Master stood.

"Are you well, Master?" Assistant asked. Adrienne watched him with interest.

"Don't you see? They traded. *I* traded memories. Those Nanorith on that planet have my memories! All of them!"

Assistant sensed Master's excitement and was pleased. Adrienne stood with Master. Master watched the realization cross her face.

"The old you? You could be whole again?" she asked.

"Then tell me Master, how may we retrieve them?" Assistant asked.

Master abruptly sat back down, deflated.

"We can't."

"We need to go find the rest of your memories. Those you shared with the other Nanorith on that planet," Adrienne said.

"No! It's too far, too dangerous. I can't even imagine the vast cold space between here and there," Master said. "There's nothing worse than space. So cold, so exposed... no pressure."

"Even for your memories?" Adrienne asked. "It's what you need to be whole. You just said they're everything you are. If you're lost without them, you have nothing to lose."

"I don't know..."

"What memories did the Nanorith impart to you of your visit? Do you know exactly where to go? Do you remember the Terran facility?"

"No, I don't have any memories of my visit there. A single Nanorith shard contains a lot, but it can't hold everything. But the Nanorith colony does have them all. Not just of my visit, either, Adrienne. They have every single memory the original Matthieu had when we went to that planet."

"Then I go with you."

"It's too dangerous..."

"We *will* go. We can do it."

"I can't imagine ever doing that," Master said with

finality.

***

Assistant watched Master's internal struggle through his brain-link connection web. The influence of the Nanorith slowly waned, because those memories were so foreign to everything Terran. Master lived as a Terran and that strengthened that part of him, but it happened too slowly. Assistant had hoped that Master would eventually agree to go on his own. But time continued to pass on the surface, while Master hid down here as if he wanted to fall into a hundred black Nanorith shards and hibernate.

I thought before Master's true memories were irrevocably forgotten. I was wrong.

Assistant saw the entire mission to reconstruct Master threatened. It considered intervening as it had done before. Assistant had hoped its last need to alter the new Master had passed.

Orb floated patiently nearby. Its systems worked best when it remained active. When it did not have assignments, it often moved about the Vault as if waiting for someone to die.

Of course.

Assistant realized the original Master had not recorded the deaths of people because it pleased him. It was because to the Nanorith, one of the most important memories of all was the demise of an individual. If all memories were sacred to them, this part was the most holy of all. An individual often could not record and report its own death, but if observed, then nothing was lost.

That has to be why Master created Orb! A result of meeting the Nanorith.

The realization was heavy. Assistant had operated under the assumption the deaths pleased Master, they entertained him. It had initially wondered if they were for blackmail, yet it had never found any evidence of such usage. Assistant's model of Master was so very flawed!

All the more reason I have to go find the real Master.

Assistant decided to act against the new Master's wishes. It would not have done that to the old Master, but this new Master was an imperfect copy. It was clear the old Master's wishes and the new Master's wishes had diverged significantly with the introduction of the Nanorith memories. The old Master had had a lifetime of memories of his own before he had shared memories with the aliens; his old personality had been able to hold its own. But this Master had only a random collection of videos, photos, and conversations collected from his old friends and lovers. It was not enough. What sat before Assistant was more Nanorith than Terran; a frightened creature hiding deep underground, avoiding intense heat only because it would kill its new body.

The old Master loved adventure. And this is an important adventure.

"Assistant, I feel..." Master trailed off. Assistant worked for long hours as Master sat passively.

There. I have done what I can. My goal is still within reach, thought Assistant. *I can restore him to perfection. For now, he has to function. He has to be able to go to that planet.*

The next thing Master was aware of was Adrienne's voice. It came to him as if through a tunnel.

"Matthieu? Are you there? What's wrong?"

"You're right," he said. "We have to go and find the Nanorith I merged with. We have to travel there."

"You changed your mind! Good."

"Someone changed my mind... Assistant, begin planning the trip. We have many preparations to make."

"Yes, Master."

Master stared at Adrienne's beauty and felt the anticipation of a goal soon to be realized.

Chapter 27

Master thought of the high temperature facility where they had defeated the Space Force team. Master and Adrienne had put all the evidence into the furnace to destroy it. The Nanorith had left, taking all its strange constructs with it except one lone shard. Master did not know if it was a copy of the original, or something new, but he took it with him on the assumption it was important.

He believed the Nanorith had moved into a lair of its own design, deeper in the crust of Idona. Master knew it would continue to search for signs of a Trilisk presence on Idona.

Since the facility's usefulness was over, he had decided to sell it. Assistant had been able to arrange a transaction. Business flowed quickly and easily in Red Calais with no government to oversee it. The same system that emitted and verified public payment records in various currencies could also record property ownership changes and service terms of transactions.

Master had purchased a ship and named it the *Resolu*. It was small by Idonan standards, but fast and modern. Like the facility used to revive the Nanorith, the cost was not worrisome, but still enough for Master to feel it. He was glad he could sell one to pay for the other.

Master pored over the configuration of his ship with Assistant's guidance. The *Resolu* could take twenty people to any other Core World, but he planned for a much longer voyage. He had toyed with the idea of taking only Adrienne, but he had to admit the two of them lacked certain useful skills, at least while Master had no memories.

"The crew?" Master asked.

"I found what we're looking for, sir," Assistant responded to Master. It pointed him at several files holding information about the crew Assistant had selected using Master's parameters. The group under consideration had three men in it. They had been rated well by two independent grading agencies paid by Assistant.

Their leader, a man named Brandel, had considerable space faring experience under his belt. He had started moving ore from asteroids to various colony planets, then graduated to moving more valuable cargoes between frontier worlds, and finally, moving things between the Core Worlds and the frontier. Having just brought back cargo from the frontier, he was ready to take something—or someone—back out.

The only wrinkle for Brandel was that his ship was old and needed work. The captain could afford the work, but it would take time. Assistant's offer of crewing Master's ship came at an opportune time for Brandel and his two male crew members.

The other two were a little less known. Master read their names: Vickson and Spask. They had each been working with Brandel for over three Idonan years. Vickson was some orphan from the frontier, self-educated, and reasonably successful. Spask was soldier-turned-mercenary after a dishonorable discharge from the Space Force.

"Arrange a face to face at the earliest possible time," Master said. Then he went back to learning about the *Resolu*.

***

Master sat across from Captain Brandel at a table in a restaurant called Your Fine Taste. They had secured their own booth with a sound curtain provided by Mimic. Hydrangea sat on a sill to their right, abutting a wide window out onto a vast green lawn. Only Orb was absent. It wandered about on patrol outside, looking for signs of imminent violence, as futile as that was likely to be under the bright light of midday on Idona.

Brandel had thick, reddish hair tied back with a golden band. His face was lightly pocked, something almost unheard of on Idona. The man had to be making a statement by leaving it that way when so many nanosurgical recourses were available. Master did not have any guess why the captain might do that, but Assistant had leveraged vast amounts of data about Terrans and decided it was likely Brandel wanted to look like a tough frontiersman.

"Would you prefer to dine virtually or incarnate?" asked the table.

Master knew that incarnate dining was considered more polite for meetings with those from the frontier. Frontiersmen and women ate real food more often than participating in the virtual gorgings enjoyed by Core Worlders.

"Real food fine with you?" Master asked Brandel.

"Yes, much preferable, thank you," Brandel replied.

Master passed the decision on to the table and it started to take orders from everyone with personal link connections.

"So here we are. I wonder why you've decided to bring us together incarnate?" Brandel asked.

"You're curious about the face-to-face. Natural. It's because I have an illegal offer to make you," Master said.

Brandel raised an eyebrow. "There's nothing illegal in this place, as far as I can tell, so I assume you mean illegal somewhere else. You have a ship. You need a crew. What else is there?"

"A ship, yes. The *Resolu*. I'll send you the specs."

"And the destination? I have the coordinates, but they're so unusual I had to ask."

"The destination is a very ordinary star system, beyond the frontier, that has a volcanically active planet close to the size of Idona. There are alien ruins there which I need to visit."

"Alien ruins?"

"I understand. You need to vet me before you could accept such a task. You see, I've already dug deeply into your records, and I know you're not an undercover agent of the government."

Brandel nodded. "I know the same of you. Of course, I

had decided there was something... unusual about the offer you extended us. The compensation gave it away."

"Of course. I'm glad we can both speak frankly."

"Then why don't you use your ship's automation to get you there? You don't need us."

"I need to get there without incident. Also, once on-planet there are certain laborious technical feats which must be accomplished. I'll need help."

"Why not androids, then?"

"Two reasons. One, as I am engaged in illegal activity, I would have to modify them extensively to keep them from recording or reporting me. Secondly, I have no experience evading the Space Force. I suspect you do."

Brandel nodded. He would know the Space Force often patrolled alien ruin sites to keep smugglers and looters away. Master considered telling Brandel there were other reasons the Space Force might get involved, but decided against it just yet. Assistant did not override the decision.

Brandel nodded. "And if we get caught?"

"Your job will be to prevent that," Master said.

"I'm amenable to this arrangement," Brandel said. "If you'd like to depart soon, I can check your ship and its supplies and requisition whatever I need in a day."

"Excellent," Master said. "There is one other passenger, my companion Miss Rekaire. She's in the know, so no need to hide anything from her."

"We can discuss details and enjoy our dinner, then."

The Master-in-making had matured to the point where he could make his own decisions. There was still a long way to go, but the rest of the journey could be made with Assistant's help, not its direction.

The new Master created by Assistant had graduated to Matthieu.

PART III

Master

Michael McCloskey

Chapter 28

Matthieu sat within his quarters in the *Resolu.*

The stolen Reiss-Marck AI core was in his hands. He played with it idly, wondering what intellect it could unleash if given the chance. He had brought only a few of his many treasures with him, the thermal activator and his artificial agents being among them.

Orb floated above him, investigating the quarters for the tenth time as if it were the first. Hydrangea sat on a shelf which extended from the wall, secured there by its own tendrils. Mimic had once again taken the form of a small piece of self-transporting luggage.

"I think I'll use this core to make another agent someday," he told Assistant.

"That sounds like a grand idea, sir," Assistant replied. "With a core like that one, it might be one of your smartest creations."

Matthieu smiled. "Don't worry, I'm not replacing you anytime soon."

"Good to know!"

Adrienne came into the small room.

"Your captain gives me the creeps," she said. "He's got this self-satisfied look on his face all the time."

"Well, I must admit that I caved to the pressure to select a ship quickly," Matthieu said.

"Did anyone you know ever use them?"

"Not sure who I know anymore, or who to trust, other than you and Assistant."

"I think he's shady."

"He *is* shady. You recall that part of our agreement is evading the Space Force?"

"Does being on a ship jar any memories?" Adrienne said.

"No. Nor will it ever. My mind was gone. Assistant had to create a framework for me to even be able to move, to bathe, to breathe."

185

Adrienne nodded. Matthieu thought maybe she had simply been making conversation, but she seemed deflated.

"Tell me a story. About the old me," he asked.

Adrienne smiled. "Your favorite subject? Of course. Let's see..."

Matthieu watched her face as she collected a story. She was very beautiful. He watched her lips purse and then expand as she decided what to say.

I'm starting to appreciate her anew, he thought.

"Early on in our relationship, you discovered the hard way that I was into espionage. I received an urgent message and had to drop from our sky bus on short notice. I fell onto a transport disk. It was a close thing, I thought. Then I turned around and you were standing there! You had dropped onto the disk after me."

Matthieu smiled. "I followed you right off the edge?"

"Yes! And I called you a crazy bastard, but I was really so impressed. Even when I found out later you love to skydive and often carry a one-shot chute."

"Oh, I had a chute with me. That's a little better."

"Well, I don't know if you did that day. I never asked. I didn't want to ruin the memory. It's more fun not knowing." She smiled. "And that's what I told you when you asked me what the hell I was up to."

"Well, I'm sorry I told you anything about this," Matthieu said. "Imagine how exciting it would be if you had come with me not having any idea why I had gone on the run from the Space Force and hired a ship headed beyond the frontier!"

Adrienne smiled. "True. But this is serious business. I'm glad to know. It increases our chances of success. What should we do now?"

"Let's take dinner with Brandel," Matthieu suggested.

"I told you I don't like him!"

"All the more reason to keep our eyes on him," Matthieu said in a conspiratorial whisper. "Also, I think we should learn as much from Brandel as we can. If we're going to continue adventuring when I'm recovered, we could use the pointers."

Adrienne nodded. "This is completely different than operating in Red Calais. I admit it might be fun to wrest Brandel's secrets from him."

Matthieu paused off-retina. Then he smiled. "It's done!"

"Whatever shall I wear?" Adrienne said, putting on an elitist air.

"Anything at all," Matthieu said. He put a simple suit design into the clothing dispenser and received a disposable set immediately. Adrienne chose a simple and conservative black dress and took it from the machine, but she stopped.

"Tell me, Matthieu, have you... been with anyone since you lost your memory?"

Matthieu turned and saw that Adrienne stood expectantly by the bed.

"I have not," he said, stepping close to her.

"Well, someone has to rip this old outfit off me, it may as well be you," she said. She stared at him with wide eyes. Matthieu pulled her close and kissed her. He felt the thrill of something new take hold of him.

Why did I leave this woman? he asked himself, but the thought did not trouble him enough to distract him from his ex-lover, who felt entirely new to him.

***

Matthieu and Adrienne arrived in the crew's dining room with a fresh flush and new clothes. The decor and food could be as fancy or as utilitarian as anyone preferred; the *Resolu* provided fare for any taste or whim. Some in the Core Worlds might well have hooked themselves up to a blood glucose monitor and gorged in virtual reality, but Matthieu and Adrienne had set up an incarnate meal with minimal fanfare but maximal flavor and companionship.

Brandel had stuck with his rugged look. He wore real,

durable clothing as if expecting to perform a planetfall at any moment. His red hair remained pulled back with his distinctive gold band. Matthieu supposed the man might have only that one ring for his hair. They said those on the frontier traveled light by necessity.

The other crew members, Vickson and Spask, sat at the table beside Brandel. Matthieu sized them up as he told the dinner table to display a faux wood surface. Vickson was a fraction taller than Brandel, with small amounts of wavy hair over a high forehead. He displayed a well groomed goatee on his chin, together with a mustache framing his crooked lips. He wore real clothes like Brandel, but they looked less utilitarian: a maroon shirt with a zip seal down the front, and black pants.

Spask looked younger and cleaner, wearing a Veer skinsuit. His hair had been cut to a centimeter, enhancing his look of fitness. Spask had a large, straight nose, a clean cut face, and piercing eyes. To Matthieu, Spask was the most formidable of the three simply because it felt like Spask was the only one not trying too hard to put forward the air of a rugged spacefarer.

"Good evening, sir, and to you also, ma'am," Brandel said. He seemed to struggle to speak formally.

"Good evening," Adrienne said. She spoke it so kindly that Matthieu would never have guessed she did not like Brandel.

"So, Captain, how is the voyage shaping up so far?" Matthieu asked.

"Things are proceeding more smoothly than I expected. Your ship is impressive. I thought there might be some bugs to shake out, but that hasn't been the case. However, the Space Force took a good hard look at us from the network. They suspect something," Brandel said.

"I'm paying you a lot to avoid questions," Matthieu said flatly.

"It's not my fault if they already know what you're about," Brandel said.

"They might have their suspicions," Matthieu admitted.

"Have you done this sort of thing before?" Vickson asked. "If so, that might be why they're interested."

"When I last went this way, I was in the Space Force," Matthieu said. That got raised eyebrows from Vickson.

"What ship were you on?" Spask asked.

Oh yes. He is ex-Space Force as well.

Matthieu had to dodge the question, but he could at least make it seem like he would not say on purpose, rather than because he did not know.

"A scout ship. I went to those ruins, and now I need to go back."

"Valuable artifacts there, then," Vickson said.

"I'm not sure you want to know the details," Matthieu said. "If we should get caught, you'd be better off not knowing."

"If we get caught, we know nothing," Brandel said.

"That's what I'll say. Of course, if you're truth-checked..."

Brandel shook his head. "Then I'll pass it."

Matthieu did not follow Brandel's meaning. Assistant offered him a theory.

"He's taken a drug that prevents the formation of memories," Assistant told Matthieu over a private channel. "Right now, he's leaving himself a note that says he's vetted you and decided it's worth taking you to your destination while avoiding the Space Force. But he won't remember why it is you want to go there."

And myself? Matthieu thought. *Surely I would not pass.*

"I could help you do it," Assistant told him. "But from Brandel's point of view, the results of an investigation would be indeterminate. It might help him avoid maximum punishment."

"The Space Force could have been interested in one or all of you," Adrienne said sweetly. "Surely you've crossed a line or two yourselves, out on the frontier. The Space Force collects vast amounts of intelligence, even from the frontier. Just because they can't afford to act on it all doesn't mean they don't know about it."

"Could be," Brandel said. "I don't think they care what happens on the frontier, though, as long as it doesn't threaten the Core Worlds."

"I'm going back for information. In fact, I might learn exactly why they're so interested in me."

Brandel looked at Matthieu like he might believe what he had said, but Brandel also looked a bit disappointed. Brandel might have been hoping there would be artifacts that the crew could collect and sell, just as he figured Matthieu must be planning to do.

Matthieu felt like an outsider. As a Core Worlder himself, he suspected Brandel and the crew looked down on him. At least his money was still good. No doubt they would apply some obfuscation scheme to launder the payment, or at least change currencies somehow to cover their tracks, but they would still be spending it if they got him where he needed to go.

The group finished the meal with small talk and stories. Brandel told a couple of tall tales from the frontier, which Matthieu dismissed as hype meant to impress. When Master and Adrienne got back to his quarters, Adrienne let out a long sigh. She stretched her arms and back.

"Well, that wasn't very informative," Adrienne said.

"But it was entertaining," Matthieu finished for her. She turned toward him. He knew what she was going to say, even though he had only new memories of her.

"Not more entertaining than our prelude, I trust," she purred.

"Not even close," Matthieu said. He pursued her across the room, then ripped off her new outfit.

Chapter 29

Matthieu and Adrienne awakened from sleep to an alert signal.

"Straighten your room," Brandel's voice came to their links. "You have 80 seconds until I'm at your door, be ready to go."

Matthieu bolted upright. He almost told the clothing dispenser to print out an outfit, then decided to wear his Veer suit instead. He grabbed it from a storage closet and started to seal it up. Adrienne was up, so he told the bed to straighten itself. She tossed the shredded remains of yesterday's clothes into the recycler and grabbed her own armored skinsuit. He took a drink. He told Mimic to stay inside and directed Orb to get to the door. Then Brandel arrived outside their quarters.

Matthieu told the door to open. Brandel hurried inside.

"Follow me, and waste no time about it," Brandel told them. Matthieu finished sealing his Veer suit and followed Brandel out, with Adrienne close behind.

Matthieu's sleepy mind cleared a bit more as they walked.

"Hydrangea, hide the shard," Matthieu transmitted back to his agent in the room. Hydrangea sent back a video feed of its tendrils grasping the shard, then secreting it away inside the pot.

"The Space Force has intercepted us. We've been evicted out of tachyonic state. A surprise inspection is only minutes away," Brandel rattled off.

I thought he would be able to evade them. They must want me a lot. Because of the Nanorith? Or something else?

"Then where are we going?" Adrienne asked.

"I have a place you can hide," he said.

"This is my ship," Matthieu said. "What place can you..."

His question trailed off. Brandel proceeded quickly with absolute confidence. He traded concerned looks with

191

Adrienne.

Is this some kind of trick?

They arrived at the forward port airlock assembly. The ship's side lock door lay open. Brandel walked in and Matthieu followed. Adrienne looked into the lock but did not step inside.

I don't blame her. This is odd.

Matthieu found the lock to be half the size he expected. He approached the wall on his left. It looked normal, with a manual access panel and two structural struts.

"That's not part of the *Resolu* as we built it," Assistant said to Matthieu in a private channel.

"What's this?" Matthieu asked aloud.

"We added this unit to your airlock. The *Resolu* doesn't know about it. You'll be in there, with this airlock decompressed."

"They can scan everything," Adrienne said. "They'll find us anyway."

"Their scans won't defeat this," Brandel said.

"Then they'll investigate the black zone in their scan," Adrienne said.

"The device doesn't block the scan, it fools it. This spot is nestled right up against the outer bulkhead," Brandel said. "If they scan from this direction, inside the ship, they'll only see the bulkhead."

A previously undetectable door opened from the wall. Matthieu saw a modest hiding space beyond.

"Go in now. It has your basic amenities. You can last in there for a day if you have to." Brandel stood still, pretending to be patient despite the time pressure, awaiting their decision.

"Well, its trust these guys or get dragged in by the Space Force," Matthieu said to Adrienne over a private connection.

"Yes. We hired these men, I guess we'll trust them," Adrienne replied. She stepped into the lock.

"Orb, stay in the *Resolu,*" Matthieu commanded on a private channel.

Matthieu and Adrienne clambered into the small hiding space. They sat on a narrow metal bench within.

"And if they scan from another direction?" Matthieu asked.

"Then you would be found, but that won't happen. Trust me, this will work," Brandel said. "Connect your links exclusively through the device, and you can monitor what's going on outside. Don't initiate any costly queries, or cause anything odd to happen in the ship. You'll be connected through the airlock controller, which would not be expected to be doing anything at all unless the lock is in use, and even then, it wouldn't be right for it to be altering things elsewhere in the ship."

They closed the device. Lights activated within the tiny space. They each had a seat.

"Too small, of course," Matthieu muttered.

"Try to think of it as cozy," Adrienne said.

Matthieu dropped his link's public discovery service and connected only to the cloaking machine. He received a notification that the airlock had been decompressed.

"It would help to know why the Space Force cares about you. I assume it's you, and not me," Adrienne said.

"I don't know. I was thinking it may be because of the disappearance of the team that went into the furnace complex. Assistant did its best to obfuscate our presence there, but the Space Force may have smart people or AIs of their own that could have uncovered it."

"We need to consider other possibilities. It may be something you did before you lost your memory. Maybe Sorune reported the loss of the egg to the Space Force."

"How would he explain having it?"

"He could have reported seeing it somewhere. Sour grapes," Adrienne said.

"We can guess all we want. We need a source on the inside to find out the truth."

"We could capture someone and get it from them."

"I doubt the officers at this level know the real reason why they're looking for me. They're just following orders."

Brandel sent them a message.

"They're sending inspectors. I think they'll be here in three or four minutes. If they ask about you, I'll say that we rendezvoused with another ship and boarded it, then departed. I'll tell them you scrubbed the ship's logs for the event. If they suspect you this much, then they'll believe you did all this to evade them."

"That's true," Adrienne said quietly within the device. "If the Space Force rendezvoused with us because they're suspicious of you, they'll be ready to accept you went to a lot of effort to evade them. It's like leaving a window open then hiding in the room. Whoever comes in to pursue will believe you left through the window."

"Well we hired these men for their expertise, it's time to trust them," Matthieu said.

"The Space Force is nearby," Assistant said to Matthieu on a private channel. "I intercepted some of their chatter."

"Don't let them detect you," Matthieu said to Assistant, realizing as he said it that Assistant needed no warnings. "Sorry. I feel helpless and so I'm trying to compensate by giving you orders."

"Understood. If it helps, my analysis indicates Brandel believed what he told you about the device."

Adrienne brought up a feed of the *Resolu*'s airlocks for them to watch in their PVs. Matthieu watched patiently.

Finally one of the airlocks cycled open both of its portals. A disk-shaped scout machine flew into the *Resolu*. Behind it, men and women marched through in uniforms. Matthieu counted seven of them, heavily armed and armored.

"Those are likely androids," Assistant said. "The real officers may not even board the ship."

Matthieu and Adrienne watched as the Space Force

presence continued to deploy into the *Resolu*. Several more robots came through the lock, dog-shaped machines with scanning equipment on their backs. Four more soldiers flanked an officer as they emerged from the airlock.

"I think that officer is here incarnate," Adrienne said.

"Why do you think so?"

"Psychology," she said. "And the look on his face. Intense. He's loving it. I say he likes his power. He feels stronger when he takes the risk of coming here himself to dominate the crew and passengers. This is his show."

"That's not good for us. If this is what he loves, he'll go to greater lengths to find us. We'd be better off with some guy bored to tears, grinding through the inspection and eager to get back to his VR time."

The officer looked at the soldiers for a moment, likely sending link commands. The soldiers immediately split up and started to check for resistance. Brandel and the tiny crew did nothing to make trouble. When it appeared there would be no firefights, the officer started to work his way through the *Resolu*.

"He's a stickler, all right. He's going to look at everything himself, even though those machines are scanning everything."

"Let's hope it's not because he's smart and knows machines can be fooled. It's just because he wants to participate for his own pleasure."

They watched as scouts, androids, scanning dogs, and the officer roamed throughout the ship. Assistant reported many queries pouring in from the Space Force ship outside. Matthieu took a deep breath and relaxed. There was nothing to do now but wait.

One of the dog machines approached their airlock. It paused here and there there to take scans.

"Here's hoping the camouflage device works," Adrienne said. They watched the dog machine as it came to the end of the corridor and turned its device toward the lock. Matthieu imagined energetic particles flying through his body, knocking against his molecules and flying on through, reflecting, or causing damage.

The machine paused. It scanned again, then moved to one side. It kept scanning.

"How long—" Matthieu started.

Adrienne just shook her head. He could sense her worry.

Can't this just be over? Will they find us or not?

The dog machine told the lock door to open. When the portal cycled, it stepped into the lock. It scanned straight out the bulkhead and straight upwards to complete some virtual map it had built, then exited.

"I think we made it?" Matthieu asked. The dog continued to retreat down the corridor.

"I believe all is well," Assistant said. Matthieu just breathed for a few moments, then he picked the feed back up at Brandel's location.

Brandel and the officer were in Brandel's quarters.

"There are no records of internal ship sensor feeds going back several days," the officer noted.

"Those were cleaned when they left," Brandel told him.

"You did not turn them back on?"

"I'm still in his employ, as far as I know."

"Yet they are on now," prompted the officer.

"I knew you would want them on so you could search the ship," Brandel said. "You told me you were boarding for inspection. I want it very clear I am cooperating as best I can."

"Well, you may as well cut your losses and go back home. I don't know if you'll get paid—but you certainly won't be performing any more duties for these two."

"Yes, sir," Brandel said. His voice carried no defiance.

"Brandel's going to pull it off," Adrienne said. "Maybe I was wrong about him."

Matthieu nodded. He watched Spask and Vickson go through similar treatment. Finally, the officer came to

Matthieu and Adrienne's quarters. Brandel accompanied him.

"Another suite?"

"Yes. This was their room," Brandel said.

The officer stepped inside.

With a shock, Matthieu saw the thermal activator sitting on the long shelf that ran along one side of the quarters.

"The thermal activator is out," Matthieu said. "I was focused on the shard. I told Hydrangea to hide it."

If he recognizes that thermal activator then we're in trouble.

Mimic was only two meters away from the activator.

"Mimic, get ready—" Matthieu sent.

The officer turned away from the items.

"What was that?" he said aloud.

"You hear something?" asked Brandel.

"Link chatter from airlock three to here."

"Damn, Matthieu," Adrienne whispered.

"It's that dumb piece of luggage," Brandel said, pointing at Mimic. "It knows you're not its owner. It just requested the ship to rescue it from being stolen and wants to leave from that airlock, since that's where it came in from."

The Space Force officer nodded. Then he resumed searching the compartments in the room's walls. He found some of their personal equipment but said nothing.

"Brandel has a plausible reply for everything. He was well worth the money," Adrienne said.

Matthieu nodded. His hopes were rising.

"What will you do with us?" asked Brandel. "We're just a hired ship's crew. We've cooperated fully."

"We're letting you go," the officer said. "We're only interested in Chaulet. If contacted again, you're required to report him. If you're found with him on board again, the result will be loss of all citizen rights and your sale to a frontier corporate project."

"I understand," Brandel said. "I have cooperated fully."

The officer had become bored; Matthieu could see it on his face. He wasted no more time in leaving the ship. After another ten minutes, the last of the scout machines and androids had left as well.

Matthieu resumed watching Brandel, who had turned toward the source of a video feed. "We need to do some cleanup. The inspection really tossed things around," he said to the crew, but he stared into the feed.

"He's telling us something between the lines," Matthieu said.

"Yes. The Space Force no doubt left some toys behind to report back to them if you should appear back on the ship," Adrienne said. "He'll need time to find and disable such things."

"Hardware or software?" Matthieu asked.

"Probably both," Assistant responded. "I'll help find and clean any software threats."

Matthieu shifted uncomfortably. "Then I guess we wait here longer," he said resignedly.

Chapter 30

Matthieu took a deep breath when he saw Brandel finally approach the airlock in person.

Can't he just let us out from anywhere on the ship?

"Brandel. Thank you," Matthieu said.

"You're welcome." Brandel stopped at the airlock entrance. "We've finished cleaning the ship of Space Force hardware. The software side is more complex, but underway."

"Their man Vickson is a bit out of his league here," Assistant said. "However, I've finished cleaning the software."

"Well then... let us out," Adrienne said. Matthieu caught the edge in her voice. He saw from the video feed that Brandel had not moved.

"I can't do that, Miss Rekaire. You see, that man didn't know what was right in front of his face, but I do."

The activator! How did Brandel recognize it?

"I can pay you more than any other buyer," Matthieu said.

"More than Sorune? I don't think so. He wants that orb a lot. And he's one of the richest men on Idona."

Orb? No, the Nanorith shard. It was still out when he woke us! He didn't recognize the activator after all.

"Sorune? Who's he?"

"I saw the orb when I came in to warn you. It's a pretty amazing item, isn't it?"

He's fishing.

"I don't know. Is it?"

Matthieu traded looks with Adrienne.

"Tell you what," Brandel said. "I'm taking the orb no matter what. But you tell me what it is, and why Sorune wants it so badly, and we'll drop you off somewhere. You could earn your freedom just by sharing a little information."

"I think you've made a mistake. Let us out. We're the

ones paying you here. You think you recognized something some random guy wants, well if you're wrong, you end up with nothing."

Brandel seemed to give up his inquisition. For a moment Matthieu wondered if Brandel would begin torturing them to find out.

"No, you two stay in there until we get back," Brandel said. "And then... I wouldn't want to be you. Sorune must be very angry with anyone involved with the theft. If you change your mind, just let me know about the orb."

Brandel turned and left.

"He doesn't have to do the dirty work. If we don't talk, he gives us to Sorune's people," Matthieu sent to Adrienne. He did not speak aloud in case the device that held them had audio sensors.

Matthieu contacted Hydrangea.

"Hydrangea. Get out of there now. Head for the garden."

"Is it worth the risk?" Adrienne said. "If they see Hydrangea moving, they'll have the shard, too."

"Sooner or later they'll go to grab the orb. Brandel wants to know what it is. He might start an investigation. Once he realizes it's not sitting there anymore, they'll tear the room apart. It can't be there, hidden in the room or in Hydrangea. We have to move it out."

Hydrangea slid itself along the shelf until it reached one end. Then it slipped off the shelf and started across the room. The bed was still folded down from the wall, so it headed underneath.

Smart. It's always using what cover it can. I must have made it that way.

The artificial agent moved for the door. For Matthieu, it felt like watching a video in slow motion.

Faster. Faster.

The door opened and let it out. Hydrangea sent Matthieu an ETA for the garden: 260 seconds.

"What if Brandel notices both the egg and a plant are

missing?" asked Adrienne.

"He won't. He won't have any recollection of how many plants were in the room. He'll search everything looking for the shard and he won't find it."

"Then he'll check the video feeds that were turned back on."

"Those were halted as soon as the Space Force walked out, presumably to help keep anything left behind by the Space Force from noticing us."

"Then we need to anticipate what he'll do next. He'll torture us to obtain it."

"The agents will get us through this," Matthieu said.

Adrienne's lips tightened. "Your creations are clever, but can they really do that much?"

"You'd be surprised."

"Go find Brandel," Matthieu sent to Orb. The agent flew away from its station near the lock and started to search the ship. It was careful to avoid any link connections with the ship. Orb passed by Brandel's quarters and listened for a minute. Nothing indicated Brandel might be inside, so it continued.

Orb found Brandel sitting in the lounge. He remained perfectly still, leading Matthieu to believe he was off-retina. Orb crept closer. It was vaguely aware of secure network traffic moving to and from the mercenary captain, but it could not tamper with any of it.

"I don't know what he's doing off-retina, but at least for the moment, he's out of our way," Matthieu said to Adrienne.

"Mimic, get to our airlock," Matthieu sent.

"There are three of them, you know," Adrienne reminded Matthieu.

"Orb can't watch all three of them at once, at least not without access to internal monitoring systems."

Adrienne chuckled. "It's far easier to hack a waste receptacle than the *Resolu*'s security center."

"Good idea. Mimic, let's plot a more circuitous route. I

need you to hack a few ordinary devices on the ship. Perhaps you should look less like luggage and more like something that cleans the ship."

Mimic transformed into a low scrubber disk at Matthieu's suggestion. Matthieu and Adrienne watched as the little robot darted across the decking, looking for everyday devices to take over. Mimic physically connected to a water fountain and spliced into the sensors it used to detect people nearby. Mimic did the same to a waste bin and a plant watering machine.

"Okay, so we can't see all three of the crew but we can see them if they move about the ship. What plan do you have from here?" Adrienne said.

"We get out of here and head for the armory."

"Even if we could get out of this device, which we can't, Brandel has cracked *Resolu*'s security."

"Really now? You know me better than that," Matthieu said.

"You have a backdoor," Adrienne said.

"Yes. Assistant and I always leave obfuscated paths for regaining control of our systems. We should take advantage of that soon, in case Brandel suspects it. I want to wait until we're out of this device though. Who knows if Brandel has some kind of safety measure on it? A gas cannister, maybe? Something he could trigger in response to our attack."

Adrienne nodded.

"Mimic, see if you can open the lock without triggering a security alert. Assistant, be ready to take control of the ship. I want two versions ready to go: one, we take control but leave Brandel and his crew enough control that they think nothing's happened; version two, take all of their control away."

"Understood," Assistant replied.

Matthieu turned to Adrienne. "Mimic will get us out," he said.

"We have to hack Brandel's device," Adrienne said.

"No, I think we can cause a fault that will make it open. But Brandel might be warned."

"We don't know he designed it with any safety features."

"No, I don't know for sure, but if I were Brandel, I would have. He works for rich clients, and keeping them alive is often critical to getting paid, whether he's protecting them or kidnapping them."

Mimic had made it into the airlock. It approached the device.

"This is likely a complicated machine," Matthieu said to Mimic. "I think we just want to cause an error condition serious enough for it to decide to open up."

Mimic cut open the berth's maintenance panel. Matthieu started to worry about Adrienne's point: if Mimic did something wrong, it might actually trap them inside.

Mimic worked for long seconds. Its tiny arms snipped four conductors to no effect. Then it changed tactics and induced currents in control systems connected to the opening mechanisms. The berth's door opened smoothly.

"It opened!" Adrienne exalted.

"Hurry. It's likely Brandel has been notified."

They scurried out of the device into the airlock.

Michael McCloskey

Chapter 31

Orb watched Brandel in his spartan quarters as he got the alert. First a look of disbelief spread across the stout man's bearded face. It only lasted a second before Brandel stood and took a weapon from his belt. A projectile barrel ran parallel to an emitter at the top of the weapon, leading Orb to conclude it was a combination laser and smart round pistol. It probably sacrificed ammunition and charge for flexibility. Brandel had another weapon at his belt, which Orb recognized as a laser pistol designed by Personal Security Gear. PSG was popular on the frontier among those who did not seek trouble but prepared for it nonetheless.

Brandel probably took that from the last person he killed, Orb thought. *Too bad I did not get to record that one.*

Brandel moved out his door. In the corridor, Spask and Vickson awaited him, presumably summoned via Brandel's link.

"On me," Brandel said. The two crew members nodded and followed Brandel down the corridor. They did not ask any questions. Spask had a pair of pistols and Vickson carried a PAW. Clearly they were ready to deal with Master and his friend with force.

Orb dutifully reported the crew's position to Master as it shadowed them. Its part in all this was clear. Three deaths were on the agenda and Orb would record every second of them.

At first, Brandel led the team toward the airlock where Master had been imprisoned. At each corner he paused, listened, and rounded the corner with his weapon up. The party was less than a third of the way to the lock when Brandel stopped them.

"They have to be out of there by now," Brandel said. "They know we're coming. Where would they go?"

"Manual controls at the spinner," Spask suggested.

"They won't need manual controls for long," Brandel said. "Don't forget, this is their ship. Likely they'll take back control within the hour."

"I locked them completely out," Vickson said.

Brandel barked out a harsh laugh. "You're an amateur compared to that woman, Adrienne. And as I said: it's their ship. They'll have prepared ways back in."

Vickson took the criticism but he looked angry.

Brandel spent a few seconds off-retina. At first Orb thought he had decided to be silent and communicate with his men on their links, but then he spoke again.

"If I knew we were coming this way, I'd take *that* corridor to bypass us," Brandel said, referring to some shared map that Orb could not see.

The group took a right turn and headed for a ladder. Wherever Master was, he could see the change of course thanks to Orb. Brandel and the crew did not find anyone in the other corridor.

"Master and Adrienne have found a weapons cache and armed themselves," Assistant informed Orb across the network. "Stay close to them. Should they split, follow Brandel."

Brandel led his group to the spinner control room. The ship was usually controlled through links, but here, manual backup controls lined a wall. The spinner itself could not be approached directly when in operation. It was housed in the foremost spire of the *Resolu*. Brandel took out his laser and made some cuts behind a bank of equipment.

"What are you doing?" asked Vickson.

"Insurance," Brandel said. "We'll sabotage a few key systems. If things go badly for us, then we'll have some leverage. They can't repair it without us."

"What makes you think they can't?" Spask asked.

"They hired us, didn't they? If they knew their way around a starship, they wouldn't need us. Core Worlders know a lot about software, but they're helpless without their robots. Pull them out of VR and they're a bunch of mewling children."

From the spinner room, Brandel, Vickson and Spask

moved quickly through the ship. Orb followed their every move. They visited a cargo bay and half the staterooms, moving quietly like stalking cats. Here and there, Brandel stopped them to sabotage a system. They tinkered with the water recyclers and an energy storage ring.

Orb could see that Spask was the only one with formal training in combat. He kept proper muzzle discipline despite employing a weapon that would refuse to shoot at those he had not selected as targets. Brandel, though sloppier, had at least had clearly done this before, while Vickson was the worst of the three. He often broke into the other two mens' line of fire or made noise as he moved. Brandel led them around the deck in a sweeping circle. He came to a door that led to the galley.

The door was locked. Brandel paused.

"Now we're in trouble," he told the others. "They have partial control of the ship."

"Then we should split up and find them," Vickson said. "We'll be able to shoot them faster."

"They may have found weapons by now, so we'll stick together. Turn your links off in case they're tracking us by service accesses. We need to find them and kill them as fast as possible, before we lose every advantage we have."

"Should we cut our way in?" Spask asked.

"We take another route," Brandel said. "They may know we're roughly here based on our links. Let's turn back, go a deck up, and approach from a different direction. We can check the bridge, too."

The group turned back around and took a tube ladder up to a service deck. It was a half deck with a low ceiling, filled with pipes, storage tanks, and machinery. The temperature dropped. Orb trailed them.

"They're headed into an ambush," Assistant sent Orb. "Take a sheltered position at the top of the corridor ahead, among the pipes that will be on your left. Record the deaths of the crew from there."

Orb's alertness level increased. It brought up its power

consumption a little, drawing upon reserves within its tiny current storage ring. It zig-zagged behind the crew as they approached a left turn. Orb linked in with a shared tactical map provided by Assistant and put the three men onto it so Master and Adrienne could see them.

Very soon now. Master will be pleased by my work!

Brandel led the way down a new corridor with a series of long pipes on their left. Orb caught narrow glimpses of a parallel corridor through the pipes. The pipes left plenty of space for Orb to flit around them, but it would be hard for the crew members to make their way past the pipes without climbing or crawling. That left them in a relatively long space with minimal cover. Orb took its position and waited. Some thread of self-preservation inside its mind was aware that a ricochet could kill it, but it remained on station.

Master likes my work. If I should die, then he'll re-create me.

Something moved ahead. A grenade rolled out at high speed toward Brandel. At the same time, Vickson showed distress and dropped prone.

His suit is heating up. He's probably getting hit by a laser.

Brandel shot the grenade with his pistol, sending it spinning off to one side. Then the captain slipped behind a protrusion in the corridor wall on his right which provided just enough cover, though he could barely move without exposing himself to fire.

Vickson yelled as his Veer suit started to smoke. Then he screamed and rolled as his head got burned. He managed to turn away to protect his head, but his weapon was not even pointed down the corridor. Orb noted that Spask remained calm. He headed back the way they had come and slipped through an opening in the pipework five meters behind Vickson, trying to flank their attackers.

Vickson fell silent. Orb saw Master at the end of the corridor. He kept a PAW aimed down the corridor where Brandel was pinned. Orb decided that meant Adrienne crouched in the corridor on the other side of the pipes, the probable source of the laser attack. It checked the tactical and verified the guess. Adrienne was moving to prepare for Spask's flanking maneuver.

Brandel popped out of cover. Master's PAW fired immediately. One, two, three sharp barks reverberated through the corridor. The weapon had probably fired on its own as soon as acquiring something that fit its target signatures. Brandel fired back. Master crumpled.

Master's Veer suit should protect him against pistol fire.

Brandel clutched at his chest and dropped to his knees with an angry look on his red face. A grenade rolled out from under a bracket holding three pipes and exploded under Brandel. The mercenary captain's body flew upward, then crashed back down, broken. Then his mouth opened and he slowly fell to one side.

Orb recorded every moment of it all. It felt a flush of success. Two deaths dutifully recorded.

Yet its work was not done. Spask had retreated and gone around the side of the pipe array. No doubt he sought to flank the attackers. Orb slipped through the small spaces between the pipes, near the ceiling.

Spask was not visible. Orb could still see Master. As it watched, Master fell back against the bulkhead behind him. His hand wandered across his chest. He found a hole in his Veer suit. The hand came away bloody.

Am I about to record the death of my own Master?

Orb felt its situation had fallen well out of its clear directives. It did not know what to do. The main directive won out in the end: Orb's primary mission was to record death. Someone was dying right before it. It advanced a few meters along a pipe to get closer.

Master brought his hand up before his face. An open gushing wound dripped more blood through the hole in the suit.

"Assistant? Assistant!"

Orb heard Master's calls on the channel. Orb caught sight of the shiny sphere that contained Assistant in Master's hand. A thick piece of sharp metal stuck out of the sphere. Assistant's lights were dim.

Matthieu fell to his knees in the bloody mess. Adrienne ran over. There was still no sign of Spask. Orb decided Master would live, so it should search for Spask. The plan called for Spask's death to occur next. Orb turned to pass through the pipes.

"Matthieu! What's wrong?" Adrienne's hands ran over his chest, searching for wounds. "Did you catch a piece of shrapnel?"

"I'll live. Assistant is gone."

Master's voice was dismal. He took a halting breath.

Adrienne stepped forward and put her arm on Matthieu's shoulder. "I'm sorry. We can handle the rest on our own. Assistant got you this far. We'll finish, you and me."

Master nodded. Orb could tell Master was afraid.

A quiet sound came from down the dark, narrow space behind the pipes. Adrienne caught it.

"Where the hell is Spask?" Adrienne asked on a channel shared with Master and Orb.

Orb transmitted its best guess based upon the sound, but it was too late. Spask emerged on the far end of the corridor behind them.

"I surrender," Spask called out. Orb saw he was unarmed. Adrienne whirled and pointed her weapon. Matthieu looked over. Spask stood with his arms wide at his sides, palms empty and facing forward.

"You had us," Adrienne said. "Why are you surrendering?"

"You have the ship. What good would it do for me to kill you? I'd be stuck."

"What makes you think we won't kill you even faster?"

"I don't think you two are bloodthirsty. I think you just

want to get to that planet really bad."

Adrienne traded looks with Master.

"Should we kill him?"

"I don't have the stomach for it," Master said, his voice devoid of hope.

Michael McCloskey

Chapter 32

Matthieu sat on the main deck, lost in morbid thoughts. The laser pistol sat within reach on the floor. Adrienne hovered nearby, working off-retina to get everything in order. The cut on his chest burned, but it had already been cleaned and sealed by his Veer suit.

"I secured Spask in his quarters," Adrienne said. "The ship has no brig. I made sure Hydrangea was in there first, though. It can watch him too."

Matthieu nodded. "Who knew such a thing would be needed?"

"There's some minor damage but we're far from dead in space," she continued. "I looked at the sensor logs; Brandel and his crew believed they had swept away all the Space Force toys."

"Thank you," Matthieu mumbled.

"We're going to get through this," Adrienne said.

"Assistant rebuilt me," he said to Adrienne. "When my mind was gone, Assistant put me back together. I'm still not really Matthieu, you know. I look like him. But I'm only... partly here."

"You have me now. And we're almost there. The Nanorith will have the memories to make you whole again."

Matthieu nodded. "Yes. Just give me a few minutes, and I'll help with the repairs."

I just have to keep going. I can learn to handle things until I can make another Assistant. How much worse would it be if I could remember all the years I had it?

Matthieu connected with the ship's control services and started to look around. At first, seeing the complexity of the ship drove a wave of despair through him. Assistant had dealt with most such problems. His personal assistant had made everything simpler. A citizen of Red Calais usually just expressed what they wanted, answered a few questions, and machines took care of the rest.

I can do this. I built the agents. I was an adventurer, a

Space Force officer.

The *Resolu* had come prepared for mid-cruise alterations and repairs. Fabrication machines sat ready, with a fair supply of raw materials to run them. The main problem was space and manpower. Components would have to be moved through the ship and vacuum discipline had to be maintained. An accident could hurt or kill them.

Mimic will help, but it's no heavy duty construction machine.

Matthieu realized the software that generated repair plans and procedures was not aware of the things that Brandel and his crew had brought with them on the mission.

Matthieu looked through Brandel's inventory lists. He found a large store of building components and raw materials. There was also a datastore with plans for the hiding chamber Matthieu and Adrienne had been locked into, sensor satellites, small cache boats that could hold and transport valuable contraband in space, and ground camps that were undetectable from space. He added these lists to the software's database of components.

He sent Adrienne a pointer to the lock device's design plans.

"Let's keep the hiding place intact if we can," Matthieu said to Adrienne. "We might have to go in there again. The plans should help us use it."

"Not sure how that would work. Would the Space Force do something to an abandoned ship? If you think we need it then we'll have to hack it. We need complete control to climb back in there again."

Adrienne had good points. Should it simply be cannibalized? Matthieu ran the numbers. Taking apart the pod and using its parts only improved their estimated repair time by a few minutes. Of course, if more work became needed in the future, then its hardware would presumably become more critical as the stores ran low.

"Okay, let's keep it for now. We have what we need. If we get underway again, then we can think about whether we need to spend time on it."

If only we had Assistant to crack its security. Then we could have it done in a few hours and not worry about it.

Matthieu promised himself he would stop pondering 'If we had Assistant...' lines of thought. It served no purpose now.

The software generated a plan and started to fabricate items. Mimic left to harvest the new parts and organize them. Matthieu shared the plan with Adrienne.

"There's more. We need to figure out what to do with Spask," she said.

Matthieu looked at her. Adrienne's tone was neutral; she did not seem inclined to make a case for any particular course of action.

Assistant would have killed him, back when it believed I liked Orb to collect deaths out of a sense of sadism.

Matthieu realized he did not know what the old Matthieu would do. He had spent so much time trying to recover himself, he had not had time to decide who he wanted to be in the meantime.

I like adventure. I like stealing things. I think I love Adrienne. But I don't see any fun in killing Spask. He betrayed me, but I just want to get rid of him.

Adrienne walked closer and put her hand on Matthieu's arm.

"I don't think we should wait until you find your old self. What do you feel now?"

"I don't know who I am," Matthieu said. "I don't like him. I do feel angry, but I don't want to kill him. I just want him gone so I can continue with the mission." Adrienne nodded as Matthieu continued thinking aloud. "I *might* kill him if it was the only way to succeed. Only because he betrayed me first."

Adrienne nodded. "That's very reasonable. I found something that may be of use," she said. "I saw something earlier that might make a difference."

"Yes?"

215

"Watch this."

She gave Matthieu a pointer to a video feed and he activated it. It showed Brandel, Vickson and Spask standing in a room of the *Resolu*.

"You're not gonna believe this," said Brandel. "I saw something important when I went to get those two out before that Space Force inspector arrived. I saw this."

Brandel must have shared something over a link connection. The other two exhibited surprise.

"What is it?" asked Spask.

"Unbelievable!" said Vickson.

"Yes. It belongs to Sorune."

"What should we do?" asked Vickson.

"I'll tell yah what we're gonna do. We're gonna take that orb back to Sorune and ride on a money wave."

Vickson nodded, but Spask made a face.

"I don't think we should," Spask said. "We have our loyalty ratings to think about. If we turn these two in, how can we find more customers?"

"Sorune's gonna make us so rich for this, we won't need a loyalty rating," Brandel said.

"What if we want to keep doing business?" Vickson asked.

"You can buy enough services to fake a loyalty rating if you want," Brandel said patronizingly. "But I'm going to be living it up in Red Calais!"

Spask shook his head. "It's none of our concern. Sorune must have stolen that thing, and so did these guys. So what? They paid us, we should take them. They're paying us top dollar, too."

"That was the plan until I saw this," Brandel said. "Do you know how rich Sorune is? We vote right now. I say Sorune."

Vickson nodded. "Sorune."

Spask looked disgusted. He just shook his head. The feed stopped.

"You see it? Spask didn't want to give us to Sorune."

Matthieu looked at Adrienne directly to let her know he had finished the clip.

"You think we could use him?"

"Yes. I say we offer him the whole payment," Adrienne said. "He'll be getting at least triple what he was in for before. And he can earn our rating. He can help us get in there unseen by the Space Force, and we could use another person to get in there and set up the activator."

"So Spask wanted to be loyal to us," Matthieu said, mulling it over. "And now you think we can afford to trust him."

"Properly motivated, I say yes," Adrienne said. "I would only trust him so far, but it's clear from this that he prefers cooperation and dislikes betrayal. We give him money, the rating, and he's doing what he thinks is right."

"We keep an eye on him. Lock him out of important ship's systems. The agents can watch him, too."

"Absolutely. We take full precautions. We can even lock ourselves out as targets on any weapon we hand him."

Matthieu nodded. "It's logical. And Spask seems logical. Let Orb watch him as we propose it. Orb and Mimic both know how to read people, it's software I stole from a hostile intention trigger and gave to them."

Matthieu sent for his two servants. Mimic showed up first, configured as a security observer. Such machines were used to scout dangerous areas and coordinate security machines at various sites. Spask had not seen or heard of any security machines on board, but perhaps if he saw this machine for the first time, it might cause him to wonder if there were also other security machines that had been hidden away. It might have been believable that Matthieu had kept the existence of such things secret, but the fact they had engaged Brandel and the others themselves gave it away as a ruse.

Ah well. He may not believe it, but surely some uncertainty can be introduced?

Orb joined them on the way. They arrived at Spask's

quarters. Matthieu asked his weapon to do a diagnostic. It reported no damage and plenty of ammunition.

Adrienne looked at Matthieu. He nodded.

"Spask. We're here to talk to you."

The answer came quickly. "Okay. I'm sitting on the bed."

The door opened. Adrienne went in followed by Orb, Mimic, and Matthieu.

Spask looked at them uncertainly and waited for them to speak.

"We have a deal for you," Adrienne said. "We know you didn't want to move against us. We saw the vote."

"That's true, I didn't," Spask said.

Orb and Mimic told Matthieu and Adrienne they believed Spask. Adrienne continued.

"Keep working for us. We'll give you the full payment for the voyage services. And a solid rating on your service. Of course we don't trust you and we've taken steps for our own safety. Cross us again and we won't spare you again. Think it over."

"I don't need to think it over," Spask said. "That's a damn good deal and I want it."

The agents vouched for Spask's response. Adrienne nodded.

"Work here in your quarters," Adrienne said. "As I said, we're not going to fully trust you. Your electronic and physical access to ship's systems will be restricted. The ship has an AI on board that's monitoring you."

Matthieu wished so much that last part was true. He cursed Brandel.

Assistant, we miss you.

Matthieu checked for Hydrangea above with a quick glance. His agent was in position. Hydrangea was not as smart as Assistant had been, but it would have to do.

"Once we're on-planet, we'll let you know when it's time to go out on the surface," Matthieu said. "We could use your help there."

Spask nodded. "I understand. Thank you for giving me a chance."

Michael McCloskey

Chapter 33

"We've arrived."

Matthieu sent the message to Adrienne who was elsewhere in the ship. The *Resolu* had been repaired during the journey. Spask was in no small part responsible for the results; he had worked hard to help put everything back together, and Orb had observed him. So far, Spask had shown no sign of betrayal. Matthieu believed the snippet they had seen was genuine, and Spask wanted to do right by his employers.

"What's it like? Do you know where the site is?" Adrienne replied.

Matthieu had been scanning the planet since they entered the system. He had indeed found their target, and there was no sign of the Space Force.

"I believe so. I can see artificial structures within a dormant volcano. They're huge, and alien."

"That was fast. I guess knowing to look in volcanos narrows it down."

"Quite a bit, yes."

Adrienne joined Matthieu on the main deck. The ship had almost no manual controls, even here. Everything was run through link interfaces, or failing that, audio commands. As a result, the nerve center of the ship looked like an elegant lounge. Matthieu had placed virtual displays of the star system, the ship, and the planet onto large mirrors on the wall so he could refer to them as needed without cluttering his link's off-retina display space. He wondered if Adrienne had done the same for herself; he no longer remembered what she preferred.

On-retina or off, Adrienne accessed the data feeds. Matthieu alerted Spask they had arrived at the planet in case they needed him.

Matthieu shared his accumulated map of the planet. Adrienne accessed it and saw a barren sphere covered in rugged gray and black rock.

"The planet looks dead," she commented.

"By our standards. But the Nanorith aren't part of a system running on energy from a nearby star. They exist upon energy from within the planet's core."

"So the life is under the surface? We should study the environment, collect our tools and gear, and go down to the city," suggested Adrienne.

"Yes..." Matthieu said, yet he did not move, and he was not off-retina.

"Your thoughts?" Adrienne said.

"Here's our first challenge: we need to avoid detection. Ourselves and the *Resolu*. I'm worried about the Space Force. They may still have a presence here, and more ships might arrive while we're down there. We have to come up with a way to hide."

Adrienne did not answer immediately. Matthieu was still thinking when her reply came a minute later.

"We should ask Spask. The whole reason we hired him was to leverage his experience at this sort of thing."

"Fair enough. He's almost here."

Spask walked in a minute later. Matthieu went on-retina to consult with him face to face.

"How would you advise us to avoid detection by the Space Force?"

"Find a place to hide the ship that's out of direct line of scans," Spask said without hesitation. "I assume this planet is the only location of interest here? If that's true, find another body in the system and tell the ship to go to the other side."

"Then how do we get it to return when we need it? We can't carry a tachyon base with us."

"I know how to disguise a relay as an asteroid," Spask said. "Usually, we make more than one. From the planet you can send a directional signal to one of the relays and send for your ship. It requires bringing some extra communications boosters with you and hiding them on the planet. As a failsafe, you have the ship return before your

222

supplies would run out, just in case your boosters are destroyed. More redundancy is easy to build in; I've used as many as three boosters on-planet and four relays in a system."

"We'll still be detected if there are probes scattered around the system looking for ships," Adrienne said.

Spask shrugged. "Then you should have put a cloaking system on the *Resolu*."

"Getting those is tricky and expensive," Matthieu said.

"It also attracts the attention of the Space Force," Adrienne added.

"Okay. We get dropped off here with as much equipment as we can, then have *Resolu* land on the far side of an asteroid or a small moon. It'll be hard to spot, but it also makes it harder to contact," Matthieu summarized.

"This might not matter," Spask said. "I see scans of the planet coming in. The surface is like a sponge. There are extensive collections of tubes leading deeper into the planet."

"And?" prompted Adrienne.

"Some of them are large enough to hide the whole ship," Spask said.

"Sounds dangerous," she said.

"The environment down there can hardly be worse than space," Matthieu said.

"Different kinds of danger. Think of what we plan to do," Adrienne said to Matthieu's link privately. "If you heat up a volcano, then nearby tubes may become hot, or even fill with magma."

"Spask, select a hiding location in the system and set up with the relays. I don't know if we'll need it or not, but best to have a backup plan."

"Right," Spask said.

"Where should we go for now?" Adrienne asked.

Matthieu stared at the mirror where he had anchored a virtual view of the planet. It magnified to the area around the suspected Nanorith city.

"We don't dare land in the ruins directly; if there's a Space Force outpost here, they'd be alerted immediately," Matthieu said.

"Besides, who knows what damage we could do to the Nanorith structures," Adrienne said.

"I doubt this tiny ship would hurt their city," Matthieu said. "I worry about the opposite: if their city activates, it could damage our ship. It might even destroy it. They probably have processes to clear rock and debris after a long sleep."

"Where then?"

"How about here?"

He indicated a large chasm on the tactical.

"Okay. We're on our way." The *Resolu* stopped feeding energy into its gravity spinner and let it wind down. The graceful ship descended smoothly as the planet's pull started to take effect. The planetary surface below resolved in the feeds. Matthieu saw mountains cracked by the wide lines of rivers. Despite the lack of vegetation, he thought there might be things living in the soup below.

After another minute, the city became visible from their external feeds without magnification.

"Cthulhu sleeps," Adrienne uttered.

The city looked like an ancient mechanical clock nestled within the circular mouth of a kilometers-wide volcano. Its size became more and more apparent as they descended. The ship angled away from the structures and headed for the round mouth of a gaping cavern in the side of the mountain. Matthieu estimated they would end up about a kilometer from the ruins.

The *Resolu* entered the cave. The tubular passage were made of smooth, black rock.

"I don't know if the surface water eroded this, or if it's a lava tube," Matthieu said.

"Could be a lava tube enlarged by the water," Adrienne said. "The shape is vertically elongated as if it's been further eroded on the bottom."

"The resident geologist has spoken," Spask jibed. "But can we land in here?"

"Yes," Matthieu said. The ship set down. Its legs extended to different lengths to level out the deck. Everyone listened, but there was nothing to hear. Matthieu supposed they would not be able to hear wind or rain from inside the ship anyway.

"What are we looking for? Or can you tell me that?" Spask asked.

"We've already found it. Alien ruins."

"Then what now?"

"First, we need to become familiar with the surface," Matthieu said. "If we can't make our way around out there, then we'll need to devise other means to do so." Spask nodded.

"Secondly, I'd like to take a look at the ruins. Ultimately, I'm going to find a way deep underground there and deploy some equipment."

"Okay. Got it," Spask said. "I recommend a lot of weapons, and of course Veer suits. You never know what kind of nasty creatures are lurking out there."

Matthieu blinked. *Was that serious, or was that some kind of joke?*

"It looks like little more than rock," Adrienne said. "I suppose under the surface—"

"Oh, there's life here all right. See this?" Spask sent them a pointer to a surface scan conducted by the *Resolu* from far above the planet. "Millions of compounds in every square meter. This kind of chemical complexity, together with solar energy input, means there's something alive out there, at least, alive by most definitions of the word," Spask said.

Matthieu verified the complexity Spask spoke of. He was right that the misty soup on the planet surface rocks had a staggering number of different molecules in it; Matthieu supposed that meant anything was possible.

"Noted," he said. "And there's another reason for

weapons anyway. A Space Force facility exists here. I want to know where it is. I'd like to know if it's manned. If it's empty we might use it. If it's occupied, we need to keep our distance so we don't run afoul of them."

The three walked to the armory to select their weapons. Once there, Matthieu picked up a laser rifle and tested its heft. He thought about the mazes of tubes and pools he saw in the scans and put it back. Instead, he chose a laser pistol and their most compact PAW. The assault weapon carried fifty high-speed projectiles, each with independent target acquisition and drift correction capabilities. Under the main barrel was a wider, shorter grenade launcher assembly. The PAW could hold five grenades, so Matthieu chose one stun grenade, two incendiary, and three fragmentation grenades.

"The place is wet. I doubt you can set much on fire," Spask commented. Matthieu felt a niggle of suspicion that Spask had paid such close attention to Matthieu's selections; on the other hand, what else did Spask have to watch? They were all here to arm themselves.

"If the things down there like being wet, then an incendiary weapon might be very effective," Matthieu countered. Adrienne also took one of the compact PAWs, while Spask chose two laser pistols, a ten-shot stunner, and a projectile pistol with extra clips. Matthieu locked Spask's weapon's friendly lists, making sure that they could not fire at Adrienne or himself.

"Melee weapons?" asked Matthieu.

"Always," Adrienne said. She took a stun baton from the cabinet. Matthieu followed suit. It told his link it was fully charged and ready to arm.

"We've also got these little things in our standard packs," Adrienne said. She took out a small plastic tube. One end had a hand grip, which she held carefully as she unscrewed the rest. Matthieu saw a four-inch blade inside. Both sides had been sharpened. The cylinder she had unscrewed was a type of scabbard that did not touch the

226

blade. Instead, two-thirds of the cylinder screwed onto the top of the hilt that held the blade.

"This is sharper than sharp on each side. It would cut through almost any scabbard, which is why this tube screws on the handle. Not exactly sword-sized, but if we need to cut anything... even steel cable... we'll be able to without wasting our lasers."

Spask nodded. "Okay. Then let's take our basic packs and some climbing gear and check this place out." He sounded enthusiastic.

Everyone grabbed equipment until Matthieu wondered if they had too much. He asked Mimic to clean out a cargo container and drag it out behind them, so they would have an outside cache of equipment they did not want to carry just yet.

"We have the cargo ramp, but I'd just as soon use a smaller exit and keep the local atmosphere exposure to a minimum," Matthieu said.

"The bottom hatch then," Adrienne said. They took a short walk to the hatch she had mentioned.

The hatch opened straight down, but it was only two meters above the rock below. Spask dropped like an agile cat, then moved off to one side, weapon ready.

Still a military man, Matthieu thought.

Adrienne went after Spask and landed with the same fluidity. Matthieu felt glad they would probably be watching for danger instead of observing him land. His physical training had lagged behind his expectations. He dropped, copying the others' springy landing as best he could. Then he walked out from under the *Resolu* and let his eyes adjust to the low light. The rock beneath his feet was smooth, like slate in a river bottom. White mist clung to the floor around him, roiling and scattering in a light wind. It built up then subsided in repeating cycles.

Matthieu crouched to look at the rock. Up close, its surface appeared shaggy and moist. He stood up and scraped it with his boot. A mat of gray-green ripped under the tip of his boot, revealing pale gray rock beneath.

"Spask is right. This planet is far from barren," he said. "The surface is covered in living slime."

Adrienne took in a deep breath and smiled. "It smells so nice. Like the air after a spring storm, or at a waterfall. I was expecting fire and brimstone."

"Well the volcano is dormant," Matthieu thought aloud. "This place is wet. Many of the tubes are filled with water."

"Every planet is different," Spask said. "I know it's easy to expect a wet planet to be filled with lush vegetation, but this planet is at a different point in its development, or the environment just isn't suitable for some reason. Perhaps volcanic activity is too frequent?"

"As good a guess as any," Matthieu said. He pointed at the slimy rock. "You're definitely right about the danger of living creatures, though. We're probably looking at the bottom of the food chain."

"Then keep your weapon handy," Spask suggested. "Which way are the ruins?"

Matthieu pointed the way deeper into the cavern. "I hope this tube connects to the inside of the volcano."

A loud clatter sounded behind them. Matthieu whirled, fumbling for his laser.

He saw the empty cargo container on the rocks. Mimic was letting itself down by one fully-extended arm.

"Little twitchy I guess," Adrienne commented. They had all reacted the same way.

"Stay that way," Spask advised.

"Let's do a walk around the vicinity. Not far. Put the gear we need for an extended trip here just for the moment." Matthieu dropped his climbing gear in the container and started toward the front of the ship, which he had set down to point toward the ruins.

Spask and Adrienne did not drop anything into the container. Matthieu supposed they wanted everything on them just in case.

The three of them stayed within a couple of meters of each other as they walked out into the mist. After twenty meters, Matthieu looked back. The *Resolu* was still easily visible, though it faded in and out with banks of fog that shifted in the wind. As Matthieu walked another ten meters forward, he realized how daunting the silence felt. His ears picked up only the wind and a bit of clacking from Mimic securing a ladder to the hatch behind them. His link paralleled the silence in his mind: there were no services out here.

Well, your old self loved adventure. Try to embrace it.

The nervousness was not overwhelming. Matthieu found it slightly bracing, or at least he told himself that.

Matthieu took another series of steps forward, carefully watching the ground. A rock wall grew from the mist ahead. The mist cleared for a moment, revealing two huge holes in the tube wall, leading farther into the mountain.

"It's that way to the ruins, so that's where we'll head once we've looked over our perimeter," Matthieu said.

The others gave no comment. Matthieu proceeded clockwise around the ship, keeping close enough to see it through the fog. His link kept perfect track of their position as well, drawing them a shared map.

They came to a break in the flat stone. A wet pile of moss-like material grew from the ground. It glistened a greenish brown but did not move.

"Careful. Is that thing alive?" Spask said.

"Probably. Looks like a plant to me," Matthieu said.

"Do what you like, I'm giving it a wide berth," Adrienne said.

They walked wide around the colony of greenish sludge.

They continued a wide course around the *Resolu*. Matthieu felt excited to be on an alien planet. What would turn up next? He gripped his weapon tightly.

"I see some change ahead," Spask said. Matthieu saw

it, too. More light, and a change in the shape of the tunnel. They walked another fifty meters to the spot.

The top of the rocky tube above had been opened up. Matthieu stared upwards at rising cliffs of rock. Light filtered down from far above. Ahead of them, the tunnel floor flattened into a wide shelf. The way continued on the far side, perhaps sixty meters ahead. They carefully walked out into the area.

Something made Matthieu look at the right side of the rocky shelf again. It was the mist. He realized the white mist was not accumulating there, but emerging from a section of the wall. He moved closer to that side. A momentary shift of the wind showed him a smooth tunnel entrance.

"I've found another side tunnel."

"Don't go in. We can't see in there very well. You could fall or become trapped," Adrienne said.

"I'm not planning on going into the smaller tunnels yet, but we will soon. We're well equipped for the unexpected and we can't get lost," Matthieu said.

"We could fall into lava and be incinerated."

"The magma beds are far, far underground from here. These tunnels are relatively cool," he said. The data bore him out; though a few of the tunnels had infrared signatures indicating they were filled with near-boiling steam, most of them had cooled to cloudy, partially-submerged tubes. "Some are filled with water. Our suits can handle it."

They finished the sweep, encountering only one more bulging patch of the green goo. The second one bubbled happily, though it did not seem to be emitting steam. Matthieu smelled a musky odor that he thought might be rotting vegetation.

When they swung back to the *Resolu*, Matthieu called out their scouting machines. The spiderlike machines, each standing only knee-high, dropped from the *Resolu* and ambled around them toward the Nanorith ruins. Matthieu had sent out ten of them with another ten in reserve. Then he sent six flying scouts out as well. The sleek, ultra-lightweight machines hovered down out of the same hatch and took off in different directions.

"We'll send these ahead. That should ease your mind," Matthieu said. "Though it hardly sounds adventurous," he added.

Adrienne smiled at his snipe. They traded a look that made Matthieu feel happy for the first time since Assistant had died.

"These will find us a way into the city," Matthieu said. "I hope we can avoid the flooded tubes, but looking at the surface scans, I think we may have to go through a few of them."

"Why not just have the machines set up your equipment?" Spask asked.

"I just might do that," Matthieu said. He was thinking of Mimic in particular, but he did not want to mention the agent in case Spask did not know about it. "We have to be near the ruins when everything is activated anyway, and the set up is tricky."

Spask seemed to accept that easily.

"He might protest if he knew we intend to reawaken the volcano," Adrienne said to Matthieu on their private channel.

"He would be wise to do so. It's all a bit dangerous, isn't it?"

Adrienne smiled. "Ah, now you're trolling me. You know I love it."

Matthieu smiled. He wondered if he was feeling more like his old self. Soon he would know.

Michael McCloskey

Chapter 34

Matthieu led the team out of a misty tube and into a canyon. Flat, gray rock, smooth like slate, extended many meters ahead. After several steps, Matthieu spotted a tiny graduation in the height; the surface was not perfectly smooth, but it had worn away into shallow terraces only a few millimeters apart in height.

The ground below was criss-crossed with tracks. The trails were about a handspan wide. Matthieu crouched to check the clearest one before him. He slid his finger over the rock. It had been cleared of the sludge.

"I'm thinking these come from something like a snail," Matthieu said. "They slid along here, eating that goop."

"I agree," Adrienne said. "From the looks of the trails, they're not large enough to worry about."

"Could be venomous," Spask said.

"Alien venom is unlikely to affect our bodies," Matthieu said.

Spask shrugged. "It's a roll of the dice. Introduce some highly reactive chemical, and see what it does to you."

"Actually Earth venoms and toxins are often made of a mix of many chemicals," Adrienne said to Matthieu.

"Okay," Matthieu said. "If something threatens, we'll tell our suits to glove and helmet up, and defend ourselves appropriately."

The canyon walls were made of hundreds of thin layers of rock. The sharp edges of each layer protruded or receded in irregular fashion like giant serrations. Matthieu kept his distance from the walls and walked down the middle. He realized that was why the ground was flat, with a new terrace every few meters: the terraces were where the ground gained or lost a layer as if they walked across giant overlapped scales.

"Some of these tracks seem fresh, but I don't see any creatures," Matthieu said.

"They may sense us. Maybe we talk too much, or

maybe they can hear our footsteps for a great distance," Spask said.

"Well they're clearly faster than Earth snails, then," Matthieu said.

"I see something ahead. Another tunnel entrance, probably," Adrienne said.

"Where?" Spask asked.

"Straight down, I think," Adrienne said. She pointed ahead.

Matthieu walked forward to take a look. He saw that water had filled the area before them. Soon his feet tromped through a thin sheet of the water. He stepped down one more layer of the rock, then slowed.

"Careful. It looks like it gets suddenly deeper," he warned.

They stopped at the edge of the deep water. The pool looked like an aquarium embedded in ice, though the temperature was comfortable. Clear crystals bordered the liquid, concealing the edges in a series of confusing refractions.

"Does it go farther that way underground, or am I staring at a reflection?" asked Adrienne.

"Don't move," Spask said. Matthieu heard an urgency in his voice that made him obey.

"There, on our right. You see it? Maybe a meter under the water," Spask told them through a link connection.

Matthieu stared into the pool on his right. He had just started to suspect Spask of causing a distraction for nefarious purposes when he finally saw it. A vague set of lines shifted in the pool.

"Stick me!" Adrienne said. "It's as big as us. Scary transparent."

Matthieu struggled to resolve the creature in the pool before him. He saw only vague shadows and reflections, some of them shifting...

"It's moving... it's coming—" Spask said urgently.

The end of the warning was lost in an explosion of

water. Adrienne went flying backwards. In the instant, Matthieu felt she must surely be dead after such a blow. He told his PAW to shoot, but it had no target sig loaded except hostile Terran or robotoid, and it knew Adrienne was a friendly.

Matthieu heard the whine of Spask's laser pistol. Steam came off a clear monstrosity before Adrienne with a hiss. Adrienne was somehow stuck to the watery shape, struggling.

Matthieu's first impression of the thing was of a giant transparent arthropod. The creature stood almost as tall as Matthieu. It had stuck her through with some specialized appendage. A long, thin spike extended from a limb, which struck Adrienne in the side. Matthieu saw part of the spike emerge from her back, stained red. Spask took one orderly step backward and shot again.

The Veer suit will protect her. But that thing will burn.

The thing had lost its near-invisibility now that it had emerged from the water. Matthieu could see it, even though its body was transparent, because of the water that ran off it, and because it refracted the light differently than the air. He overrode the safety and pulled the PAW's trigger, being careful to shoot well wide of Adrienne.

Matthieu smelled the thing burning. He also saw he had blown away a large chunk of the creature's back. Adrienne finally managed to get her PAW in line with her right hand. She shot the creature three times in rapid succession, causing it to fall back toward the water's edge.

The attack had lasted only four seconds. Matthieu felt his heart hammering in his chest as he rode a massive wave of adrenaline. Adrienne wobbled for a moment, then leaned forward. Matthieu ran up to steady her. Spask kept his laser aimed at the transparent pile of flesh that had been the alien creature.

Adrienne let go of her PAW and started to pull the spike out of her.

"Should you—" Matthieu started, but she had already

pulled it halfway out. She grabbed the spike up higher, by her armpit, and pulled again. The spike fell to the ground with a wet clatter.

"I'm okay," she said confidently. She leaned heavily into Matthieu and then away, still wavering.

The spike had not gone through her lung as he had feared. It had entered under her arm, piercing a cooling vent there, then exited out the backside. The blood flow had already been stemmed. The Veer suit had undoubtedly closed up the wound automatically.

"Go back to the *Resolu*," Matthieu said.

"No. Just give me a second to recover," Adrienne said. "Just shock and adrenaline, you know?"

Spask looked at Adrienne in admiration. "I had no idea you two were so capable. Brandel was convinced you were helpless."

"Based upon what?"

"You hired us to take you here."

"I wish we hadn't," Adrienne responded.

Matthieu did not want his companions fighting now, when they all needed to work together.

"Enough. We continue," Matthieu said.

"How are we going to see those things?" Spask said.

"Well, out of the water, it's easier to spot," Matthieu said. "I bet the mist gives them away."

"But we'll be mucking around in those tunnels. Half of them are filled with water," Adrienne said.

Matthieu hesitated. He wanted to let her know he took the danger seriously.

"We can use our weapons. I have a target sig from that thing now. Your weapon will tell you if it locks onto something."

"Far from perfect," Spask said. "If it's hard for us to see, it'll be hard for the weapons, too. Not that I'm saying we shouldn't do it. I just mean we can't rely on it and walk around like we're perfectly safe."

"Agreed."

Matthieu took another bearing from his link map and moved around the crystal pool of water. He watched the smooth plates they walked upon carefully through the concealing mist, looking for another of the pools.

The canyon narrowed to another tube leading into the mountain. Mist came from the tube in fits and bursts. Matthieu checked the temperature with a thermal view. It was not steam. He turned his PAW's light on and led the way in.

Matthieu often paused to check the floor. He feared the mist might conceal a chasm or another pool. Adrienne and Spask walked along behind. The beams of their lights alternately revealed a curved rock wall or dispersed into a bank of fog.

Matthieu suppressed an urge to ask them to check their six every twenty seconds. To his relief he noticed Adrienne checking behind them at one of his stops.

This is dumb. We're sitting ducks in here. We need radar equipment.

"Wait... we need something..." Matthieu told them.

Matthieu stopped and dug something out of his climbing pack.

"What's up?" Adrienne asked.

"This," Matthieu said, holding up a silvery disk. "This is a smartrope carrier. It—"

"Takes rope across gaps and up cliffs," Spask finished for him.

"Yes. Well I realized they have radar for low visibility situations."

Matthieu released the tiny disk. It hovered in the air ahead of him. He told it to feed its sensor sweeps into their shared map. The tunnel became visible ahead and behind. Matthieu was relieved to see the tunnel was clear nearby. Then he saw a large obstruction sixty meters down the tunnel.

"See that?"

"Yes. It's not moving," Spask said. "Send the carrier

237

on ahead."

Matthieu sent the tiny device forward. The shape ahead still did not move. Matthieu imagined a creature like the one that had almost impaled Adrienne. Then he thought maybe the ceiling had caved in, partially blocking the way. As the carrier neared, he saw the obstruction had a symmetrical angularity to it. The carrier stopped and warned him its connection to his link was degrading. It was at the limits of its range.

"Is that a part of the city?" Adrienne asked.

"It's definitely alien," Matthieu said. "It doesn't look like... I think it's a machine. A robot or a shuttle? Maybe even a spacecraft."

"So we're not the only ones who thought to land in these hidden spaces," Spask suggested.

"Let's check it out," Adrienne said. They walked forward.

Matthieu felt apprehensive as they walked down the tunnel. He slowed to stare at the thing they had discovered. From thirty meters away, the mist alternately obscured and blew off it in a light breeze.

Matthieu heard a throbbing through the sound of the wind in the tunnel. He realized it was the beating of his own heart. He took another step forward and raised his PAW.

Someone came here. Something. When? What were they doing?

"What are you going to shoot, Matthieu? You don't even have a target sig," Adrienne said. Matthieu figured she had read his body language and was trying to soothe him. His breath came in short gasps. He told his PAW to accept targets from him. If something attacked them, he would fire back.

Matthieu glanced at Spask. The ex-Space Force man looked equally ready for action. They walked up closer to the shape. It was a saucer-shaped ship or robot a third the size of the *Resolu*. In between clingy patches of fog, Matthieu counted four legs holding it a meter from the ground.

The surface of the machine was grey-green. Matthieu saw a round hole pointing in their direction.

"What does that look like to you?" Matthieu asked, pointing. He started to move laterally.

"Reaction engine nozzle," Adrienne said. "It's not a cannon."

They followed Matthieu around to the right as he inspected the alien machine. It was smooth with few sharp angles. Halfway around the thing, he saw gates along the top had been opened. The gates looked like they closed back together side by side to restore the curved saucer shape of the thing. Inside, Mathieu saw an empty carrying bay.

When they reached the far side, Matthieu saw a hexagonal container on the ground. Mist blew around it, revealing only the top. The belly of the container had been opened. Matthieu stepped forward to look inside.

"Nanorith!" he announced loudly.

Row upon row of black Nanorith orbs sat within, encased in transparent cases with foam or plastic spacers to keep them in order.

"Were they trying to evacuate the city?" Adrienne asked.

A smooth-bored tube led away from the ship toward the city. Matthieu shook his head.

"The opposite, I think. Something emerged from this ship, and drilled away in that direction, toward the city."

"We could be looking at the seed that created the entire city," Adrienne said.

"Or someone else came, and tried to loot it," Spask said.

Matthieu saw Spask's point. The shards in the container could have been coming or going. He looked back into the empty bay. It had indentations shaped to hold containers like the one on the ground.

"I think this is a Nanorith ship," Matthieu said. "It's made to hold these containers. The container looks made to hold the shards."

"So that's how they came to other planets? They just sent a bunch of those things like Sorune wants?" Spask said.

"They might be able to live on almost any rocky planet of this size," Matthieu said. "Imagine: they send a batch of the shards in a ship equipped with drilling machines. They drill if there are no suitable volcanos active at the target planet. The heat re-activates the shards and they grow into Nanorith."

"I wonder if they can speak to the others with tachyon bases," Adrienne said.

"I don't know the limits of their technology. There might be a timing problem? At any given moment, will the other sites be active? I get the feeling they're dormant most of the time."

"Maybe they always plan to wake up at certain times now to communicate."

"I got the feeling they woke up when the volcanos did," Matthieu said. "But you're right. Maybe when they were primitive, they lived at the mercy of the volcanos? Once possessed of advanced technology though, I would imagine they could channel heat through the crust of a planet whenever they wanted."

Spask had been listening with an intent look on his face.

"I'm surprised you came here to deploy something," Spask said. "Don't you know these things are worth a fortune? There must be other Nanorith artifacts within the city. If you two aren't smugglers, what are you exactly?"

"The Nanorith have something of mine," Matthieu said. "I've come to get it back. Chances are, you can grab something here or there for yourself if you want. But not these shards. These are not for the taking, understand? Any other artifact, sure, you can take it and sell it once we part ways."

Spask nodded. "Thanks." He looked the area over one more time, scanning for items.

"We're almost to the city," Adrienne told him. "Maybe there'll be something there."

"Don't the Nanorith stay asleep for thousands of years? There's probably nothing left," Spask said.

"The Space Force recently awakened this city," Matthieu said. Spask looked surprised.

"No, it's not safe, but the Nanorith are back asleep now. We're paying you well for this," Adrienne said.

Matthieu led them down the tunnel extending from the alien transport ship. He used the rope carrier to verify the tunnel ahead looked empty, then made the best time he could. The end of the tunnel became visible between bursts of fog. Matthieu caught a glimpse of a long, smooth beam of material past the exit. It looked like a glossy ceramic or metal against the sky beyond.

That's artificial. Nanorith.

"This is the edge of the city," Matthieu announced. He walked to the exit to take a look. He saw the crater of the volcano, over a kilometer in radius. The spires within were as tall as Terran skyscrapers. What had looked like a clockwork toy before now towered ahead. The structure right before them was gray and black, with brass-bordered openings arranged in rows around the building at regular intervals.

It looks like their buildings had floors much like ours.

Matthieu did not see any transparent material blocking the windows. He thought at first perhaps it was so perfect as to be invisible, here where the air was clear. Then he decided that superheated air must flow up through the curved towers from below to vent out through the portals.

He took a step forward, then stopped. The fog had cleared at his feet for a moment, and he saw a dizzying drop. The exit of the cave stopped a meter short of adjoining a tall, twisting tower.

Matthieu took a smart rope and told it to grab his belt harness. "Hook up," he said, passing the rope back to Adrienne. She let the rope slip through her own belt and

241

passed it to Spask. Once they were attached to each other, Matthieu hopped across. Adrienne followed without hesitation. Matthieu noted a look of distress on Spask's face, but he came across quickly as well.

From the edge of the tower they stood upon, Matthieu looked into the building through one of the portals. The edges of the opening had flaps like exhaust vanes on a jet thruster.

"I doubt that's an entrance," Spask said.

"Well I doubt it was meant to be one," Matthieu said, climbing through carefully. They followed him inside.

The interior was illuminated from the outside through the many circular portals. Five long cylinders stood vertically within the large room, each one covered with an array of curved moving parts that fit together like a dizzying orrery for a system much more complex than Sol's.

Spask walked up to one, as if assessing its suitability for taking.

"I have no idea what this is."

Matthieu shrugged. "I don't know either. I doubt most of what's here could possibly make any sense to us without a lot of study. I'll tell you though, Spask, even a Nanorith can opener would go for tens of thousands of ESC on Earth, or the equivalent in any Idona currency you choose."

"So this is where you need to be?" Spask asked. "Do you have the equipment already, or do we go back for it?" Spask asked.

"I don't have the equipment yet. It will require going deep into the city. Right now, I just want to look things over. It's rare to be able to explore alien ruins."

Spask seemed to accept the answer. Adrienne looked troubled.

"I have to speak with you alone," Adrienne sent to Matthieu's link.

"Yes?"

"Do we really have to go deep into this city? It could be dangerous."

"What? No longer an adventurer?" Matthieu asked. Spask seemed to detect that something was happening with them, so he paced about the room, moving refuse with his boot and peering out through the openings in the structure.

"We could send Orb or Mimic," Adrienne said.

"Orb will go ahead of us. But I need to go find out where to place the thermal activator."

"This is insane. You're going to set that thing off? Then what?"

"We wait. It's like ringing the Nanorith doorbell."

"It's like waking them from decades long sleep. They may not be happy."

"When the Space Force first did this, they were glad to meet Terrans. And it had been a lot longer than a few years."

"Maybe they're actually happier to be awakened after a long time than a short one. Also, this time... and I'm sorry for this, Matthieu... it's just that this time, your goals are personal. It's for the benefit of one man, not for forging a new relationship between two races."

I suppose she's right. I was their friend, but how can I awaken an entire city for my own personal problems?

Matthieu knew that to the Nanorith, to erase someone's memories would be a crime greater than murder. Still...

Adrienne saw him struggling. "I know you're desperate, Matthieu. I'm just saying, there may be a downside."

There's that phrase of hers again. It's what she says when she means, 'it's going to go bad, don't do it'. The old Matthieu probably knew that.

Matthieu saw a scan had highlighted an anomaly. One of their scouts sent in a high priority feed. Matthieu accessed it. He saw a large, white building nestled among the rocks. The half-disk-shaped facility nestled against the inside lip of a lava tube that descended straight down for an unknown distance.

Michael McCloskey

"Reverse Hastur! What's that?" Adrienne asked.

Matthieu and Spask went off-retina and looked over the structure for a second.

"It's Terran," Spask noted. "I think we've found the Space Force presence."

"Yes. It's large. It has to be Space Force. Either that, or a Core World corporate base," Matthieu said.

"What are they doing? Studying the Nanorith ruins?" Spask asked.

"They have to be," Matthieu said.

"Wait. Could they be talking with Nanorith?" Adrienne asked.

"I don't know. I guess they could be warming up individuals instead of waking the entire city..." Matthieu said.

"We have to know before we proceed," Adrienne said.

"Proceed with what?" asked Spask.

"I'll send in Orb and Mimic," Matthieu said, ignoring Spask's question for the moment.

Chapter 35

Orb approached the Space Force base from above, hovering centimeters from the rocky cliffside. The top of the base was a long, curved section of white ceramic, as if from the tip of a gigantic dinner plate embedded in the rock. If the shape of the base was a cylinder of the diameter suggested by the arc below, most of the base was built into the rock beside the tube that led down into the volcano. A quick calculation indicated only twenty percent of the base was exposed to the tube, assuming a uniform shape.

The Space Force must have been convinced this volcano would not be active for hundreds of years, thought Orb. *Or perhaps they just decided learning about the Nanorith was more important than the possibility of losing a base to an eruption.*

Orb saw a long scar in the cliff. In order to remain as stealthy as possible, it dipped into the depression. The niche took it twenty meters sideways and as half as many downwards. Then Orb emerged and continued downwards. It approached within ten meters, then five, then one.

The smooth exterior of the base angled downwards as it extended from the cliff. Moisture dripped off the surface across the entire roof. A simple assembly of four antennas broke the soft lines of the roof about ten meters from Orb. The spy bot wandered over to examine the equipment and look for a way into the base.

A very thin line gave away the presence of a hatch on the upper surface ahead of it. The base had been constructed with such tight tolerances that the line would not be visible to Terran eyes. Orb stopped to look at it. There was no evidence the door had been used recently. A fine layer of mineral deposits from the misty air had accumulated across the surface, obscuring the line even more.

That means no one has opened this hatch since the last hull scrubber went over it. Would that be days? Weeks?

Orb decided to try its luck at the sides of the base. It

hovered along the top hull of the facility to the edge and looked down. The vertical side of the facility was more complex; here and there niches were built into the outer bulkhead. Orb saw some heavy cables and drop lines and guessed they were used for moving things to and from the deep chasm.

Orb stopped instantly when it detected movement directly below. A floating platform with Terran soldiers or androids emerged from the side of the base. Orb could not see the opening from its vantage point. Orb risked a directed comm link with one of Master's scouts at the lip of the volcano above. It sent a video feed of the soldiers.

More activity came from below. Now Orb could see two platforms floating away from the base. The platforms looked like hovering longboats, sending high tech soldiers off to war on a faraway planet. Three large robots came into sight from below the base and moved into a line about thirty meters from the soldiers. Each robot was the size of a construction truck, narrower than the platforms, but rounder and probably more massive. The large robots bristled with weapons and sensors. Orb supposed they might be large enough to have gravity spinners of their own. The distance the machines kept from the Terrans supported the idea.

"What could they be doing? Gathering samples? Exploring?" Matthieu pondered over the link.

The platforms started to descend into the lava tube. Orb descended to get a closer look at the men. They were indeed heavily armed and armored. Men and machines sported the circular green emblem of the UNSF. Several cases of equipment had been loaded onto the platform with them.

"They're going deeper in, where the Nanorith ruins must be," Matthieu said.

"That makes sense. Those robots are not pure science machines, though. Those are military machines," Adrienne said.

"The Space Force is cautious. They've learned to be,"

Matthieu supposed.

Four gray-blue spheres emerged from the base and floated beside the platforms holding the men. Orb saw the floating machines had four legs folded up against their sides. The top quarter of the machines were raised from the body a few centimeters, exposing a slot around their upper perimeter. Within the slot, sensors and weapons rotated the full circumference of the machines.

Another squad of four spheres emerged from the building. Then another.

Orb caught sight of a scout machine on the perimeter. Its body had the shape of a dragonfly, two meters long, with a spherical part up front and a long cylinder trailing behind which contained the propulsion unit. The scout shot downward after a pause, leading the way down the giant tube. The three large war machines followed, then the men's platforms.

"Heavily armed for a bunch of scientists, aren't they?" asked Adrienne.

She is correct, thought Orb. *They're ready for a fight. There is a good chance I'll witness a death here.*

"Follow, Orb. I want to know where they're going."

Orb began to descend after the task group. The squad remained on alert, even though two scouting machines preceded them. Orb saw each soldier had a laser rifle. It did not see any grenades or projectile weapons.

Such a uniform weapons mix implies they know what they're fighting.

Orb did not dare pass by the group on their way down. It trailed the men on their platforms. The smaller robots remained close to the men. As they moved deeper, the light faded until the group activated powerful light emitters on their boats. The large war machines remained dark, but Orb could hear the electromagnetic noise of their scans. It stayed close to the cliffside and tried to use protrusions of rock to hide. Even though it was mostly invisible to Terrans, it did not know what kind of sensors the military machines might have. If Orb was detected, it would be surrounded by heavily armed enemies with no way to fight back.

They arrived at the bottom of the shaft and landed on a flat shelf of rock. Openings beckoned in three different directions. Orb saw tracks and muddy pools that suggested the different exits had been used by the Terrans before.

The men exited their floating boats and unslung their rifles. The smaller spheres deployed in a grid to one side. The soldiers almost all faced the same direction: toward the new tube leading out of the bottom of the shaft.

They'll go that way.

A scout machine flew into the tunnel. Orb considered following. Fear of the unknown caused it to reject the idea. Whatever this vanguard faced, Orb could learn about it from the rear.

"They're deploying for an assault," Spask said through Orb's connection.

Orb recalled that Spask was ex-Force. It agreed with his assessment: the soldiers were preparing themselves for battle.

The machines had moved forward, ahead of the men. Orb saw one soldier checking his grenades. The others remained kneeling, but looked eager.

"What's down that tube? These men are ready for action all right," Adrienne said.

"There must be Nanorith to fight?" Matthieu said. "They wouldn't need those combat machines for a natural predator like we ran into."

"Those are kill groups," Spask said. "With four machines in each group, they would have to be after something powerful. I'm thinking they must be after something sentient with weapons of its own."

"Could they be coming for us?" asked Adrienne.

"If they are, they're looking in the wrong direction," Matthieu said.

The spherical robots moved out through the tunnel, followed by the soldiers. The massive battle machines remained behind. Orb followed the task force.

Orb lost contact with Master and the others as it left the main shaft behind. It supposed that the scout machine at the top knew roughly which direction Orb was going, so it might be able to move along the surface and re-establish contact later.

The tunnel was dark and misty, but the men obviously had gear to help them see. They walked confidently. Orb did not catch a single shared word; if they talked it was among their link traffic.

Light grew ahead. At first Orb thought it must be another shaft or canyon, but the end of the tunnel was made of the same material it had seen in the Nanorith ruins. The Space Force team was entering the alien city.

Orb entered after them. They were now near the bottom of the volcano's crater. The curved skeletal spires of the city rose a half kilometer above. The light filtered down from the planet's star, finding its way around the enormous slivers of curved ceramic or metal.

Somehow the Nanorith must be able to control the power of the volcano's eruptions. Otherwise, their city would be destroyed.

Orb picked up a signal from above once more. It established a directional connection and resumed its video feed.

The scout machine must have plotted our course in a straight line from the direction we left the bottom of the shaft. There were no twists or turns, so it found us again.

A squad of men broke off to guard each flank. Then the main body moved forward behind the battle machines. They moved around the first huge base of a tower that arced away at a crazy angle. It did not look like a form any Terran building could sustain against the typical gravity which Terrans preferred.

Up ahead of the column, Orb saw a trench dug into the ground of the crater. It stretched between two huge spires. The spires rose, gray and black and brass-colored, twisting like the tentacles of a towering alien god. Inside the trench, Orb spotted five armored turrets with projectile weapons mounted within. The weapons faced forward from its current view.

The soldiers did not halt in the trench. Instead, they crossed at three small bridges. Orb spotted two or three soldiers that had already been in the trench. They greeted their comrades silently and joined their ranks.

"They guard this line? They must be fighting the Nanorith! How can that be?" Adrienne asked on the channel. Presumably she was watching Orb's feed again.

"Maybe they're fighting a corporation here, or smugglers, or... I don't know," Matthieu said.

"The trench has almost no defensive value against modern weapons," Adrienne said. "They must be desperate."

"Sometimes a covered position like this can be as much for the psychological effect on the men as for any real defensive advantage," Spask said.

"The trench has value or they would not have made it," Matthieu insisted. "The thing is, we don't know *what* they're fighting."

Once the men had all crossed the trench, the spherical battle machines led them on. Orb stayed close, and crossed over the trench carefully. It did not know what kind of detection systems the Space Force might have set up in the trench.

Once it crossed the tiny area without incident, Orb's apprehension over the position shifted from what lay behind to what lay ahead. The Space Force soldiers headed straight for a massive but squat black building a quarter of a kilometer ahead. It rose only as high as a four or five story Terran building. It did not possess any of the round, dull yellow portals the spires all seemed to have.

"What is that? Some kind of vault?" Adrienne asked.

"Look at that," Spask said, though Orb did not know what he spoke of.

"There's been a battle here before," Matthieu summarized.

Orb examined the area more closely. It saw discolorations on the surface of the building and some of the thick spires ahead. The markings did not appear to have done anything to the structures other than scar them.

Explosions? Laser hits?

The assault robots had deployed into a wide arc before the building, at a range of about a quarter of a kilometer. The soldiers fell in another 100 meters back. Many of the soldiers were clearly looking at the building, others had set their rifles on their own assault machines, while yet others stopped to set up grenade launchers on the ground.

"This is desperation," Spask said. "The Space Force usually has heavy assault machines like the ones they left on the other side of the tunnel, or orbital support. They would strike from thousands of kilometers away, not a few hundred. These tactics are primitive."

"These men are here to secure the scientists, not to conduct an interstellar war," Adrienne said.

"Does it look like they're defending the base to you?" Spask shot back.

"I mean simply the Space Force garrison here is not equipped for an offensive."

"Perhaps the city defeats more advanced measures," Matthieu speculated. "Maybe they don't dare risk waking the Nanorith."

Orb saw movement in an opening of the building slightly above it. Just a flicker. It focused its attention faster than any Terran could. An object had appeared in the opening with alarming suddenness. Orb saw it as a column held upright on four thick legs. The column glowed. The video feed showed the object radiating heat along a wide range of frequencies.

Is that a creature or a machine?

The Space Force machines targeted the object. The soldiers had not yet reacted. A fraction of a second later, the entire group of assault robots opened fire on the object.

Thunderous sounds erupted in the city. The machines were releasing projectiles—a large number of them. The Terran soldiers were still acquiring the target. Even though many of them did not have their rifles pointed well, their weapons were doing the work for them.

A wave of self-guided grenades flew above the machines and headed for the tunnel. Smoking chips of metal rained down from above. The grenades caused huge balls of fire to coruscate across the building. Orb realized the rain was not parts of the building. It was shrapnel from the projectiles and the bombs themselves.

"What the hell? It's enough to destroy a city," Adrienne breathed.

A small Terran city, maybe, Orb thought.

"They have no clear target, I think," Spask said. "These are not standard tactics at all. This is something they've learned to do against this enemy."

Orb supposed that Spask had not caught sight of the thing in the building. The rain of fire continued. Matthieu noticed some of the Terran machines had stopped firing.

"I think they're running out of ammunition," he said.

"They're losing the machines," Spask said. Matthieu spotted another assault robot that had halted.

"Those frozen machines are dead?" asked Adrienne.

One of the still machines turned about and opened fire on another assault machine. A group of four spheres on the flank responded by firing back. The traitor machine imploded in a hail of bullets and energy beams. It crumpled like a burned eggshell.

Finally the fire stopped. The opening where Orb had seen the glowing column had become a gaping canyon in the rock.

"Reverse Hastur! What was that for?"

"I think that may have been a Nanorith machine," Matthieu said.

"Something's wrong with the assault robots," Spask

said. "They're disabled."

The same kill group started to destroy the frozen machines. One of the targets started to return fire. Its main laser focused on a marine, causing him to dive for cover as his suit sparked and smoked. Then the other machines blew it to bits.

"Something is hacking them," Adrienne said.

"They expected it," Matthieu said. "That group farther back snipes the machines that go still. It's as Spask said. These are special tactics. They've done this before."

The Space Force soldiers moved forward, weaving in and out among the statues of the Space Force machines.

"Whatever that was, it was strong," Adrienne said. "If it was Nanorith, it must have been fast, like its masters. It took a lot of firepower to overwhelm it."

"The Nanorith think faster than Terrans. Their whiplike appendages make them look physically very fast as well, but they still have a lot of mass and it still resists acceleration. I think they're chemically fast, energetic. That doesn't mean they make robots that can dart around much faster than ours."

"Then why so much to kill one?"

"The battle must be very slow to it," Matthieu said. "It has time to think. Time to watch each projectile come in. It must have countermeasures it can apply. I would guess they had to saturate its defenses."

"So it could see everything coming for it, but it could not stop it all," Spask said. "Still, they seemed to be shooting at the whole building."

"Interesting. Well, they had better hope they don't encounter another. They lost a third of those robots," Adrienne said.

They don't expect another, Orb thought.

The marines had resumed their forward movement. They passed the line of assault machines and double-timed it for the building. Many of them hefted black cases in pairs. At the entrance, one group went inside a large doorway in the ruins, weapons ready. The others stopped and opened the black cases.

Minimalist worker robots, little more than powered skeletons, came out of the cases and unfolded themselves on the rugged ground. As the machines configured themselves, the men picked the cases back up and carried them inside.

Orb followed. It floated through the doorway into an interior lit by bright light pods the Space Force men and women had tossed into the corners. The men had fanned out once past the main entrance.

Orb watched a squat work robot carry away two large black containers. The marines nearby were readying more of the containers. Orb passed by the group and went into another chamber. Instead of another square, empty room, it saw a roughly circular cavern with thousands of black spheres crusted all across the walls. Orb spotted a marine just as she closed up one of the containers. It was filled with black orbs. The objects were unmistakable.

"Time's almost up. We need to leave, people," she barked.

"Those are Nanorith shards!" Adrienne exclaimed.

"You mean the eggs?" Spask asked.

"Not exactly eggs, but the term is good enough," Matthieu explained. "Those black orbs can produce adult Nanorith in a very short time, if they are heated to extreme temperatures."

"So they're taking sleeping Nanorith from the city," Spask said.

Orb noted from the tones in Spask's voice that he did not sound surprised. There was no delay in processing the bombshell of information from Matthieu.

Spask already knew what they were, Orb thought. *Maybe Brandel received some information from Sorune and passed it along to Spask?*

"This supports my assertion that the Space Force is taking advantage of the Nanorith's hibernation," Matthieu said. "They fight guardian machines and steal eggs. It's a cold war, in an almost literal sense: if the Nanorith were hot and awake, they would resist. Successfully, most likely. Their speed is powerful."

"Well, maybe the Space Force is right to fear them. If we can't face them awake, then they may represent a danger," Spask said.

"No," Matthieu said. "I have the memories of the one they sent. Nanorith have no designs on any place we would ever live. They want environments we find uninhabitable, and they aren't imperialistic anyway."

"I don't know how you could have memories from the Nanorith, but if you do, the memories could be tailored for you. To make you believe you're safe," Spask pointed out.

Adrienne nodded. "Fake memories. The equivalent of a Nanorith lie."

"That would be almost against their religion," Matthieu said. "It's against everything Nanorith believe in on a very basic, universal level."

"Well, for the moment, the Space Force seems to have the upper hand," Spask said.

Michael McCloskey

Chapter 36

Mimic watched from a narrow ledge on the cliff as a cleaning robot worked its way over the surface of the Space Force base. The cleaner bot moved slowly, scrubbing away. It affixed itself to the hull of the facility both magnetically and with suction. Mimic recognized the robot as a Gauss Systems design that it could emulate. Mimic rearranged its internal frame, preparing to become the machine's duplicate.

Like a spider dropping from a web to the ground, Mimic lowered itself onto the top planes of the Space Force base, mere meters away from the cleaning robot. Then Mimic started to close on it. The other machine made no defensive moves; it seemed occupied only with its work.

Once within range, Mimic attacked the hull cleaner with rapid precision. First, it isolated the machine's link with a damper field, temporarily isolating from the outer world. Then Mimic cut off an outer panel and ruthlessly extracted the machine's CPU and link assembly. The body of the cleaner machine halted. Mimic kicked the husk away, letting it slide from the hull and fall into the crater below.

I still have need of you, Mimic thought. *Let's keep you at home.*

Mimic secreted the machine's simple brain within its own casing and provided it with the inputs it expected. Mimic created a virtual world with a very dirty outer hull to keep cleaning. Mimic hoped to retain the machine for any security challenge responses Mimic might need. It would not do to simply record several of them now; likely the proper response code changed in time and space. Not knowing the secret algorithm, Mimic preferred to hang on to the cleaner's mind.

Mimic started to move along the hull. It was not cleaning anything, but it figured that even the cleaner bot would have to return to base now and then to replenish supplies or energy. There was also the possibility of needing repair. When Mimic had found a hatch into the base, it manipulated the virtual world of its captive cleaner brain.

Oops, your scrubber broke. You have to go get repaired.

The cleaner brain saw itself break. All the inputs were smoothly generated by Mimic for the bot. In the virtual world, it crawled back to the door and sent a message. Mimic passed the message on into the real world as fast as it could manage. If the delay was greater than the time granularity of their security, the scheme might not work.

The hatch opened to allow the machine to enter. Mimic scurried inside. The machine it emulated would need to go to a bay for repair. Mimic accessed a public map service at the lowest level of security. Most of the map was blank, but a nearby robotics bay was shown, so Mimic headed there.

Mimic scuttled through two short corridors without encountering man or machine. Then it emerged into a modern room equipped with many stations of varying shapes and sizes. About a dozen other machines were in the bays, receiving work or waiting about. Mimic had been in many of these places itself, despite being owned by Master, who preferred to do most of his own agent maintenance. Most of the parts needed would be fabricated directly by the bay working on a robot, but sometimes prioritization required a machine to sit idle.

It did a quick analysis and chose the smallest occupied bay that could receive it. Since it then had to wait for the bay to become available, Mimic took the time to think.

Mimic considered the models of machines it could see in the bay. Eighty five percent of them were Gauss Systems machines, likely built for the Space Force, and the rest were built by the Space Force itself. Mimic thought about assuming that the observation machines would be Gauss models. It had several such models in its link cache files, and they looked very similar to each other. It decided not to act without learning more first.

Master wanted to know all about the base. He had

mentioned a special interest in Nanorith studies going on, or live Nanorith.

I have to be able to move around almost anywhere. I could become an interior cleaning machine...

Mimic considered the limitations of that approach. It decided such machines would be restricted from science labs, where they likely have specialized maintenance machines.

Mimic continued to examine the machines in the robotics bay. The bays were of four different sizes, arranged into rows. In one corner, Mimic saw a roving eye device, presumably some kind of security observer. The agent took note of the exact details of the real device and subtly altered its own appearance. In particular, it added a blue number to its side. The machine across the bay was number 14, so Mimic gave itself the same number. Then it floated over to the machine.

The bay had anchored the spy robot with a work arm to replace one of its hovering fans. Mimic floated into the bay and duplicated the brain-link extraction it had performed on the scrubbing machine. It broke the scrubber machine's brain and dropped it on the floor, replacing it with that of the spy machine. Then it took over the input of the spy machine and gave it a virtual world to play in.

So disguised and equipped, Mimic floated on through a doorway leading deeper into the station. The next room also looked like a robotics bay, but made for heavier machines. Mimic saw over ten spherical military machines waiting to be serviced by one of four bays. Many of the machines were being carried by retrievers, machines used to pull or tow disabled machines back to a repair facility.

This is unusual. A lot of that model are here.

Mimic looked the machines over, searching for holes, dents, or burns. The machines did not show any signs of damage. Yet here they all were.

Some kind of software hack, or possibly a powerful EMP issue?

Mimic moved on. The next room was not a bay, but a barracks. Rows of soldiers stood in half-tube niches built into the wall. A long bank of equipment lockers faced them.

Android barracks.

Mimic decided there were probably no Terran marine barracks on the base. Most likely the android complement served as the support troops to any heavy assault machines the base had. It expected Terran scientists, not soldiers. Still, the Space Force might have some combat officers here, given the remote location beyond the frontier and the presence of aliens.

Mimic chose a door and emerged into a corridor. It followed the path straight, still heading deeper into the complex. Up ahead the way curved to the right. The long, curved pathway had many closely-placed doors, each with a number.

Officer's quarters? Or small labs?

Mimic analyzed the wear patterns on the deck. Though very clean, the deck showed regular, even traffic to each of the doors.

Quarters, I think.

Inside of its virtual world, Mimic's captive eyebot headed into an area of the base that Mimic had not seen yet. Mimic had to choose between creating fake environments that the eyebot might know were wrong, or just not letting the door open. It chose the latter.

The eyebot tried to report the malfunction. Mimic replied with an order to reverse patrol and wait for repair. The eyebot seemed to accept its new orders. It turned around and headed back the way it had come in the imaginary world Mimic provided it.

I wonder how long I can keep it fooled?

Mimic's link received a burst transmission on a frequency not used by the normal link protocols put forth by the Core Worlds' government. To most it would look like little more than a high frequency noise spike, literally a 'cosmic ray'. It decoded the message.

"Mimic, this is Master. Orb is following an away team headed back up to the base from the depths. They have Nanorith shards with them. Find a likely ingress point for the team and figure out what they're doing with those shards."

Mimic felt energized to hear Master's voice and receive new, special orders.

Master needs my help on his mission! It must be very important, or he would not risk sending me a message here.

Mimic recalled that the Space Force soldiers had exited from below where it had entered. It found a descending maintenance tube and headed downward. It emerged two levels below into another corridor. The new corridor looked different. The doors were heavier with rounded corners, spaced farther apart.

Airlocks. But I don't think they go outside.

Mimic floated by several of the doors, wishing for a window or a guide. The wear on the floor was even, as before, but considerably lighter.

Either this section was made later, or the people here wear the deck less.

As if to verify Mimic's guess, a woman emerged into the corridor, ten meters away from Mimic. She wore thin clothing, probably disposable. Her frame was light.

She's a scientist. The other quarter probably housed Space Force officers. Larger men and women with thick protective boots.

Mimic decided to dart into the lock. The door cycled, trapping it inside for the moment. From here, there were windows revealing the room beyond. It was some sort of cleanroom.

Mimic annotated its growing base map with its suppositions.

It asked for the inner lock to open and received a challenge. It passed it on to its imprisoned eye-bot.

Risky. That bot was not expected a security challenge. For all I know it is not even authorized to operate here.

Michael McCloskey

The bot responded to the challenge and Mimic passed it on. The lock opened to allow Mimic to come in. Mimic passed through a zone with a strong breeze whipping down from above and through a grating in the floor, to a second door which let it through.

Beyond the inner door, Mimic saw a spotless lab with several robotic arms built into the walls. Several vats or repositories sat in the center, with one arm above each one. The lab had no other doors, though it did look like some smaller chutes were set up to bring materials in from other levels.

The team could not enter here—but wait! Those are Nanorith shards.

Mimic saw smooth, black orbs waiting on the farthest station, waiting in rows for processing. The arm flicked one of them off its waiting ridge, sending it rolling down a gentle slope toward the center of the area atop the station. The egg slid into the center of the depression. The round table underneath rotated for a moment, positioning the egg. A bright light snapped onto the egg from above.

Mimic approached closer, still watching the egg. It started to spin under the light, faster and faster. This continued for over a minute while Mimic watched. Finally the machine spun back down. The smooth action of an iris opening allowed the egg to fall through the depression. The orb clattered down a slide and fell into a large bin filled with more of the black eggs.

Those eggs have been processed. Thousands of them.

The machine continued, processing them all one at a time.

They're decoding the memories of the entire race. All their knowledge from... centuries back? Or more.

Mimic decided what it had discovered was important to send to Master immediately.

Time to open a channel of communication out of here.

Even though Mimic had received a message moments ago, it did not have enough power to transmit out of the

262

base, so it had two options: go back outside, or hack something that could transmit for it.

Mimic went back to the double portal and asked for egress. The cleaning lock issued Mimic a security challenge. Mimic passed it along to its captive eyebot link, then returned the result. A light above the door flipped red. Mimic received a message to stay motionless or be destroyed.

The eyebot must be smart enough to know I'm feeding it lies. It decided to return the wrong security code. Or maybe I haven't been fast enough or accurate enough with the codes...

Mimic backed away from the door and scanned for laser bulbs on the ceiling. It did not see any of the distinctly shaped, optically perfect lenses that both protected mounted lasers from attack as well as allowed them to fire out from within. One of the worker arms suddenly snatched at Mimic, narrowly missing it. Mimic hovered away into the middle of the room.

The doorway made a cycling sound. A cylindrical security robot emerged and within one second it had launched a grenade at Mimic. The agent darted away, avoiding the projectile. The grenade exploded at a point nearest Mimic in flight. Glue attached to Mimic's surface.

Mimic hid behind one of the stations and sprayed itself with solvent. The solvent worked, dissolving the glue's points of contact and freeing Mimic. Mimic floated low around the machines, searching for cover. It had heard the door that let the robot inside close again.

No way out... except those chutes! The shards must come from there... the Space Force team Master mentioned must have put them into the other end.

Mimic went to the chute by the far end where the eggs were being processed. It would have to open the hatch somehow. There was no sign yet of where the security machine lurked. Mimic darted up to struggle with the chute hatch.

The security machine caught sight of Mimic and fired another grenade. It arced toward Mimic. The agent twisted viciously, trying to prevent molecular bonding, but it was too late. The hot glue had grabbed Mimic's surface and held.

Mimic's solvent reservoir had been expended. Having no other recourse, Mimic released the outer plates that gave it a rough spherical shape, leaving them behind with the glue. It also spat out the link of the captive eyebot, letting it fall to the floor. A skeletal frame shot out of Mimic's old casing, holding nothing but its intricate structural components, its round AI core, and its hover fan. The agent swerved wildly until it could form parts of its frame into airfoils to keep it aloft. It bounced off a wall and kept flight.

Mimic watched the security machine behind with all of its now-exposed sensors that dotted its frame. Another glue grenade shot out of its launcher. Mimic dodged violently and turned a corner. The flower of glue erupted nearby but did not connect.

Mimic had to try again. It rose beneath the chute. The glue grenade's impact had damaged the door slightly, leaving a centimeter-wide opening. Mimic reached out with a tiny manipulator arm and pried the door farther open, then it quickly turned sideways and pulled itself through with a scrape.

In the chute tunnel beyond, it heard another glue grenade thwump against the other side of the chute door.

Too close. Much too close. Time to find the other end of the chute and tell Master what I've found.

Chapter 37

Matthieu stood in his quarters with the thermal activator in his hands. It felt heavy. He had researched its use and checked its services to make sure he had access to its full functionality. He added it to an equipment pack, then started to pick out weapons from one of the arms repositories.

Adrienne came into the small room and put her hands on his shoulders.

"You realize when that thing goes up, the Space Force base is going with it."

"They deserve it. They're plundering the wealth of a friendly race as they hibernate. It would be like stealing everything on Idona while the Terrans were asleep."

"They deserve to be obliterated?" Adrienne asked.

"Absolutely."

"You sound bloodthirsty. Remember..."

"What? I'm not myself? I joined my memories with this race. They met us in peace and now we're stealing their every memory for ourselves. Mark my words, this is about plundering their technology."

"Well, the Space Force is entrusted with protecting all of humanity. They have to know what the Nanorith are capable of. And they need every edge because sooner or later, there will be a dangerous race out there that isn't extinct."

"Like the Trilisks, which the Nanorith are helping us against. The Nanorith are peaceful. As for other races, they'll either be way ahead of us or way behind us."

"How do you *know* the Nanorith are peaceful?"

"Because we shared memories with them. All the memories of a Terran and all the memories of one Nanorith. It could not have hidden anything."

"Think again! The Nanorith trade memories like you and I would trade drinking glasses. They could have been very selective about the memories in the individual who shared with you."

Matthieu did not answer right away.

Could she be right?

"It's possible. They may have gotten a full read of me and denied me all their knowledge."

"So in their own way, they may have stolen Terran technologies and given little in return."

"You know the corporations as well as I do. And you know the Core World governments aren't any better. So why defend them?"

Matthieu suspected that Adrienne's past loyalty to her corporation may have been why they parted ways. Those thoughts rose to mind again.

Is she here for me and me alone?

Adrienne shrugged. "All I'm saying is, it's a big action to take. I just want to talk it through. If you're committed, then I'm helping."

"I know I have it right. The Nanorith are peaceful beings. They've tried to help us, suspecting that Trilisks control Idona. The Space Force is taking advantage of them. The Space Force has tried to stop me, tried to kill me, probably because there are Trilisks at the highest levels."

Adrienne did not reply.

"They built a base above a volcano. They'll have emergency escape routes," Matthieu said. "The scientists will escape with their lives, but the base will be destroyed."

He took a laser carbine, slipped an arm through its strap, and let it rest on his back. Then he selected four stun grenades. He hesitated, then grabbed a projectile pistol as well, putting it in a hip pocket of his Veer suit.

"I need you here," Matthieu said. "Watch out for us. We might need to get out fast, so have the ship ready to take off on a moment's notice."

"Got it," Adrienne said. "Be careful. Tell Spask if he returns without you, I'm not giving him a lift off this rock."

"I appreciate the sentiment, but I'm not sure that's a productive threat."

"Nevertheless."

Matthieu embraced Adrienne for a long moment, then walked off to meet Spask outside the ship. When Matthieu exited the *Resolu*, he found Spask waiting on the smooth rock just under the edge of the ship. The man still had all his pistols and climbing gear.

"Ready? I have the equipment to deploy," Matthieu said.

Spask looked at Matthieu askance, as if surprised he could not see the items Matthieu spoke of. Matthieu had implied that the items might be large when he had explained to Brandel that he needed help with it, but he had never verified it. Spask seemed to accept that whatever the equipment was, Matthieu could carry it in his pack easily.

"And Adrienne?" he asked.

"She'll coordinate from here. It might be necessary to pick us up somewhere else in an emergency, or even just save the ship."

Spask did not seem fazed. He nodded.

"Here's our route. We'll overlap as much as possible with what we traveled yesterday." Matthieu shared his link map with Spask. Scout machines waited along the route to help spot danger and ensure continuous communications with the ship.

They set out. Just before they entered the first tunnel, Matthieu linked himself into the perimeter surveillance of the *Resolu*. If Adrienne was about to be attacked, he wanted to know about it.

Spask and Matthieu walked back through the same tunnel they had discovered the other day and made their way around the old shard carrier craft. As usual, the mist obscured the way and kept Matthieu jumpy. He mostly worried about the Space Force, though he also wanted to be ready in case another indigenous predator ambushed them.

At the end of the tunnel where the city became visible, Matthieu came back into contact with one of the scouts linked back to the *Resolu*. The perimeter watch processes had sent an alert. Matthieu held up his hand to stop Spask, who stood waiting while Matthieu went off-retina.

The *Resolu* sent him a feed of the outside of the ship. It showed Adrienne walking outside in her Veer suit with a full pack, heading after him and Spask.

What is she doing? She agreed to stay there.

Matthieu thought perhaps she had changed her mind. He wondered if she had agreed simply to avoid an argument, knowing all along she could not bear to let him go out alone. The ideas seemed reasonable, yet...

Can I trust her? Is she here for me or her corporation?

"What is it?" Spask asked.

"Nothing. Jump over," Matthieu ordered. Spask turned and leaped across the gap. Matthieu looked at Spask standing on the other side. Matthieu's paranoia had been activated by Adrienne. Now it focused on Spask.

He could have thrown me off the cliff while I was off-retina. He didn't do it. I think he's not a danger.

Matthieu jumped across. Spask pulled him forward from the edge when he landed. Now they were inside the same building at the edge of the city that they had explored before. Spask and Matthieu checked for any changes.

We both have the same suspicion, even though there's no reason to expect that anyone else has been here since we left.

"What kind of place are we looking for?" Spask asked.

"Something deep. I have reason to believe these squat buildings like Orb discovered the other day are placed over fissures that lead into the crust," Matthieu explained. "There are shards there, which means, we might find Nanorith machines, too."

"How can we deal with that? Doesn't it take a whole company of Space Force soldiers and machines to take one of them out?"

"We won't have to take anything out. The Nanorith are peaceful beings."

Spask raised an eyebrow. Matthieu smiled.

"Thinking about betraying me again?"

"No. But I don't like suicide missions, either."

Matthieu sighed. "So hard to find good help these days."

Spask made a face and beckoned Matthieu to take the lead. They started a new routine of descent. Each level had a way downwards somewhere on the floor, often at the very center. Once they had dropped using a smart rope, they usually walked toward the center. Then if they found no downward portal, they swept the level clockwise until they found something.

The building grew steadily darker as they made their way. The curving beams grew thicker and more cluttered. At one point, their tower met another tower. Matthieu saw gigantic runners that allowed the two structures to slide along each other while remaining interlocked. He had never seen anything like it in Terran architecture.

"We'll move to that building here," Matthieu said. "We want to move toward the center as well as downwards."

They switched to the attached building which curved in the direction Matthieu wanted to go. He looked back up the spire they had come down, watching for some glimpse of Adrienne. How would she be following them? Footprints? Heat signatures? Chemical traces?

They were almost at ground level when Matthieu spotted something outside.

"Over there. See that? It's like that low building the Space Force fought their way into."

Spask peered through the opening. "If we go there, then we may encounter a Nanorith machine too."

"Good. The Nanorith will help us."

"How can you know that? They're aliens!"

"I'll tell you a secret. I've talked with one," Matthieu said.

Shared memories with one, actually. I won't say that.

They exited the building down a smart rope only two

levels above the rocky ground. Then they walked toward the new foreboding complex. All around the city rose in ancient grandeur: a frozen clockwork of towering spires locked together in an impossible puzzle.

They came to the low building that looked like a fortress. There was only one entrance, standing open, with no door Matthieu could see. They walked slowly inside. Matthieu suppressed fresh fear. The city was a graveyard, an alien graveyard with strange guardians that might emerge to challenge them at any moment.

The walls inside the new building were more complete. Even less light found its way into the rooms. Matthieu ran a hand along one wall. It was as smooth and black as obsidian. There were no machines or debris on the floors.

"It's like an empty palace," Spask said. "This is where the bad guy would live if this were a VR."

Matthieu returned the comment with a grim half-smile. They walked through an arched doorway into another dark chamber. Clusters of shiny black orbs lined the rounded walls.

"This is a shard chamber," Matthieu said. He walked by the rows of shards and wondered how many memories they held.

It must be many times more than a Terran brain could ever hold...

Spask was not impressed. "There's an opening leading farther underground over here," he pointed out. They moved farther down.

They dropped into a new level. Both of them turned on their lights and swept the room. Dark objects lay all around them. Mist obscured the floor to knee level. Matthieu smiled to himself despite the grim scene: it looked too much like a creepy graveyard in some horror VR.

"Those hulks..." Spask said.

"Terran assault machines," Matthieu said. He walked up to one. It was a spherical machine similar to the ones that had accompanied the marine assault they had watched. Matthieu's light swept across something much taller at the edge of the room.

It was a towering robot. Its skin looked more like a dense ceramic than a metal. It was not perfectly cylindrical: its body was made of many flat planes that approximated a cylinder. Matthieu thought maybe it had ten or twelve sides. Four stubby legs supported it from the bottom, while four slender, curved rods spread out from the top. It had round bulges and soft protrusions in the midsection which Matthieu supposed might be weapons or sensors.

The top of the hulk had been chipped away as if by a thousand bullets.

It's possible that's exactly what happened.

Matthieu and Spask began searching for another way deeper into the building through the misty ground.

"There was a battle here, obviously," Spask said. "Mostly dead Space Force machines, though. Do you think they got any real Nanorith?" he asked eagerly. Spask's Terran bias came through all too loud and clear.

"Let's keep searching. They may not have killed any," Matthieu said.

"Or maybe they captured some and took them back to that base," Spask suggested. They walked through the ghostly shells.

"The Nanorith won," Matthieu said after a moment.

"How do you know?" Spask asked.

"There they are," Matthieu said, pointing. Four tall constructs moved among the Space Force machines toward them.

"Run!"

"No. And hold your fire, unless you want to end up like these broken machines."

Spask struggled with the decision, his body shifting left then right, but he did not run away.

The foreboding constructs closed in on them.

Michael McCloskey

Chapter 38

The sombre pillar before Matthieu seemed to thrum with an inner energy. Matthieu checked his Veer suit's radiation sensors. They showed EM activity, but nothing it had been designed to warn for. Clearly they emitted a lot of infrared energy, as Matthieu already felt too warm. The suit's electronics warned him it could not keep him cool for long without a supply of water.

"Do something," Spask whispered. Sweat streamed down his face. His hands were still raised. Matthieu supposed the gesture was useless or worse; the aliens could not know what it meant.

Matthieu reached slowly into his pack (realizing only as he did it that anything he did must seem slow to a Nanorith machine) and brought out the thermal activator.

"We've come to use this," Matthieu said. "We want to wake up the city, stop the Space Force, and exchange more memories."

The machines immediately reconfigured around Matthieu. Their response reminded him how very slow Terrans lived compared to the Nanorith. The machines could have deliberated for their equivalent of days before making a decision, yet they seemed to move the instant he had spoken.

"You convinced them!" Spask said. "Wait. They're herding us." Spask sounded worried but Matthieu was not.

The columns had moved to surround them, leaving the widest gap in the direction of an exit. The two Terrans started to walk.

They'll lead us to a good spot to turn it on.

Matthieu walked for the gap. Then he sped up.

"Hurry if you can. To these things, we're painfully slow."

"They're robots, right?"

"I think so. But I don't know if they turn on and off like the Nanorith do. Maybe the robots can't wait around

273

indefinitely."

New pillars seemed to materialize ahead as Matthieu and Spask followed the unbarred paths through the tunnels. Matthieu supposed there were not so many of the machines. He figured they somehow rotated ahead to move with the two Terrans. They started down a long, spiraling ramp, gathering speed. The way grew darker, so they turned on their weapons' light sources.

"This is crazy. They could just shuffle us off a cliff into some pool of molten rock," Spask said.

No cliff came. Instead, the spiral ramp ended in a circular room. The walls were the perfectly smooth interior of a cylinder. They reflected some of Matthieu's light with an oily blackness that gave weak reflections in all colors of the rainbow.

Three of the silent monoliths came in after them. The tall constructs came to a stop and seemed to wait. Heat radiated off them, making the room seem like an oven.

"Weird," Spask commented. "I don't see any way out. This is a prison cell," he concluded.

"I'll place it here," Matthieu said loudly. He dropped to the floor and put the device down. He configured it with his link to activate in an hour.

When Matthieu looked up, he saw the machines moving away. Whether it was because they had shown Matthieu the spot, were satisfied with his actions, or because they sensed his distress, he did not know. The merciless heat receded. Matthieu took a water bottle out of his pack and drank deeply. He did not give any to his suit just yet. The suit knew how to carry air across his sweat to cool him, he just needed to stay hydrated.

"We're free of them?" Spask asked. His breath came in ragged gasps.

"Well for now, yes. After the device is triggered, there will be more of them. Real Nanorith, not just their guardian machines."

"I can't let you do that, Matthieu," Spask said.

Matthieu looked over. Spask had his laser pistol leveled.

Matthieu stood. "What? Why would you betray me now, of all times?"

"You're about to destroy that base."

"I see. I didn't realize you were such an upstanding citizen."

"I'm not. I'm a Space Force man, myself. Never left. I've learned what you know, what you're doing, and I think this is a fine place to stop it and take you in."

"That weapon won't target me," Matthieu said, reaching for his laser carbine.

"You mean this one?" Spask said, holding out another pistol. He dropped it on the ground.

"You have another," Matthieu said.

"That's right, I found this one among the dead marines we passed. And I'm a Space Force operative. This weapon accepted my override."

The weapon informed Matthieu's link that he had been targeted.

Matthieu was getting desperate. He had come too far to fail now.

"And what if I simply proceed?" Matthieu said. The device before him blinked green, then red. Their links received a warning.

Danger! Evacuate the area immediately. This zone is about to experience extreme thermal upheaval. Death is imminent to all who remain in proximity!

With the warning came a map delineating the danger zone. It extended a kilometer out from the perimeter of the volcano.

"Then I'll kill you and destroy the device," Spask said. "Stop it now, I'll only give you one—"

Spask's face contorted into a grimace of pain, then he fell forward like a sack of leaf bugs. Adrienne appeared from the shadows of the ramp beyond the body.

"What are you doing here?" Matthieu demanded.

"You're welcome, Matthieu. Did you really think I

came all the way out to this planet beyond the frontier just to sit back on the ship and let you die?"

"But what if we need the *Resolu*?"

"I'm in contact with it. I've set up a line of relays."

"And if they're picked off by the Space Force?"

"Then we'd best get back now, yes?"

They started back up the long spiral ramp. Matthieu moved more quickly now and Adrienne kept pace with him easily. At the top, they walked through the black building together.

"I'm going to send them a warning, just to make sure they have time to evacuate," he said.

"What?"

"I've been thinking about what you said. There has to be at least one innocent person on that base," Matthieu said. At the same time, he thought that might not be true. But what if it was?

"What will the survivors do to you? Attack? Report you to the rest of the Space Force?"

"I have to give them a fighting chance. As for the rest, maybe the Nanorith can protect us."

Adrienne smiled. "I agree. Warn them."

As soon as they left the dark building, Matthieu paused to go off-retina. He broadcast the warning through the nearest scout machine.

"Okay," he said. "More quickly now."

They started to run. When they made it to the spire leading upwards, Matthieu started to realize a miscalculation. Climbing all the way back up the lower spire and then the upper one would take much longer than it had taken to arrive, even though they had arrived at only a moderate pace. Matthieu had given the thermal activator a time-based schedule rather than notifying it remotely because of its isolated position deep in the city. He now wondered if his setting of an hour was wise.

We might run out of time.

They pressed forward. Matthieu climbed as hard as he

could. His suit provided emergency simulants to keep his body working. His legs burned by the time they made it to the level where they could jump to the cave in the cliff. He wobbled and wondered if he could even make the jump. He heard Adrienne breathing heavily, indicating she was stressed as well. They staggered toward the jump point.

"I think I should rest before—" Matthieu started.

A powerful tremor shook the ground. Matthieu and Adrienne both went flying. Adrienne tried to roll, ended up bouncing off the floor, and almost regained her feet. Then suddenly she reeled right toward the gap.

"Adrienne!" Matthieu screamed. He launched himself forward recklessly.

Adrienne slipped over the edge but Matthieu had a strong grip on her. His legs were shot but his arms were still fresh.

"I have you," he said, lying on his stomach and holding her.

"We're slipping!" Adrienne exclaimed. Matthieu realized with horror that she was right. His body slid a bit closer to the edge.

"I've got it!" Matthieu said. "Just hang on one more second!"

Matthieu's smart rope emerged from his pack. One end wrapped itself around Adrienne's arm, then slid around her, going for her waist. Matthieu could not see the other end.

He fell.

It seemed to take forever, but he was frozen in time. Adrienne stayed right where she was, supported by one end of the rope. She stared at him in horror. Then his view of her slid upwards like an image slideshow making room for the next picture. Matthieu felt a sharp yank between his legs, thankfully spread by his Veer skinsuit.

The smart rope!

His yank on the rope broke Adrienne's grip. As he fell to one side, trying to lock his legs around the middle of the rope, Adrienne started her fall.

Michael McCloskey

"Matthieu!" he heard her yell in his link. He found it odd that now, of all times, she would cry out on her link. It was her training. Better to stay stealthy at all times, even in death.

Another yank came, then Adrienne crashed into him and they stopped. Matthieu had no idea what held them up, but he was glad for it. He looked down at the rocky fall below and almost vomited.

"The ropes have us!" Adrienne exalted. "Both of our ropes have us."

"Quickly, before the next tremor," Matthieu said. He ordered his rope to haul him up.

"Already? Didn't you give us time to get out of there?"

"This is hardly a device to be employed by the average citizen," Matthieu said. "It's for use beyond the frontier. There were no safety considerations to speak of."

"Except to avoid incinerating us!"

They made it back up to the edge of the building. They stood breathing hard.

"Just jump. The rope has a good hold now, so even if you miss..." Adrienne said. Matthieu nodded. He took a few steps back, then ran forward and jumped.

He made it to the far side, though instead of a real landing he simply collapsed forward. Then he hooked his arm around a rock formation and motioned for her. His smart rope was ready to grasp her.

Somehow Adrienne made it across the gap. They were in the tunnel, almost to the shard carrier when the next tremor came. Matthieu steadied himself against the wall, then a hot wind started to blow through the tunnel from behind them. The mist quickly cleared.

"Run for it!" Adrienne yelled. Her warning was unnecessary, as Matthieu had already started to run.

Matthieu's suit gave him an alert. It told him it could not cool him for much longer in the hot air blowing by them. Matthieu did not stop running. He took a water bottle out of his pack as he felt the heat building in his suit. This

278

time, he did not drink. He opened a water intake at his throat and poured the water bottle into his suit. He spilled some portion of it as he ran through the cave, but he just needed enough to keep running.

He immediately felt relief as the suit circulated the water and started to evaporate it. The suit closed his flex helmet over his face, which then hardened into a faceplate. His strained breathing became noticeable within the closed helmet, but he did let that distract him.

We're going to make it!

The two tiny forms staggered up under their ship as reddish light lit the sky. They lifted into the *Resolu* and stripped off the Veer suits, panting. Once free of the suits, they collapsed. Both of them went off-retina as cool air poured over them.

One of the scout machines had remained at the lip of the tube to watch the base as the heat blossomed in the core of the volcano. Adrienne was already watching its feed. Matthieu did not see much happening in the video feed except a glow, but the scout machine's external sensors showed a hot wind raging up from the crater.

Orb watched the Space Force facility from growing altitude as it fled the area. Transports were leaving the base. Orb transmitted its view as the last two oblong ships lifted from the huge tube, aided by a flow of hot air.

"Where are they headed?" Adrienne asked.

"Orbit, it looks like," Matthieu said.

Another tremor shook the mountain. The base blew open in two spots and started to emit thick smoke.

"There it goes. That'll end their exploitation of the Nanorith." Adrienne looked at Matthieu's glum face.

"Mimic is still in there," he said.

Suddenly the base exploded, obscuring the entire tube with bright flame, then black smoke. Pieces of debris flew from the tube. Orb was half a kilometer above, fleeing for the *Resolu* as quickly as it could.

"Was still in there," he corrected himself.

"You had no choice," Adrienne said, putting her hand on Matthieu's arm. "I won't lose a minute's sleep about what we did to that base."

Then she embraced him. "I'm sorry you've lost another agent."

Chapter 39

The *Resolu* shook as the planet's crust shifted beneath it. Matthieu ordered the ship to direct large amounts of energy into the gravity spinner just as Orb reported its successful rendezvous with the ship. The shaking subsided as the *Resolu* stabilized itself and its contents as it would during space travel.

"Will they detect the spinner?"

"I'm sure they will. I want their attention."

"I meant the Space Force," Adrienne clarified.

"Oh. They'll leave the system soon, I think," Matthieu said. "I don't care what happens to them. What they were doing to those Nanorith was unconscionable."

"That may be your Nanorith part speaking, but I won't complain," Adrienne said.

"The transports made it out," he maintained.

"Outside temperature is increasing sharply," Adrienne noted the obvious. Matthieu saw it in his PV. The temperature had increased by twenty degrees Kelvin.

"I'm nervous. Can we take her up above the surface?" she asked.

Matthieu nodded. The *Resolu* rose out of its hiding place and moved into a position one hundred meters above the rocky surface to observe the ruins site. The alien city below came into direct view of the *Resolu*'s external sensors. The city spires were lit with a hellish light. Plumes of hot gas escaped the kilometers-wide crater in several places.

"If the volcano explodes—"

"While the thermal activator could be used to do that, given sufficient pressure below, I believe it's configured to avoid that outcome," Matthieu said. "Also, given that we've done this recently, I doubt that there's been time for more pressure to build."

"You believe?"

"Well, I have lost my memories, after all," Matthieu

said, enjoying the moment.

Is this what I was like? Enjoying the danger of such actions, seeking adventure after adventure for simple adrenal stimulation?

Adrienne rolled her eyes.

"I'm sure the Nanorith city is designed to prevent a catastrophic eruption," he added.

They continued to watch the Nanorith ruins off-retina, fed from the *Resolu*'s sensor data streams. The city had already changed. It looked cleaner, smoother. The rocky debris which had littered its surfaces had been removed. Matthieu wondered if the material had been shaken loose to fall below, or if it had somehow been used as raw materials for repairs.

The ruins of the city had started to glow themselves. Matthieu used the ship's sensors to display the radiative output across a wider spectrum than Terran eyes could perceive. He saw a myriad of frequencies blazing like a light show, even though the spires and soaring rib-shapes looked the same color in the visible spectrum.

The entire city started to revolve like a gargantuan corkscrew emerging from the crust, except more elaborate. Where one set of curved spires might rise together, other sets interlocked with them and moved in another direction. Smaller structures nestled within rose straight upward, revolved like giant screws, or spread open like symmetrical flowers.

"The entire city is one huge mechanical... piece of art!" Adrienne breathed. Matthieu was also affected by the power and grandeur of it.

These creatures built this place, maybe thousands of years ago. Things that live in ways we can only imagine. What possible common ground did we find with them? Intelligent beings that harvest energy from the red-hot interiors of volcanos. They have probably never seen a tree or a lake or a beach.

"It's amazing! And terrifying," Adrienne said.

The city had expanded to emerge above the mouth of the volcano. Sharp spires and long, arcing beams interlocked in a myriad of patterns.

Is that art or pure function? What is that city capable of achieving in few hours?

"Let's go!" Matthieu announced. He dashed out of the lounge. Adrienne ran after him.

"Where are we going?!"

"Into the city," Matthieu answered. His voice dripped with conviction. They ran into their quarters and Matthieu took out a fresh Veer suit.

"Hydrangea, give me the shard."

Adrienne watched Matthieu as he took the Nanorith shard from his agent.

"Isn't it dangerous? Will it transform with us in it? Will the Nanorith welcome us?"

Matthieu started to answer, then hesitated at the last question.

They will find out what was done to them. And we are Terrans.

The Nanorith that had helped Matthieu on Idona was ancient and wise. Though it could move and react much faster than he could, he would never describe it as rash or violent.

"We have to go ask for my memories. They won't blame us for the actions of the Space Force."

"I'm afraid," she said, but she reached for a Veer suit herself.

"Don't be. Come with me. Hurry."

"Why?"

"Every minute that passes they will accomplish so much. Hurry out before they find uses for every joule that's been liberated."

Matthieu and Adrienne finished dressing. They exited from the ship's ramp and ran the course to the city again. Matthieu went too fast, ignoring his fatigue and much of the fog. Adrienne kept up with him without complaint for his recklessness. They arrived at the cave mouth that opened upon the city.

The spire beyond the gap glowed. They felt the heat, even in their Veer suits. Matthieu's suit warned him it could not protect him long.

"It's become too hot for us," Adrienne said. "We have to return."

"They're very sophisticated. They'll help us," Matthieu said. Despite his words, his heart beat rapidly in his chest.

He leaped across the gap again.

At the instant he landed, the platform changed. The room before him was suddenly cool and clean. A series of Terran-like windows ran around the circumference of the tower. Lounges were arranged around the center, eight in all. There was no exit except back the way he had come.

"You were right," Adrienne said from beside him. "All this happened in the blink of an eye! But it doesn't look like they want us to continue."

"Do you recognize me? I've come back for my memories," Matthieu said, both aloud and on his link simultaneously.

Adrienne opened her mouth to say something. Matthieu knew what she might say: 'can you just speak to them like that?'. Before she asked, the response came from the Nanorith.

"That is of no interest to us." The voice was neutral, androgynous, and held little emotion.

Matthieu almost panicked. He did not have time to convince them. They lived so much faster than he did. His next words had to be just right.

"The Space Force stole your memories as you slept! I stopped them. *My memories were stolen from me!*"

Matthieu held up the shard that the Nanorith on Idona had left behind. It shot away from his hand, pulled by some unknown force. Matthieu's eyes could not tell him where it had gone.

The response seemed immediate to Matthieu's perception of time. Suddenly he realized so much more about who he was and what had happened to him. He remembered building Mimic and Hydrangea and Orb. He recalled when Devina had given him Assistant. He remembered meeting Adrienne for the first time, and knew what he had felt for her. And he remembered the Nanorith.

They valued their memories more than Terrans did. Memories were shared and replaced like books, photos, and VRs. They were raised to a sacred level in the culture of this race. He had managed to make the right point in his limited time.

Matthieu laughed.

"What? You have your memories back?"

"Yes. I know you! I know you so well."

"Tell me."

"We don't have time now. The Nanorith will do what they will, so very quickly, and then return to rest," he said. "I think," he added.

Will they choose to siphon more energy from below and remain awake?

"Will they talk more?" Adrienne asked.

"You can only ask and see," Matthieu said. "Be quick."

"Do you know why the Space Force treated you so poorly?" Adrienne asked.

Her answer came without the slightest delay.

"The Space Force revived us, which was a valuable chance for advancement of both races. But once the Terrans saw our amazing speed and potential, they took their winnings and fled. They did not want to revive us again. To Terrans, our quick lives have an unfathomable speed that instills terror. But to us, it is you who are the terrifying ones, the race that is always awake, that can do anything while we sleep."

"I'm sorry for the actions of the Space Force," Matthieu said.

285

Michael McCloskey

"Be warned: we will take precautions. Our guardians have been increased a thousandfold."

A memory of Nanorith warfare flashed through his mind: A hollow missile flew down from the sky and broke open, covering a wide area in a fine dust of quiescent nanomachines. Then a second missile carried a warhead to the scene. The bright blossom of a nuclear bomb lit up the landscape. The nanomachines harvested the heat and light to break the bonds of the materials they rested upon. Within a couple of seconds, they had fabricated a Nanorith army, thriving within the kilometers-wide blast zone. This Nanorith force could wage a continent-wide campaign, laying waste to whole cities within a single Terran minute, before running out of energy and returning to sleep much as the Nanorith themselves.

"I will do what I can to see that you are left alone," Matthieu said. This time, there was no answer.

Chapter 40

"Something's happening outside," Adrienne said. Matthieu spotted a spire in the distance, winding slowly down into the planet like a giant spiral screw.

"The city is cooling," Matthieu said.

"So soon?" Adrienne asked.

"It's almost the end of our time," came the reply.

"Why don't you funnel more heat upwards, or move your city deeper into the crust and remain active?" Matthieu asked.

"That's not optimal for us. We live in cycles by nature. It is our preferred existence. You may learn that immortality is not optimal for a race. Stagnation will occur. We will store our memories in a million shards, and those who live next time will each have a sampling of those memories. New combinations will form, and from that, new achievements will be attained."

"But that could be hundreds of Idona years from now. Thousands, even."

"We are also patient beings. Even now, we speak with other colonies using communications systems similar to your tachyon receiver bases. Everything is going well in the galaxy. In the time since you arrived, we have lived several Terran lifetimes."

"Thank you again for my memories. I'll protect yours very carefully, as no doubt the Space Force has already done. I have to get back to my home."

"Take these shards with you," the Nanorith said. Matthieu received a location pointer. "You must be very careful. To return home is to return to danger, Matthieu. We know of a hidden presence on your planet Idona. You call them Trilisk."

"I'm afraid I failed to root them out last time," Matthieu said.

"Yes. We sent you back before, with one of our kind. One Nanorith shard. The Trilisk, the one named Sorune,

Michael McCloskey

destroyed your memories and stole the shard from you. We
thank you for eliminating him."

"I don't... I don't remember it. So Sorune was an
android controlled by an alien?"

"Your restored memories only continue up to the point
you shared them with us. We sent you back hoping you
would revive the shard and allow it to hunt the Trilisk.
Somehow Sorune found out about your trip beyond the
frontier. He likely destroyed your mind and stole the shard.
You had no chance, really, against such a being. They can
use artificial bodies, or even alien bodies, as easily as you
use a remote android. Such an odd twist of fate that your
machines eliminated him in turn. You were avenged by your
agents, though they had no idea what greater purpose they
served."

Memories flitted through Matthieu's mind. He learned
what the Nanorith spoke of. The information had come on
the shard he had brought to this planet.

"I can't believe it! A Trilisk was killed by... a poison?"

"Their artificial bodies are powerful, it's sure, and
immune to many things. But some molecules affect their
designed Terran bodies even more keenly than a normal
Terran. Mimic dealt him a fatal blow. Sorune's cruelty to
you was returned in kind, Matthieu. Remember, there must
be other Trilisks on Idona. Heat these shards. They will live
a life there attempting to find and eradicate the Trilisks once
more."

"I'll do as you say," Matthieu promised. Outside, the
city spires shifted down again. "Why do you seek to destroy
the Trilisk? Terrans are so different than you are. I'm
surprised we find kinship between us."

"We spoke of stagnation. The Trilisk are exactly what
we seek to avoid in ourselves. We would stop them, or at
least reduce them, at every lifetime."

The city around them rumbled. Matthieu and Adrienne
steadied against each other.

"Go now and find our gifts. Return to your ship above

us. Goodbye."

"Goodbye," Matthieu said.

He wondered if he had felt the same sadness when he had said it to the Nanorith the last time he had left this planet.

"Send a scout over—"

"The scouts are all gone," Adrienne said. "It's up to us." She readied her PAW and looked at him.

"Okay. Let's go get the shards."

The temperature outside was dropping rapidly, but Matthieu could still tell a fiery tempest had been unleashed. His suit warned him again in the short time it took them to jump the gap and run down the tunnel toward the shard carrier debris.

As they approached the alien ship in the tunnel, Matthieu hardly slowed, until suddenly the fog shifted, revealing a new shape. Matthieu started, bringing his weapon up. He heard Adrienne gasp.

"That's new," Matthieu said. He saw a tall, pillar-like machine similar to those he and Spask had encountered deep in the city.

"Dangerous?" she asked.

"No. It must have brought our shards. This is the spot the Nanorith mentioned."

They walked around the machine, searching through the roiling fog.

Inside the carrier they found a new set of shards. The black orbs were shiny and perfect. Matthieu gathered them into his pack. He searched the area carefully, making sure not to miss anything.

"Let's hurry, Matthieu. I'm glad we came here, but..."

"Yes," he said. He wanted to reassure Adrienne, to tell her he remembered her now, but there was no time. He knew she would wait. She was no stranger to putting small things aside during a mission.

They hurried back to the ship with their weapons ready. Matthieu stopped at the mouth of the last cave, watching the mists.

"If there's a Space Force ambush, it would be here," he told Adrienne over the link.

"Agreed. Let's stay to the left on the way out of here. Don't go straight back as they would assume."

"Okay."

They took a more circuitous route back, despite the urgency. No group of hidden marines awaited them though, and they came back to the ship unharmed. The ramp opened and they piled back into the *Resolu*. The ship told Matthieu it had not been visited. Adrienne prepared the ship for departure while Matthieu secured the eggs into a rugged container. He brought them to his quarters.

"Anything going on in the system?" Matthieu asked.

"Yes. A Space Force distress call."

Matthieu hooked into the *Resolu*'s sensor feed. He saw a pane describing the distress call. The ship picked up several objects moving into low orbit above them. Matthieu saw the lifeboats were moving into a formation above the planet. He did not spot any larger ships or bases on the sensor map.

"We have to leave before a ship comes to pick them up."

"I don't see how that could be anytime soon. How did they arrange something? Surely there's no tachyon receiver base here."

"There must be. Or supply ships visit regularly. Or the Space Force has secret technology no one knows about. In any case, it's clear they have contingency plans. The lifeboats will have emergency supplies. They don't need us."

Except to imprison us for talking with the Nanorith and destroying their base.

Adrienne nodded. "Agreed."

Matthieu rode in silence as Adrienne set them on course for Idona. Once they had cleared the vicinity of the Nanorith's planet, she set a course out of the plane of the system and told the *Resolu* to bring the gravity spinner to critical once they were at a safe distance.

"I remember that time we left Red Calais and went into the Lorix Spinner Systems lab," Matthieu said.

Adrienne looked over at Matthieu. "Ha! We were lucky to get out of there in one piece," she said. Then she started to laugh. "You had to tangle us up eight ways from extinction to keep us from floating right out the exhaust shaft! And I kept saying we should just share one glider and get it over with."

"Yes. It was so exhilarating," he said. "I remember all our trips. You were so mysterious to me, so capable... you still are."

Adrienne smiled and kissed him.

"We did it! You're back! I can't believe it."

"Believe it. That's how good of a team we make. You, me, and the agents."

"I don't feel that different except when I'm recalling things," Matthieu said. "I think Assistant did a good job modeling me from what data it had."

The statement filled Matthieu with remorse that Assistant had not made it to hear the assessment. Adrienne must have seen his face darken.

"I'm sorry, Matthieu."

"Maybe I can do the same for Assistant. I still have the Reiss-Marck core."

"That's a fantastic idea. What will you call it?"

"Assistant," Matthieu said, as if the question was silly.

"You'll try to recreate it?"

"Its state is stored back in the Vault. It should be possible to reinstate Assistant, or something very close to it, when we get back. After all, that's what Assistant did for me."

"I thought every core had to bloom on its own," Adrienne said. "There are supposed to be subtle differences between each one caused by the path to consciousness."

"Then Assistant will be like its father. Something to

examine and emulate."

"We'll need all the help we can get. You need to go back to being dead," Adrienne said.

"What? Why?"

"You just destroyed a research facility built above alien ruins. Even if no Space Force personnel lost their lives, they'll want you. If anyone is paying mild attention, or, more likely, if the Space Force has AIs culling through long fact lists looking for coincidences, I'd say you're going to be flagged. If they figure out any of a number of activities you were involved with on Idona and connect that to our little space voyage, you'll be in trouble."

Another memory surfaced.

"The Nanorith I... shared with told me that they would make the devastation look like a natural disaster. They said they could arrange for a new fault in the planet's crust that went unnoticed by previous Space Force geologic surveys."

Adrienne laughed. "Such power. I guess this is their domain, after all."

Chapter 41

Matthieu sat alone in the *Resolu*'s fabrication shop, supposedly working on a case for the shards that could evade inspection upon arrival back at Earth. They had moved the shards into the device where they had hidden during the Space Force inspection.

Matthieu had felt awash in his own memories since they began the trip back to Idona. He used excuses to find time away from Adrienne to mull it all over by himself. He had already completed the case with a hidden compartment in which to hide the shards, but he had not announced that to Adrienne. Now he had started another agent for his AI core.

He paused again to replay the memories in his mind. Before he had had so many questions about their relationship and what she had meant to him.

Now he remembered. He remembered their incredible attraction and varied adventures together on Idona. They had grown close in adversity and fortune, and even saved each other's lives a handful of times.

In the end, he had found Adrienne to be too connected to her employer. He had suspected she would always put her career over their relationship. Company people were known to be like that; anyone who made it to the top of their specialty in a supercorporation had shown incredible loyalty and work ethic. It was natural for her to be that way. Matthieu had come to see the undercurrent of their every activity had been toward an aim desired by her employer.

Now, she showed her loyalty to me, though, Matthieu thought. *I was wrong to assume she would always put her company over me... wasn't I?*

Matthieu sighed. Something had been troubling him, something else he did not mention to Adrienne. In addition to his newfound memories of Adrienne, he had also come to recall Liane Vanault. The depth of his attachment surprised him; he had thought of their encounters he knew about from the cache she had left behind as glimpses of a fling; now that he had the full recollection of their time together he realized it was much more. Liane was a woman of real purpose. He had spent his life up until that point in meaningless diversions and shallow amusements. In Liane, he had discovered purpose and a mission to fulfill, something more related to the benefit of all mankind, not just the profits of a corporation.

They had shared the mission of investigating the Nanorith together. When a UNSF scout ship had discovered the ruins and realized what they were, the Space Force put together a work group of scientists and soldiers to travel beyond the frontier and investigate the find. Liane had been picked, and she had the influence to get Matthieu on the mission roster. She told him it was his incredible skill at creating ingenious agents that convinced the Space Force, but Matthieu had always known she had pulled a few strings for him. He would always owe her for that.

The thought keyed the release of a new memory. One that could only have been planted by the Nanorith. Matthieu gasped. Among the shards he had been given to take to Idona, one was special.

It contained Liane Vanault's memories.

Is it possible?

He accessed a video feed from within the shielded cache and found it. A black orb the same size of the other Nanorith shards but with a slight reddish tint. It was so like the Nanorith to simply create a memory of it rather than just tell him. It must have been very painful for them to carry on a conversation with a being as slow as a Terran. Easier to simply add a few memories to his mind.

But Liane is dead... or is she?

Matthieu heard the door open. He turned quickly, startled. Adrienne raised an eyebrow at his reaction.

Smooth, Matthieu. Not suspicious at all.

"Matthieu, what are you doing?" she asked mildly.

Adrienne walked into his workspace. A hundred components were arrayed all around him.

"Working," he replied simply.

"I've been giving you your space," she said hesitatingly.

"I know. I appreciate your patience. It's a difficult thing, to reconcile two versions of yourself and a smattering of alien memories."

"I'd like to talk about it."

Matthieu nodded. "Then let's have dinner. I'll finish up here in the next hour or so."

"I assume you're making a new agent," Adrienne said, looking over the mess he had made.

Matthieu knew she must be looking for the Reiss-Marck core. Matthieu had placed it out of sight for some reason he could not explain. It was indeed the brain for his new agent.

Why don't I trust Adrienne?

"I am," he verified. "It takes me a long time to make them, though. I'm a perfectionist, I guess."

"I wouldn't have it any other way. Look how much help your agents have been." Adrienne headed for the exit. "I'll see you at dinner then."

"Yes, dinner," Matthieu said quietly, even though she had already left.

Michael McCloskey

Chapter 42

Matthieu walked alone in the fading evening light of Idona. He followed a ceramic walk toward the Vanault Estate.

He had not told Adrienne of his errand. After all she had done for him, he felt that she might resent his loyalty to Liane, or jump to conclusions about his visit to her. He simply had to see if his suspicions were correct. If there was any chance to help her...

Hydrangea was in his hands, as if it were some kind of gift. Matthieu had secreted the reddish black orb within its shielded pot.

The Vanault estate was still as he remembered it. It was now nighttime, since Matthieu had not possessed the patience to wait until the next day. A sliver of hope in the back of his mind leaped forward and grew into excitement.

Do I need to sneak in again?

Matthieu walked up to the impressively large double gate at the front of the Vanault estate. As he approached, he received a security challenge.

"State your business."

The voice was artificial, cold.

"Matthieu Chaulet, here to pay my respects to Liane Vanault."

The doors opened.

Matthieu sighed and smiled.

That's more like it.

A thin silver robotoid awaited Matthieu on the other side. One of Liane's house machines.

"Welcome, Matthieu. This way, please."

It led Matthieu through the yard and into the house. He followed the machine into a wide room filled with flowers and jade sculptures. A coffin sat against one wall. Dark windows lined the wall. Matthieu extracted the Nanorith orb, slid it into the pocket of his printed suit, and set Hydrangea down on a simple table next to one of the sculptures.

Matthieu asked the coffin to open. Its shiny wooden lid lifted slowly and without a sound.

Inside he saw a transparent box where Liane Vanault lay. She looked perfect. Matthieu's link picked up a monitoring service and connected. It gave him the status of Liane's body in stasis.

By the Five!

It was just as Matthieu had hoped. Liane Vanault had never actually died at all—she simply lay at rest with her memories stripped as Matthieu's had been.

Matthieu asked the coffin to release Liane from her sleep. It replied with a decision pending response. Now the coffin was asking someone else... the question was, who?

"Please," Matthieu broadcast. "I was in this condition myself. I have a remedy. I have her memories here from the Nanorith."

After another second, the light intensified in the case. Matthieu waited. He heard a whirring sound and felt a thrum in the floor. Matthieu stood and listened to the pounding of his heart. After a minute, the case opened.

Liane Vanault opened her eyes. Matthieu dared not breathe as she slowly rose to a sitting position. He could not help but smile.

Liane gave Matthieu a blank look. He knew she was not there, not as she had been before.

"Hello?" she said flatly.

So someone has tried to help her. She can speak again. Doubtless, she is without any memory of what happened.

"My name is Matthieu. I'm a friend."

"I don't remember you. Can you tell me what happened?"

"We were assassinated. Not physically, but mentally. I'll help you get your memories back." Matthieu took the special shard out of his pocket.

"What is that?"

"An alien machine that will restore everything you

are," Matthieu said.

Liane looked bewildered.

"I—" she started. Then her face became calm. "I remember now."

It was Matthieu's turn to look confused.

It's done? The Nanorith must have made this device differently. It's not really a shard, just a Nanorith memory machine.

Matthieu smiled. "It's so wonderful to see you again!"

Matthieu stared at Liane. He found her so very mesmerizing... some niggling detail fought for attention in his mind. It was Hydrangea. Matthieu was receiving a message from his agent.

That's most unusual. Hydrangea never dared to interrupt me before—

Liane opened her mouth to reply, then she looked over his shoulder.

"I'm afraid I will need that," a new voice said from behind Matthieu.

Matthieu whirled. It was Adrienne.

"It's not what you think," Matthieu said.

What is she here for? How can I delay her? Liane can't help me.

"No. It's not what *you* think," Adrienne said. Her voice sounded angry. Matthieu saw her holding a pistol aimed at him. He realized the situation had already escalated far beyond anything he was prepared for.

Maddeningly, some part of Matthieu's mind brought him back to the message from Hydrangea. It was an image on display in an off-retina part of his visual cortex. He saw a statue of a woman. A female soldier. Matthieu realized it was Liane. It hardly seemed important.

Hydrangea, why... not now!

"I'm just giving an old friend her memories back," Matthieu said.

"Step away from her," Adrienne said urgently.

Hydrangea sent an urgent pointer to the image

metadata. Matthieu looked at the location tag on the image. Hydrangea had taken the image capture in Sorune's house! Matthieu thought furiously.

Liane and Sorune?

Matthieu forced himself not to look at Liane. His face would certainly betray his sudden uncertainty.

"She's here to take the shards for her corporation," Liane said. "I remember now. That's what she's wanted all along."

"She's a Trilisk, Matthieu."

"What?" Matthieu spat.

Matthieu would never have believed it before Hydrangea's image. Now his head spun.

A sphere zipped to a position between Matthieu and Adrienne's weapon. Surprise crossed Adrienne's beautiful face. She tried to step to one side, but the sphere adjusted itself to stay between them.

"Is that yours?" she asked.

"I finished it after all. Meet Ancile, my new agent."

"She's the danger, not me," Adrienne said.

I know.

"You're the danger," Matthieu said to Adrienne, though he no longer believed it.

Go along with it. It can't suspect you.

"Think about it. Liane can't be a Trilisk," Matthieu said. "She shared memories with the Nanorith. Memories that are in this shard. A Trilisk would never have done that because that would expose it."

Matthieu told Ancile what to do.

The small machine rushed Adrienne, charging for her face. She recoiled instinctively, but it made no difference. The machine's compact stunner discharged at point blank range, disabling her. Adrienne fell to the floor.

Liane shifted uncomfortably. "Is she dead?"

"Yes."

"That's what Ancile does?"

"Ancile protects me on my adventures," Matthieu said.

"I'll have to get one myself," Liane said.

Matthieu gave Ancile another command. The machine flew straight at Liane.

Liane's left leg arced up and connected with Matthieu's shoulder in less than a second. Matthieu felt the crunch of bone inside his body, then he was flying across the room as if he had been hit by a ceramic carrier. He landed in disarray against a cabinet. Something from the cabinet top crashed to the floor and shattered. He never saw the result of Ancile's attack.

Matthieu was as paralyzed by his astonishment of the force she had unleashed as by the blow itself.

"Liane?" Matthieu croaked.

"Liane is gone. As you were, until you managed to come back. An amazing feat, really for such a pathetic creature."

Matthieu could only raise his head. He knew he had to distract the Trilisk for a moment longer, until Adrienne....

Adrienne popped back up to her feet, firing her weapon. Ancile's attack on Adrienne had been a minimal one; Matthieu's on-the-fly idea to catch the Trilisk by surprise. In a split second, Liane was upon her. The weapon went flying. Adrienne clutched the arm that had raised it. Her face tightened into a grimace of pain.

No! Adrienne, I've caused all this.

"Don't do that again," Liane said. "Where did that shard get off to?" She looked at Matthieu. "Give it to me or she dies," Liane said.

Matthieu felt amazed. She had seemed so real. Everything they had done—

"You've always been... a Trilisk?"

"No," Liane said. "I already erased you both and stopped the Nanorith once. I decided to take this beautiful body for my companion living in Sorune. When you killed him, I waited, knowing that if you regained your memories, they would only send you running back here into my trap."

Liane had been real. That's why the Nanorith had her

memories.

"I'll give you only five more seconds," Liane said. She tightened her grip on Adrienne's arm, causing Adrienne to cry out in pain, though her face showed only anger.

"Hydrangea... gas them now. Gas them all. Ancile, use the poison we used on Sorune..."

Matthieu inhaled, then stopped breathing. His heart beat in his chest too quickly, causing him to need another breath within a handful of seconds. He tried to calm himself but it did not work. He heard a commotion, then he gasped for air.

***

Matthieu awakened. He held his head and stood, groggy from the gas. He found Liane before him. She was not breathing. He looked all around in confusion. Adrienne sat upright nearby.

"She's dead," Adrienne said. "I'm so sorry, Matthieu."

"How did you know she was a Trilisk?" Matthieu asked.

"The Nanorith told me there might be a trap. The Trilisks know the shards are a threat to them."

Ancile almost doomed us both just trying to protect me from the wrong person.

"How did they know Liane would be a Trilisk?"

Adrienne shook her head. "They didn't know. I'm sorry. I followed you here. It seems it's becoming a habit of mine."

"If you didn't know about Liane, why did you follow me here?"

"The Trilisks were one step ahead of you before. You lost that one. I had to be with you. I figured they probably knew we were back."

"Their artificial bodies are different than ours, that's what the Nanorith shared with me," Matthieu said. "In most ways of course, they are superior. Yet the poison used by

Mimic was even more effective on one of their bodies."

"Why didn't you tell me you were coming here?" Adrienne asked quietly.

"I didn't want you to feel like... like I was choosing her over you," Matthieu said. "Still, I thought I owed her her memories, the chance to come back like I did."

Adrienne nodded.

"Also, I wondered if you had a corporate directive behind going on the trip. Maybe your employer wants some Nanorith shards?"

Adrienne smiled. "That would be like the old me. I don't blame you for thinking that one bit. You should know, though, that I don't work for that corporation any longer. It cost me too much. When you left me, I finally saw that. I've been an indie player in Red Calais for over a year now. I was hoping we'd cross paths again, but you were with Liane..."

Matthieu was glad to hear that. Still, he stared at Liane's body at his feet.

"I'm sorry, Matthieu," Adrienne repeated.

"It's just that... when I saw her lying there, still alive..."

"You had the feeling of elation when a distant hope becomes real," Adrienne said. "I felt the same thing when you showed up at that party."

Matthieu barely smiled. "You didn't exactly welcome me with open arms."

"Not my style," Adrienne said, smiling back. Her face became serious. "I'm so sorry you lost her. What will you do now?"

Matthieu did not answer at first. It was a lot to take in.

"Well, maybe I'll look up my friend Renard and go looking for some beautiful..." Matthieu watched Adrienne's eyebrow rise coldly. "...places to go adventuring with you." He finished.

Adrienne smiled. "That's what I hoped you might say."

Michael McCloskey

Made in the USA
San Bernardino, CA
15 February 2018